A FISTFUL of HONEY

a novel

by

MALENA CRAWFORD

A FISTFUL OF HONEY

Transformation Press

P.O. Box 829 Silver Spring, MD 20901 Phone (347) 559-4907.

This is a work of fiction. Any reference to historical events, real people, or real places are used fictiously. Other names, characters, places, and events are products of the author's imagination, and any resemblance to actual events or places or persons, living or dead, is entirely coincidental.

This book contains quotes from *Song of Increase* by Jaqueline Freeman, *The Queen Must Die* by William Longgood, *The Shamanic Way of the Bee* by Simon Buxton, *Midnight Harmonies* by Octavius Winslow, *Honeybee Democracy* by Thomas D. Seeley, and *Long Life, Honey In The Heart: A Story of Initiation and Eloquence from the Shores of a Mayan Lake* by Martin Prechtel.

For information about special discounts for bulk purchases, please contact support@malenacrawford.com or 347-559-4907.

Printed in the United States of America
Library of Congress Cataloging-in-Publication Data;
ISBN 13 Digit: 978-1-5206644-3-9

Cover design by James Egan of Bookfly Designs, LLC.

Reader's Praise for

A Fistful of Honey

"I just finished reading your book, *A Fistful of Honey*. Wow! I must say, I got your book through Kindle Unlimited. Took me approximately 5 hours. I was and am enthralled! I want to read more, learn more, etc. Thank you! Your book healed some of my wounds. Thank you, and bless you." **Pheobe S.**

"I just finished reading *A Fistful of Honey* and I must say I am thoroughly fulfilled. Even though I've already left a review on Amazon, I had to stop by and acknowledge how much your book spoke to me. The patience you took in creating each character, especially Alena, is obvious. Through Alena, you were able to illustrate the depths of the Black woman's experience in America in a refreshingly authentic way. A Fistful of Honey is a gem for people like me who are able to discern the many truths hidden in fiction. The story was beautifully layered and the ending was exceptionally rewarding. Thank you for bridging a gap for Black women and for Black women writers, who like you, have a story to share. I can't wait to read what's next!" **Tiara J.**

"I just finished reading your book and I'm so grateful for the experience! I just wanted to say thank you. I can't wait for the sequel. I'm also looking to become a part of the Movement. I've been on this uncharted journey to find my purpose and I'm struggling to get there." **Angelique G.**

"Malena Crawford your book changed my life in so many ways. Thank you for following your life's purpose. I am passing this book on to as many people as I possibly can so that we can see our true selves!" **Amy C.**

For my daughter, Adara. May I live on in you as the divine beauty and joy that you are

&

For Juanita Holmes, Roy Lee Holmes, Dacia Stephenson and all of my ancestors who took the night so that I may have the day. Thank you.

It took many years of vomiting up all the filth,
I'd been taught about myself,
and half-believed,
before I was able to walk on the earth
as though I had a right
to be here.

— James Baldwin

"From the moment of the queen bee's birth, she is destined by invisible forces. We watch the miracle that unfolds with wonder."

THE QUEEN MUST DIE

CHAPTER 1

"*Please God, heal me. Help me now or just leave me the hell alone.*" Alena Ford begged the prayer the night before, shutting her eyes with a secret wish that they'd never open again. It was a simple, desperate plea but it held just the millimeter of faith that would change her entire world.

"Mommy, you have to get up now," a small voice chirped from the side of the bed. "Mom... MOM... *Mother!* Today's my field trip, remember? We can't be late or they'll leave me!"

Alena opened her eyes to see her eight-year-old daughter Maya standing next to the bed, hands on hips, gray-green eyes shining brightly. She was fully dressed in a purple shirt and a red pleated skirt. *She looks so much like Gabe*, Alena thought, noting the stark contrast of her daughter's complexion against her own. Her café au lait skin color barely showed any trace of Alena's black African bloodline. Sometimes in the early days, when he wasn't paying attention, she'd stare at him, too—marvel at how white he was.

"Mom, can you make waffles? I want waffles."

"Okay, okay, baby, I hear you. Good morning." Her voice was hoarse from sleep. She glanced at the clock. There was less than an hour to feed Maya, fight through Manhattan's Friday morning traffic, and drop her off at school. How she longed for the nanny and the maid she'd had to let go.

"Shit," Alena said absentmindedly, loud enough for Maya to hear. "How did I miss the alarm?"

"You said the s word. That's not a nice word, Mom."

"I know, honey. I'm sorry."

"Mom, I want waffles."

"I heard you, Maya. Run down to the kitchen and turn on the TV for Mommy, okay? I'll be right down... promise. And while you're at it, go find your sneakers."

Alena slid on her robe and headed to the kitchen where Maya sat waiting. She'd turned on the flat screen (with the mute button on just how Mom liked it), and pulled out a box of frozen waffles, a plate, butter, and powdered sugar along with a glass for milk.

"You sure are Mommy's helper, Maya. You're getting to be such a big girl." Alena patted her head.

"Mom, I'm not a baby, I'm eight now," Maya said with a roll of her eyes.

Alena slid the waffles into the toaster and poured a cup of coffee. She glanced at the television and unmuted it as a newscast came on.

"There is growing outrage this morning after Keyshawn Arnold, an unarmed African American teenager, was shot and killed by police in the Brooklyn neighborhood of Crown Heights last night. Conflicting reports describe the events leading up to the shooting. Investigators report that at 8:00 p.m. Thursday night, a police officer, who has yet to be identified, encountered Arnold and another man outside an apartment complex. Allegedly, one of the men brandished a gun, and a struggle ensued. However, investigators say no weapon has been found. We will have further information as it becomes available."

Alena mashed the mute button back on.

Maybe if they stopped reinforcing their own stereotypes, pulled their damn pants up, and acted like they had some common sense they wouldn't get themselves killed, she thought.

The waffles popped up, and Alena whisked them onto a plate for Maya, who dug in with vigor.

"I'll be upstairs getting ready, okay? You need anything, babe?"

"I'm fine, Mom. Just hurry ple*eez,*" Maya said between bites.

Thank goodness this is her last week of school. Alena trudged up to her bathroom. A shiver of unease stopped her short at the top step. Then strangely, the spot between her eyes started to twitch as she took in an unmistakable scent. This was an odor she hadn't smelled since she was a girl, but her body jolted instantly in response. *Not now.* She willed herself not to panic. *Please. Not after all these years.* Her stomach knotted in pain.

When Alena reached the bathroom, she tried to calm herself. She balled her dainty hands into small fists and closed her eyes. The scent, the pain, the feeling—it was undeniable. These were the telltale signs of what she had worked so hard to overcome—and the timing could not have been worse. *Pull it together. It wasn't real then and it isn't real now.* She leaned hard over the cool marble counter, her forearms resting on the sink, and tried to put the smell and the feeling out of her mind. *Just breathe. Breathe and it will go away.* She turned on the shower, and as she waited for the water to warm, stared into the bathroom mirror at her naked reflection. She couldn't help but think that while she "still had it" lately she felt so much older than her soon-to-be thirty- three years of age.

Her cocoa skin glowed under the small light, eyes red from a night of crying. Her smooth complexion was the perfect canvas for her high cheekbones, delicate nose, and full lips. Alena's narrow waist gave way to bountiful round hips and strong, shapely legs. By most accounts, she was a beautiful woman, striking even. With her sweet as honey sashay and graceful posture, she looked far taller than her 5"5 frame. Still, her presence hid a frail, terrified girl within.

Steam filled the room, but the smell of decay only intensified. Alena bent over the sink to splash it away with water, then patted her face dry with a towel. When she turned to place the towel back on the rod, the shadow of something, or someone, caught her eye in the mirror... there... behind her. Alena whirled around, almost losing her balance. She drew up those tiny fists, ready to strike, as if she would actually know how to use them, but no one was there.

A shiver snaked up her spine, and her heart pounded wildly. The room temperature seemed to have dropped by at least ten degrees despite the steam. Alena flipped on the overhead bathroom light and searched the room.

She looked into the claw-foot soaking tub, and then into the vast walk-in closet. There was nothing there but rows of exotic shoes and tailored designer dresses. She ran back down the stairs. Still no hint of an intruder—or the visions. Maya was safe and sound, eating happily. She peered through the penthouse's floor-to-ceiling window at the panoramic view of New York City. Everything was just as it should be. Satisfied, she took a deep breath and headed back up the stairs.

Maybe I'm so tired that I'm hallucinating, she reasoned, taking a final careful look around the bathroom.

Alena stepped into the shower and let the hot spray of water rinse away the remnants of the night before. As the hard drops pounded the back of her neck, she whispered another prayer.

"Please, God. Please! Help me to forgive," she begged once more. Yet no sooner were the words out of her mouth than she said through gritted teeth, "I hate him. I... hate... every... part... of him." In that moment, Gabriel, her soon-to-be ex-husband, and her father were one in the same.

Why couldn't she just let it go? Sobs wracked her body, but there was no time for crying. It was time to wear her happy face and slide on her designer armor. As she ran downstairs, Maya's voice greeted her, jarring her out of her thoughts.

"*Mom!* It is time to *go*! Daddy never does this. If Dad were here he would—"

"Well, your dad isn't here now. Is he?" Alena hissed. "Watch your mouth, little girl, and go put your sneakers on like I told you!" Maya's stunned little face fell, and she hung her head.

"I'm… I'm sorry, Maya Bear. I didn't mean to snap at you."

It was too late. She felt her daughter's heart sink along with her own. Tears of shame flooded her eyes, and she turned away from Maya.

"Go on and get your shoes, honey. You'll make the bus, I promise."

With Maya out of view, Alena buried her face in her hands. "I said pull it together, dammit!" she whispered to herself and took a deep, purifying breath, trying to hang on to the little faith she had left.

"To produce just 1 pound of honey, a hive of bees must visit 2 million flowers and fly 55,000 miles. At the center of this miraculous chaos is the queen bee herself. There shall be no honey without the nurturing of the queen."

CHAPTER 2

Alena hadn't become Mrs. Gabriel Ford overnight any more than a butterfly could heave from a cocoon in a day. Her ascension into his world was cumulative—well-crafted moments spent erasing, overwriting, and re-creating herself. After winning Gabriel over by date number five, she'd become masterful at the introductions to his people. She'd learned precisely how to stand, smile, and hold her breath with just enough poise to seem unbothered when they asked the kind of questions that white people who had no intention of sharing their privilege liked to ask. Instead of the shortness of breath she'd first experienced when someone inquired about her family, she became the queen of the pivot. "They're lawyers, too," she would lie with a smile, "But I won't bore you with that." Then she'd use her charm to steer them right to whatever hologram they needed to see in her, which mostly involved her Ivy League law degree. On this particular hot June day though, the last of the hologram had cracked down to nothing.

At 6:30 sharp that evening, the doorbell chimed through Alena's penthouse. Michael, her first love and best friend, had arrived. She'd arranged for Maya to stay a few hours with Ms. Duluth, an older woman she hired from time-to-time to babysit after the nanny left, and ordered takeout from Zephyr, her favorite.

When Alena caught her breath and opened the door for him, the sight of Michael made her heavy heart soar. Casually dressed in a body clinging white T-shirt and jeans, it was evident in his firmly muscled, 6'4" frame why this accountant-turned-personal-trainer was so highly sought-after.

"Mike!"

Michael's hug lifted Alena off her feet. She pressed herself into him. His arms were comforting and familiar. He stepped back for a moment and eyed her at arm's length.

"Wow, you haven't changed one bit, Leen. Still beautiful as ever."

"Now that's something I haven't heard in a good long while. Don't you come over here making me blush," she said, beaming from the compliment. "Thank you. You look great, too. You don't know how good it is to see you, Mike. Please, come in."

Michael crossed the palatial living room in three easy strides and plopped down. His long limbs sprawled over her antique French armchair, dwarfing it. He was the only man that had been in her home since Gabriel left.

"How've you been doing?" he asked. "You sounded like hell on the phone."

"Hell sounds about right. Trust me, I'll tell you all about it. I picked up some dinner. Any chance you can stay and have a quick bite?"

He shrugged. "For a little while, sure."

Staring into his powerful dark eyes made her feel fragile, lonely. It made her want to cry, but she fought back the tears.

"I hope I'm not getting you into any trouble by asking you to come here. I really need to talk and I just didn't have anyone else to go to."

"No, no trouble. I'm glad you called me, Miss Upper East Side," he said soothingly, flashing a broad white smile. "It was good to hear your voice after all this time."

Alena managed a grin. "Really? Good. I was so nervous, I didn't know what to expect. Actually, I thought Lola might cuss me out for calling."

Michael smiled knowingly. "That was a long time ago, she's cool now. She knows we're just friends."

"She has no clue you're here, does she?"

"Absolutely not," he smiled again.

Alena shook her head and grinned. "Well it's probably better that way. Anyway, can I get you something to drink? Water, coffee... wine?" A strange feeling simmered up from inside her. It felt like something was watching them. She gritted her teeth and pushed on, resolved to say nothing.

"Hmm, I'll take the wine. I could use a little drink." Michael looked around the room, stopping on one of her paintings. "Ahh, Romare Bearden. *Two Women?*"

Alena returned with two glasses of Merlot and took a seat. "Yes it is, very good. I see someone's been boning up on his art history." She gave him an affirming smile.

"Something like that. Lola has me going to these art shows. Well, had me going. You always did have great taste."

Had? She recognized something then, his eyes held a tinge of sadness like hers.

Alena took a deep gulp of her wine. "How is she...They?" she ventured.

He cleared his throat. "Everyone's good. The boys are growing up fast. Malik is headed to middle school this year, and Jeffrey will be right behind him next year. Lola's doing her thing, too, although things aren't all that good between the two of us right now. It's pretty damned icy to tell the truth."

"I'm so sorry to hear that, Mike. You guys are so good for each other," Alena said, though it wasn't the complete truth.

Michael shrugged, "Well, we're not officially over yet. You know I'm a fighter. Still trying to salvage what can be salvaged. I guess that's life. Besides, not everyone can live happily ever after like you and Gabe." He was trying to hide his frown.

Without much warning, Alena's pain broke itself free and tears rushed down her cheeks.

"Whoa, Alena, talk to me. What's going on with you?"

"Gabe told me he wants a divorce. He left me for another woman," she sniffed.

Michael's eyes widened in shock.

"Yep. Didn't even bother to be original with the shit. It's not like I didn't see it coming, I did. Guess I just didn't think he'd really leave. He started with the coming home late bullshit, hiding hotel receipts, and then finally, he just started bringing his whores here while I was gone. Discretion wasn't much his thing either." Alena paused before continuing.

"I caught the last one—her—right upstairs. His cliché ass blonde secretary giving him head. That's who he wanted all along. A white woman."

"Damn. I'm sorry, Leen." He moved forward to hug her and her lips slightly grazed the stubble along his jaw. She closed her eyes and let her face fall into the cave of his neck and shoulder. It was almost shameful to her how good it felt to be engulfed in his presence like that. Remembering that it wasn't hers to savor, she sprung herself from the embrace.

"Don't be sorry. Screw him," she said, straightening herself. "It's bad enough that he left, but what's even worse, he left these behind. I found them hidden in his things."

She handed Michael a fat stack of envelopes from a drawer in the coffee table.

"Go on and open one."

Michael ripped open one of the envelopes, and his eyes scanned the emboldened first line of the official looking document. "Warrant of Eviction," he read aloud. "Wait, what?"

"Yep. Foreclosure. Son of a bitch kept it from me all this time. There's a whole string of summons and complaints in there. Looks like he'd ignored each and every one. Notice to Quit, Notice of Sale, Summons of Unlawful Detainer—and who would that be? Maya and me. I'm an unlawful fucking detainer in my own fucking home. How could he do this to me? To his own child? There was a time I would've given my life for that man and he left us with no damn place to go! With no damn warning! You wanna know the kicker, Mike? He wants Maya. That bastard is the one who leaves me holding the bag, and now he wants full custody of my baby!" A shrill cry cracked through her voice.

"Custody? Man, what an *ass*hole." Michael shook his head sadly. "I don't get it, though. I mean, I get that he wants to leave and everything, but why does this guy have it out for you like this?"

Alena was rubbing her temples wearily.

"I don't know, Mike. There's got to be more to all of this, something even bigger that he's still hiding. We've had our problems for a while now, but it was like one day he just completely turned on me and I became his worst enemy."

Another dam of tears burst forward.

"Alena, calm down, okay?" he said, stroking her hair. "It's going to be okay."

She whipped her head around to face to him.

"It is not *okay*. I lost my job today. After all I've done for them, those bottom feeders let me go!" She was on the verge of screaming. "I was one of the best damn attorneys they had, made millions for them, *millions*. All because I wouldn't sleep with that red-faced bastard, Kavitz."

"Shit." Michael leaned back pensively.

"Yeah, exactly. Shit. When it rains it pours, right?"

"Do you have anyone you can stay with?"

Alena bit her top lip and took a steadying breath. "I don't. And to be honest, I don't get too much company these days. My friends, if I can even call them that, disappeared along with Gabe. And you know I left my fucked up family back in Maryland. I still haven't talked to them since that day."

"Well what about money? You have savings, right?"

She shook her head slowly and lowered her eyes. "Not much more than pocket money. I was so naïve. Bump that, I was damned stupid. I let Gabe handle all of our money, and now he's got it all on lockdown. Everything is in his name. On paper, all of this is his! This penthouse, the other properties, the accounts, everything." Alena finally met Michael's eyes.

"And before you ask, yes, I signed a prenup. His mother insisted, you know, to protect her son's precious inheritance. It was 'only fair' she said. I was such a gullible ass fool!" Alena barely breathed through her rant.

"What am I gonna do, Mike? I have six days left to figure out a plan. Six days! How did this bullshit become my life? I'm a contract attorney for god sakes, with a J.D. from Columbia. I *knew* better. And now I have nothing to my name!"

"Leen, try to chill out, all right? You said it, you're a great attorney. You'll have another job in no time."

"At what firm? If history's any indication Kavitz and his cronies have already blackballed the shit out of me from here to Idaho. That's what they do to the ones who don't play the game, especially the token black ones like me."

Alena rose to her feet.

"I grew up poor. I don't deserve to be back here. Gabe may be rich but I've earned this life. I earned this damned penthouse and everything else. And he stole it. Pulled the damn rug out from under me in one fell swoop," Alena burned with shame and anger.

"Okay, just relax and let's think about this," Michael said. "I have a friend who owns a building. The rent's still relatively cheap and he has a vacancy, matter of fact. I'm pretty sure that if I talk to him it's yours without a security deposit. If not, I'll float you the money. I'll be honest though," he glanced around the opulent room, "it's nowhere near as… luxurious as you're used to. It may even be a little rough."

"Where is it?"

"Brooklyn." When she frowned at him, Michael held up his hand to silence her. "This isn't the time to get bourgeois, Alena. You and Maya can have a brand new start and you can get on your feet. What do you say?"

She drained the last of her wine and heaved a sigh.

"Okay. I'll do it. What other choice do I have?"

"And now the queen emerges into the swarm... At some time, she has done this before, and has a memory of flying."

SONG OF INCREASE

CHAPTER 3

Alena clutched Maya as the moving truck arrived at 119 East Church Avenue. She silently prayed that Maya wasn't feeling any of the trepidation that was rippling through her.

What had she done with her life to end up here, to have to bring Maya to this place? After clawing her way through Columbia Law and into high society, here she was in the place she never wanted or expected to return to—the 'hood. This, she decided, was defeat, but she was not going to let it take her over.

She peered through the window at the aging brick building. It was bordered by a small lot that was littered with beer bottles, Black & Mild cigar boxes, and broken toys. The block was busy with activity. There were old men playing chess on the sidewalk, a group of boys playing basketball on a patch of concrete, some older women sunning themselves and gossiping on the stoop, and a cluster of young men talking. Children were playing, scattering this way and that, screaming at the top of their lungs.

"Mom, is this our new house?" Maya asked, clutching her doll to her chest. "Why are those kids acting so crazy?"

Alena leaned in close to Maya, "Remember what I told you, baby. It's only temporary, kay? We won't be here long. I promise. I'm getting a new job soon and we'll be out of here in no time," she assured herself as much as Maya.

When the truck stopped, Alena turned to Maya. "All right, here's the deal. When we get out of the truck, you stick close to me, understand?"

Maya nodded.

They scooted out of the truck and Alena gripped Maya's hand tightly as they walked up to the building. The people on the street all turned their attention to the new residents. It didn't help that Alena was hardly dressed for a moving day in her bright blue Cavalli dress and sea green espadrilles. Her gold jewelry shone brightly in the sun. The boys stopped playing their basketball game to get a glimpse. The women on the stoop shifted on their stone seats to get a good look. With glares sharp as razor blades, they sized her up. A group of young men stopped their conversation and fixed their eyes on her.

"Yo, Bengy, check her out." One of the men nudged his friend as he nodded toward her and licked his lips. "Hey, sweetheart!" he called out. "Aye yo, Sexy Chocolate!" He shouted again when he didn't get an answer.

"My man said 'hey', Shawty," the one named Bengy called out in a deep raspy voice, almost in warning. He had a jagged scar above his brow with a teardrop tattoo etched at the corner of his eye.

"Oh I get it, you too good to speak." His gaze was a mix of lust and disdain. He let his eyes linger slowly over her behind as she passed them.

"Well it's cool, 'cause damn lil mama, you looking good for real. Do yo' baby need a daddy? Hell yeah, I'd tap that all night long."

As Bengy and his friends erupted in laughter, Alena's stomach tightened with disgust. Her face burned from humiliation. How could they catcall her in front of her own daughter? Did they have no respect at all? These, she thought, were the very type of black people she couldn't stand. Loud. Ignorant. Mean. They were the type of black people that she had vowed she would never live around again, until today.

"Niggas," she mumbled under her breath. She hurried to the apartment doors, gripping Maya's hand even tighter, careful not to meet anyone's eyes. The closer they got to the building, the stronger the stench of liquor and urine became. It was so overwhelming in the elevator that she decided to walk up to the third floor.

"Don't. Touch. Anything," she whispered to Maya.

They climbed up three flights of battered steps. The smell of Caribbean food now permeated the narrow hallway. Gruff, arguing voices echoed from one apartment. Loud Samba music blared from another. Nestled in a shadowy corner was their new place, 3B.

Alena fished a hand wipe from her purse and turned the knob with it. Stepping inside was like walking into a nightmare. The apartment was less than one quarter the size of the penthouse. The pale yellow kitchenette had peeling linoleum floors, and the counter space wasn't much better, barely offering enough room to fry an egg. It was jammed between two cramped bedrooms and a lackluster bathroom. Alena drew in a long breath.

"Well, we made it," she said to Maya.

Since announcing the move, she was impressed with how well Maya had taken it but wondered if she was just holding back to save her feelings. Maya went to look around. Alena followed close behind. The ever-growing stacks of boxes and furniture the moving men brought in made the already minuscule space feel like a shoebox. Maya's room was slathered in four coats of dull powder blue paint. Alena watched her daughter's face for a reaction.

"Do you like it, just a little bit?" She asked hopefully.

"It's dusty in here, Mom. And my room is like a closet."

"I know. Don't worry, we'll work with it. It'll look much better when we set up your bed and things."

"Mom, when is Dad coming back?"

"I don't know, sweetie. We'll try to call him again. Tomorrow, after camp."

"Why can't we call him now? I miss him."

"Because we need to get settled first, all right? Let's put some things away and then we'll get something to eat."

Maya folded her arms in protest.

"Maya, listen. I need you to be a big girl and do your mother a huge favor. We're not going to tell your dad about our new place. He doesn't need to know yet."

"But why? Why do you want me to lie to Daddy? Why can't he know we moved?"

"It's complicated, okay? It's adult business. If your dad knew that we moved here, to a place so…small, he might get upset with me. He might say that you need to go live with him instead of me, and live with him *only*. Do you want that?"

"But I want to live with both of you. I want to see my dad, and I don't want to lie!"

Alena tried to temper her frustration. "Maya, your father loves you, but he's where he's chosen to be right now. If I could undo all of this, I swear I would, and you'd have both of us. But that's not going to happen, honey. For now, so that we can stay together, I just need for you to keep this one secret for me when you talk to your dad. Once I get us a better place, you won't have to keep it anymore. Okay? Will you do that for me?"

"I guess." Maya pouted.

"Thank you. Now enough of all this sad talk." She clapped her hands together. "Why don't we organize later? Let's go get some pizza and watch a movie!"

A knock at the front door interrupted them. Alena peered through the peephole. It was one of the women from the stoop.

"Who is it?" she called through the door.

"It's your neighbor, Gloria Chukwu. Looks like you might have dropped something."

Alena slowly opened the door as Maya wedged her body next to her to get a peek. The woman's smooth, butter yellow skin belied her old age, save the deep lines etched into her forehead. Prominent cheekbones were set elegantly high on her face, framed by long straight salt and pepper hair. Around her neck dangled a brilliant purple jewel that immediately caught Alena's eye.

"Hello, I live in 3A," she said, smiling cheerfully and holding up Maya's doll. "This was in the hallway. I thought it probably belonged to you." Her eyes were kind as she turned to Maya.

"Thank you, Ms. Chukwu," Alena said, waiting impatiently to close the door. "What do you say, Maya?"

"Thank you, ma'am," Maya said, delighted to have her toy back even though she hadn't missed it.

"Maya. How fitting. A pretty name for such a sweet, beautiful girl," the woman cooed to Maya. "You must be, let me guess…ten years old."

"She's eight," Alena said.

"My goodness, aren't you tall for your age? And those eyes. She's got an old soul, this one."

"Well, thank you for dropping off the doll, Ms. Chukwu. It was nice meeting you," Alena said brusquely.

"Oh call me Gloria, honey," she said, still smiling warmly. "Right," Alena said.

Gloria seemed to sense Alena's annoyance.

"All right, well welcome to the neighborhood. I hope I'll see you around soon. That goes for you, too, Sweet Pea." She smiled at Maya, then walked away.

Alena shut the door and muttered to herself, "I hope none of these nosey nut cases think I'm here to make friends."

As soon as the words left her lips, she was embarrassed for herself. Ms. Chukwu had been nice enough, and it wasn't as if she couldn't use a friend.

During the first night in the new apartment, Alena was unbearably restless. The closeness of the walls and ceilings left her no hiding place. The last of the illusion was slipping through her fingers. This nightmare was real. This was her life. She had become exactly what she'd always feared—a black single mother living in poverty.

She paced her bedroom restlessly like a caged animal, then finally sank into bed. The lonely sounds of the night flowed around her. Self-pity swirled over her until soon she felt tears sliding down her cheeks. When she heard Maya's slippers flopping against the linoleum, she quickly blotted them away. Maya's gentle knock sounded on the door. Alena cleared her throat.

"Come in, baby."

"Mom, I can't sleep. I don't like it here. And there are bugs in the hallway."

"It's okay, Maya Bear. Come sleep with Mommy." She patted the spot beside her.

"I love you, Mom," Maya whispered sleepily as Alena held her close and pulled the covers over both of their bodies. In that sacred moment Alena silently promised that she would make it right again. She lay there for an hour more watching the rise and fall of Maya's breath until her own eyelids relaxed and she, too, fell asleep.

The orange light of daybreak scattered through the blinds and stung Alena's eyes. She woke up and got Maya off to summer camp— a two-hour long trek on the subway. On her way back to the apartment, she heard someone call out to her.

"Hey, what's up? You the new lady 'round here, huh?"

It was a young woman in her early twenties. Her short hair was slicked back with gel, and a fake auburn ponytail sprouted from the top. She was curvy, and her faded purple jumpsuit fit tightly. Her hands were jammed into the pockets.

Alena nodded reluctantly and tried to keep moving.

"I'm Takeah. They call me Tacky. That's a nice bag you got," she said, admiring Alena's black lambskin purse. "Chanel, huh?" Takeah had a Caribbean sounding lilt to her voice, and one of her front teeth was crowned in gold.

Alena clutched her handbag to her, picked up her pace, and tried to stop the scowl forming on her face.

"You gotta lot of style. I saw you roll through here the other day. You got swag. Rich girl swag."

Alena nodded again and gave her a half smile. "Thanks."

"Your little girl cute. She mixed, ain't she?"

"Yes. She is. Look, it was nice meeting you, but I really have to go."

"Oh it's like that? Damn. Yeah, they said you was stuck up. Walkin' 'round here like you the damn Queen of Sheba. Whateva."

Alena raised her perfectly arched brows and shook her head at the exchange, scurrying into the apartment building and up the stairs back to 3B. As soon as she disappeared through the door, she called Michael.

"I don't know if I can do this, Mike. I don't think I can live here," she huffed. "What happens when Gabe finds out that I've moved his daughter to the 'hood? He'll eat me alive in court. One sniff of this place and they'll give Maya to him for sure."

"Well, where else are you going to go, Alena?" he asked sternly.

"My unemployment should start coming in soon. Maybe I can pull together enough to move to Fort Greene."

"Leen, it's your life, but I'm going to keep it real with you. You're dead broke. Not forever, but right now, you are. What do you think you'll get in Fort Greene with an unemployment check?"

"But what about Maya? What about the quality of life she's used to?" she said.

"You have a home and that's what Maya needs right now. And a mother with her head on straight so she can make her next move."

"Mike, I know, it's just that—" He cut her off.

"What I want you to do is ask yourself why you care so much about a man who couldn't even be bothered long enough to let you know that all of this was coming. Seriously, where the hell is your husband? Where was he when his daughter was on the brink of having nowhere to go? Stop worrying about shit that doesn't matter and wake up. I'm sorry if this sounds harsh, but you have to open your eyes, Alena. You're not on Fifth Avenue, but you're not homeless either. Take what you've been given and make it work. You of all people can do this."

Before Alena could reply, he said, "I have to run, okay? Later." Alena heard the line click off and for a moment she still held the phone to her ear. The shock of Michael's unusually sharp tone left her dazed. She replayed the conversation in her mind. He was angry with her. He was losing his patience. She didn't want to lose him, too. She couldn't. He was the only person left in the world that still cared about her. Her last crutch was sliding from her grip. Alena's heart sank as his words echoed again, "*Wake up.*"

"A single honeybee cannot perform the many necessary survival tasks a bee needs to do, nor can a honeybee survive without her hive. If a foraging bee gets lost or trapped somewhere overnight, most likely she will be dead by morning."

CHAPTER 4

Eleven days. That was how long it took Gabriel to call Alena after the loss of their marital home. It was just one more of all the ticking time bomb secrets he'd kept from her. Alena was at a café finishing her new daily ritual of scouring the Internet for jobs when his call came through.

"What do you want?" she answered with a dose of all the pent-up anger she'd been barely holding in check.

"Calm down, Alena. I don't need you getting emotional," he said.

"Emotional? You bail on us, our home is foreclosed, we're left homeless, and you have the nerve to tell me to calm down?"

"Look, I tried to stop that. They weren't supposed to take the penthouse. I had some business outside the country that took me away, but I knew you would be fine."

"Bullshit! I hate you! You knew we were losing our home and you didn't say one damn word all this time. Turn your back on me, fine. But your own daughter? And then you have the nerve to try to take her from me? You're going to rot in hell. Do you hear me?"

"Spare me the drama," he spat. "I didn't call to argue with you, Alena. I don't owe you anything. Get that through your head. Like I said, the penthouse was a casualty, a misunderstanding, and I'm taking care of it. Anyway, I called to speak to Maya. I want to see her."

"Do you really, you selfish bastard? Did you care about your precious little girl when you left us to fend for ourselves? Or was it when you were screwing that bitch in my bed?"

"You are bitter and pathetic. I suggest you stop this little fit while you're ahead before this gets ugly. You and I were over long before Brittany came along, Alena, and you know it. Look, enough of this shit. What you and I are going through has nothing to do with Maya. You know that I'll do whatever I need to do to see my daughter. Now where is she? Has school let out yet?"

Alena's courage vanished. The terror of what Gabriel was capable of sobered her. In addition to money, his family had prestige and power, and now she had nothing. One wrong move and they could easily level her and take her daughter away. Fear replaced the anger and she shrunk into herself, the same way she had as a girl. Gabriel was just like her father—scary and unpredictable, while at the same time holding hostage what she wanted most—love.

"Where is Maya?" he demanded again.

Fear forced her to sweeten her tone. "My mother's. We moved to my mother's house."

"You moved to Maryland? You're lying! You haven't spoken to your mother in years. Don't lie to me, Alena. You know what, never mind, I'll find out myself."

Panic fluttered through her stomach and throbbed in her throat, trapping all of the sophisticated words she wanted to use to lash back at him.

"Okay, okay. Gabe, you'll see her, okay? Tomorrow. Central Park at four o'clock by the carousel."

"All right," he said.

"Gabe, please don't take Maya from me," she begged. "She's all I have left." Desperation had faded her voice to a whisper.

The phone clicked as he hung up, and then a thought flashed through her mind.

What if he takes Maya from the school? The thought sent a wave of panic, and she scrambled into action. Her mind sped past her body, and she nearly tripped over her own feet looking for an exit. *Oh my God,* she said over and over to herself. *My baby. Help me, God.*

Alena hurried from the café to the corner and hailed a taxi cab to her daughter's day camp. Her heart was still pounding even after she'd spotted Maya's face beaming in the sea of children. She didn't calm down until she was holding her in her arms. When she did, she almost collapsed with relief.

"I'm so happy to see you, Maya Bear!" she exclaimed and planted kisses all over Maya's face. "Hi Mom," Maya looked at Alena suspiciously. "Are you *okay?*"

"I'm fine, just glad to see my baby. Let's go home."

Alena tried to bury her anxiety for Maya. At the apartment, she sat at the edge of her bed and spoke gently and quietly. "You're going to see your dad tomorrow," she announced.

"Tomorrow? Woo-hoo! I'm gonna see Daddy!" Maya sang.

As much as Alena hated herself for it, Maya's excitement for her father saddened her. She wanted to be the one her daughter chose and celebrated for once.

"That's right, honey, your daddy's back." She forced a brittle smile onto her lips for Maya. "Listen, remember what we talked about the other day, about our new place?"

"Yes, Mom."

"I need you to remember to keep our little secret, okay?"

Maya nodded impatiently.

"Maya, can I ask you a question?"

"Mom, another question?" Maya whined. "Are you happy here?"

Maya looked around her room, up at the ceiling, and then back at Alena.

"Well, I miss our old house. I miss my old room, too. I don't have any friends that live this far away, and you don't let me play outside with any of the kids here. They don't seem that nice anyway."

"What I mean is, are you happy with *me*? Do you like living with me?"

"Of course, Mom," Maya said, and then nestled against her mother.

"I know this is all a huge change for you, but I promise you that I'm doing all I can so we can move soon. We'll have a great home in the city again that your friends can visit. Do you believe me?"

"Yes."

"And Maya, I know you want to live with both of us, but if you had a choice, who would it be? I mean, if your dad wanted you to live with him, would that be something you would want?"

"Ahh, Mom!" Maya whined again.

"I know this is hard, but I need to know what you want."

"Mom, I don't want to talk about this. That's adult business, remember?"

"You're right, honey, I'm sorry. I'll get dinner started. Why don't you get your clothes ready for tomorrow?" Alena weaved her fingers into Maya's and kissed her small soft hand.

The next afternoon, Alena was trembling under her rigid demeanor when Gabriel walked up to them. Her jaws involuntarily clenched, and she could barely look him in his eyes. She hadn't expected to feel such a yearning for him. How could her heart be so damned foolish? It scared and infuriated her to know that she still wanted someone she would never have, and who wanted nothing to do with her.

She'd hoped the hatred she felt toward him would have helped her stop loving him, but it hadn't. As usual, Gabriel seemed unfazed and confident. He was handsome as ever—face tanned olive, piercing gray-green eyes flecked with topaz, angular chiseled jaw just like one of those Abercrombie models she saw plastered over Times Square.

He was dressed down in steel gray slacks and a slate blue collared shirt. The sleeves were rolled up to the elbow, revealing his sculpted forearms. Alena stole a quick glance at his bare ring finger, for what she didn't know.

"Daddy!" Maya squealed, jumping into his arms.

Gabriel spun her around. After he set her back on her feet, he held Maya close as they chatted. Alena looked on. He still hadn't said anything to her. It was as if she wasn't standing there. She was no longer a part of their dynamic, ousted from their family. She was now the ex-wife. Ex-cluded. Ex-pelled. Dismissed. The realization socked her in the gut, directly behind a trace of envy. How she wished Gabriel's eyes lit up for her the way they did for Maya. Just a split second of affection was all she needed. What had she done to make his heart turn so cold toward her? To Alena's relief, he didn't ask Maya where they were living.

"Mom! Did you hear that, Mom? Daddy is taking me to see the *Lion King!*"

"That's great, honey." Her forced smiles were more like painful winces now.

Gabriel hugged Maya and planted a kiss on her cheek. "Wait here while your mother and I have a quick talk, princess."

Maya nodded cheerfully.

He finally addressed Alena. "So, where did you move to?" He asked with the coldness of an old enemy.

"It's safe and it's close, okay?"

"Where, Alena?" he demanded.

Alena looked down at the ground, silent.

Gabriel looked back at Maya, who was sitting on the bench three feet behind them. "Keep your secrets," he whispered. "They're only going to hurt you," he warned.

"Listen, Gabe. Please promise me that you'll bring her right back tonight. Please. Call me and I'll meet you anywhere in the city." She felt him reading her, sensing the fear in her.

"Of course, Alena. She stays with you. For now," he said and then walked over to Maya. Alena stood watching as he left with her, terrified.

Hours passed, and exhausted, Alena had fallen asleep in her apartment only to be awakened by a chirping smoke detector.

"Oh crap!"

She leapt off the bed. She was only supposed to close her eyes for five minutes while the chicken browned. Alena fanned thick smoke from the charred pan.

"Oh no!" she cried.

She ran water over the blackened slab of chicken breast and then slammed the pan into the sink.

"What the hell are we going to eat now?" She growled, then scraped the scorched remains of the last of her groceries into a trash bag and headed out the door with it. In her haste, the black plastic snagged on the doorjamb, ripping the bottom and leaving all of its contents in the hallway. Alena pounded the door with the heels of her hands.

"You've got to be fucking kidding me. I can't take any more of this!" she screamed.

The door to 3A opened, startling her. She looked up to see her new neighbor Gloria standing in the doorway.

Alena looked down at the mess, embarrassed. "I'm sorry, I just had a little accident."

"Oh, honey, I've had plenty of days like that. Let me help you." Gloria walked back into her apartment and returned with a new trash bag, a broom and a dustpan.

"Thank you," Alena said.

"Smells like you burned something up pretty good."

What does this old lady want? Alena thought.

"Yes, I fell asleep and, well, the whole thing is gone now."

"Why don't you and your little girl join me for dinner then?" Gloria asked.

"We can't. I'm sorry," Alena said quickly.

Gloria laughed heartily then smiled with motherly assurance.

"I don't bite, sugar."

"No, it's not that. It's getting late, I think I'll just order some takeout. But thank you, it's very kind of you to offer."

"All right, well if you change your mind I'm right next door. And by the way, I do make a mean pecan pie."

Gloria's smile was so sweetly genuine that Alena decided she could definitely use the company and the meal.

"Wait. On second thought, yes. Yes, I will join you," she smiled. "Do I need to bring anything?"

"Just yourself and that sweet baby of yours," Gloria said.

"My daughter is with her dad for a few hours," Alena said, her voice trailing off.

"Okay," Gloria smiled back. "It'll be just us girls then. Hopefully next time she can join us." Something in her voice soothed Alena, and her hesitation disappeared.

To Alena's astonishment and delight, Gloria's apartment was exquisitely decorated, a cross between a tiny palace and a museum. Rare antiques and furniture filled every stately corner. A grand piece of artwork covered almost every inch of the saffron painted walls. Most of the art was African—paintings, richly colored cloths and carvings.

"Have a seat and make yourself comfortable. Dinner will be along in just a bit," Gloria called from the kitchenette. "Would you care for some tea?"

"Yes, please. Tea would be wonderful," Alena called back.

"Very well. I've found there's something about tea that helps to soothe whatever ails you."

Alena shrugged and eased back onto the plush sofa. Taking in more of the lovely space, Alena noticed a large painting of a dark brown-skinned Mother Mary and Jesus. It was so breathtaking that it stood out from the elegant decor. "My God," she heard herself say aloud.

Its haunting radiance invigorated Alena and made her want to reach out and touch it. Life seemed to stir behind Mother Mary's eyes. It was as if this Mary and Jesus were beckoning her to join them. She smiled, mesmerized by the image.

"This painting is absolutely gorgeous, Miss Gloria," Alena called out.

Gloria ducked her head into the living room to see which piece she was referring to. She smiled and placed a palm over her heart.

"Thank you. Yes, the Black Madonna. My love. That was my husband's favorite. It's mine, too."

Gloria set a hot mug of jasmine tea on a saucer in front of Alena and leaned forward.

"She's a healer, you know," she said and gave Alena a mysterious smile and a wink, setting a pointed gaze on her as if they were in on the same secret. Unsure of what she meant or how to respond, Alena lowered her eyes and blew ripples over her steaming drink.

"Okay," she said politely, and then quickly changed the subject as Gloria returned to the kitchenette.

"Thank you for your hospitality, Miss Gloria. You have a beautiful home," she said.

"Oh thank you, honey! Decorating is one of my joys." She returned with two heaping plates of jambalaya and placed them on the lacquer table in front of Alena. Gloria then clapped her hands together joyfully. "Now this, my dear, is some good ole southern home cooking. Let's eat!"

Gloria said a prayer and Alena leaned forward to take a bite of the savory dish. The sweet and tangy flavors burst across her taste buds. It was the best meal she'd had in a long time and the pie was even more delicious, just as Gloria promised. Still, all through the meal Alena caught herself staring back at the painting, entranced by it. Trying not to be a rude guest, she pulled her eyes away from it and said, "Do you have any children, Gloria?"

"Oh yes, I have three daughters. Nneka, Olivia, and Abiola. Olivia, my oldest, was named after my grandmother. Nneka's my middle and Abiola is the baby. She's the only one still here in New York. She lives in Tribeca, into all of that Hollywood television stuff." Gloria sighed nostalgically. "My sweet babies. Of course, they're all grown, two of them with children of their own now."

"Are you originally from New York?" Alena asked.

"Oh no, dear. New Orleans, born and raised. I moved here with my husband about forty years ago. He passed away going on four years now. What a great man, my Adeyini. He was Nigerian, worked as a professor at NYU for twenty-six years in Africana Studies. When I met him, I was teaching Sociology at Sarah Lawrence." Alena could see both the joy and the sorrow in Gloria's eyes.

"I'm so sorry for your loss. It certainly seems like you've lived a charmed life."

"Thank you, honey. Life is only as charmed as you make it."

"Forgive me for asking, but how did you end up living... here? You don't seem like you belong in a place like this. I mean, you have very elegant tastes. Your apartment looks like it came out of the pages of *Architectural Digest*," Alena said.

"Not everything is as it seems, my love. The people in these buildings have just as much beauty and genius as anyone else. Not too long after Ade passed, I started a little school a few blocks from here. It was a small etiquette and empowerment school for girls. The school closed almost as quickly as it opened. Not too many bureaucrats in City Hall shared my vision of poor inner-city girls investing in themselves, so they cut off all the funding. The parents and the girls believed in the vision though. They loved it. After we closed our doors, I stayed put. I figured God wanted me here for a good reason. So what about you? How are you two settling in over there?"

"It's... ah.... different. A lot to get used to, I mean. The great news is that I've finally unpacked all of our box—"

Alena stopped mid-sentence, transfixed by the gorgeous purple stone around Gloria's neck. It had caught the light overhead and held a glorious sparkle that captivated her.

"Your necklace is stunning," she exclaimed.

"Well, aren't you just full of compliments? Thank you. It was a gift from my Ade."

"What kind of stone is that?" Alena asked.

Gloria unclasped the necklace and held it in her palm for Alena to examine. Cut into several facets, the massive stone glinted wildly. The jewel's setting was unusual, secured by five ornate gold prongs, each shaped like the wings of a vulture.

"It's an amethyst, a spirit crystal. The necklace is really an amulet of sorts. *Ulinzi.* That's the Kiswahili word for protection. He gave it to me when we went to Tanzania for his study on postcolonial cultural relations. He said it was for my protection."

Alena marveled at the gem. Like the painting, it had a strange effect on her, almost hypnotizing. Looking at it exhausted her.

"Well, it's beautiful. I hate to eat and run but I should probably get going. Maya's dad will be calling soon. Thank you so much for inviting me over. Everything was perfect."

"Why don't you both come over tomorrow? That is, if you're free. I have all sorts of movies my grandkids left behind that Maya can watch. You can help me bake a hummingbird cake, and I'll even braid her hair," Gloria offered.

"You'll *braid her hair?*" Alena teased.

"Oh yes I will, honey." Gloria said with her hands on her hips. "I have three girls, remember? I've still got it! And I still remember what a chore it can be having to do it all up all of the time. Your Maya has that fine, thick hair just like I had when I was her age."

She picked up a black and white photograph from the mahogany credenza. "See? My daddy was that pretty shade of coffee brown like you; my mama was Creole. She looked something like Lena Horne. That's me there." She pointed to a young fair-skinned girl with long raven black hair nestled between the man and woman.

"Yes. Very nice, Gloria." Alena hesitated. "Okay, we'll be back tomorrow then, if we can," she said with an awkward smile.

"Oh good, we are going to have a ball!"

When Gloria hugged Alena goodbye, she stiffened. Gloria's tenderness was so foreign that it alarmed her. Maya was the only person who had ever hugged Alena this way. The thought of her precious girl with her little arms clasped around her neck brought a tear to Alena's eyes.

"Let her heal you," Gloria whispered in her ear.

"Pardon?" Alena asked, puzzled.

"Mother Mary," Gloria whispered again. "Let her heal you."

Alena nodded to hide her confusion this time and brushed the strange comments off as Gloria's particular brand of eccentricity.

"Good night, and thanks again for dinner," she said. She flicked a glance at Gloria, who wore another mysterious smile, and crossed the hallway back to her door.

Alena hadn't been in her apartment more than ten minutes when the door creaked open, then stopped short by the chain lock. A loud banging on the door soon followed.

"Mom, open the door! Dad is here, too!" Maya exclaimed, her face pushed into the opening of the door.

Alena gasped. *What in the hell? How the fuck did Gabe get here?* "Okay, baby!" she called, her hands nervously fumbling with the chain on the door. A moment later, Maya burst in the apartment like a whirlwind.

"Mom! *The Lion King* was so awesome!" Maya exclaimed happily, her arms full of sweets and toys.

Alena saw Gabriel in the dimly lit hallway.

"That's wonderful," she managed, with her eyes steady on him. When Maya bolted for her bedroom to sort through her gifts, Alena held her breath, bracing for another barrage of insults and demands. But he was silent, mocking her it seemed.

"Thanks for bringing her back," Alena said softly.

"Sorry to hear about your job, Alena," he said. Without another word, she closed the door in his face and put the chain back in place.

With Gabriel gone, her fear and shame quickly turned into anger. "Maya!" she called. Maya came running in, still teeming with the excitement of her day. Alena breathed deeply, being careful not to let her anger seep into her tone.

"Maya, honey, we talked about this! I asked you to please not tell your dad where we're living."

"But, Mom, I didn't tell Daddy anything. He already knew. He said he knows about everything."

"The Arc of Creation opens with a blessing, a sound that names us. We dwell in that enclosed area, the interior of the hive."

SONG OF INCREASE

CHAPTER 5

Alena and Maya left the apartment early before the heat of the July morning became insufferable. Alena had decided that today would mark her new beginning. Michael was right. It was time to wake up. She had no choice in the matter.

She'd counted up the last of her savings the night before. It was tucked away in her purse—all five hundred and forty-three dollars of it. Not even enough to cover next month's rent, let alone hire a half decent family law attorney. She looked at the shoes on her feet and the jewelry on her wrists and fingers. It was time to let go of that dream life and all of its golden trappings. *Survival is all that matters now,* she thought as she purged her closet of items to sell.

It would be a full day. After dropping Maya off at camp—a final luxury that Gabriel had prepaid earlier that year—Alena would first go to the consignment shop, then the pawnshop, and then to the unemployment office.

She walked into the shop, past the black awning with "Bridgette's Couture Consignment" written in gold letters.

"Can I help you?" the brunette at the counter asked, barely sparing Alena a glance.

"Yes, hello. I have some items I'd like to sell," Alena answered.

"All right, let's have a look." She examined Alena from head to toe with a haughty scowl on her face.

Alena unloaded the suitcase she'd filled and lined up a dozen pairs of her shoes for the woman to appraise.

"These are all yours, correct? We do *not* purchase stolen goods."

"Stolen? Why would you assume that I'm trying to sell stolen shoes? No, I haven't stolen anything, of course these are all mine."

"It's policy, ma'am. I have to ask."

"Right," Alena huffed. She tried her best to stay calm, reminding herself how badly she needed the money.

"So here's how this works," the clerk explained, giving Alena a strained half smile, pinching the crow's feet around her eyes. "You'll receive 50 percent of the sale price, which will be reduced approximately 20 percent every 30 days. After ninety days, the item gets discounted 50 percent off the original selling price." The woman then examined the soles, then the heels.

"Hmm. I would list these for about six hundred dollars apiece."

"Six hundred?" Alena exclaimed. "These are mint condition Louboutins, worn maybe once, if that."

"These are all from past seasons. I'll be lucky to get that much for them."

Alena took a deep breath. "Ma'am, please. I'm in a tough spot, can't you do any better? What about these?" She held up a pair of red sequined stilettos. "These are limited edition. They were at least seventeen hundred dollars."

The woman's stony look softened a bit.

"Well, they are unique. I don't get too many of these in. I can price them for about eight hundred seventy-five dollars."

Alena was convinced that she was being cheated, but desperation left her at the woman's mercy. She tallied up the bounty. Thirty-seven hundred dollars, and that was only if everything sold. It was far from the $10,000 retainer she needed for a lawyer, but it would keep a roof over Maya's head and food in the fridge. It was a deal. On her way out, the woman assured her that she would call as soon as she had a sale.

Alena didn't fare much better at Louie's Gold and Pawn. The man bent over her emerald ring, a gift from Gabriel for their fourth wedding anniversary, and after examining it for a few minutes, he pronounced it to be worth three hundred dollars. Alena tried her best not to panic. Last was the unemployment office to see about the check she was expecting. She smoothed a stray tendril of hair behind her ear and clasped her hands in front of her as she waited her turn. Several minutes later, the woman behind the counter motioned her over.

"Hello, I'm here to find out when I should be expecting my unemployment benefits."

"When did you apply?"

"At least a month ago now."

"Name?"

"Alena Jae Ford. A-L-E-N-A."

She clicked around on her keyboard and studied the screen, then she looked up at Alena.

"You won't be receiving any benefits, Mrs. Ford," she said.

"What?" Feeling faint, Alena grabbed the counter to steady herself.

"Your previous employer listed insubordination as the reason for your dismissal. Unemployment insurance can only be collected if you become unemployed through no fault of your own. In accordance with New York State law, you are ineligible for unemployment benefits, Mrs. Ford. I'm very sorry."

The woman's face was blurred through Alena's tears. "This can't be happening. I give up. I just... give the hell up." She stepped back from the counter and slowly turned away. "Thanks for nothing." Alena whispered and walked out of the building in a daze.

Her faith was shriveling along with her strength. Exhausted and stunned, she ducked into the subway station and got on a train headed back to Brooklyn. An hour later, Alena trudged up the steps to her apartment, where she flung the suitcase in the corner, sat on her bed, and buried her face in her hands, weeping. The walls of the little room felt like they were closing in on her. She felt trapped again, suffocated.

She'd started the day with so much hope, but now it had all but vanished. On impulse, she thought to go see Gloria. She needed comfort and Gloria could at least lend a sympathetic ear. Their friendship had grown quickly, with every visit she and Maya had made. Alena went to the bathroom and washed her face. A few minutes later, she stood outside of apartment 3A and was about to knock when Gloria's door swung open.

"Come in, honey," Gloria said kindly, seeing Alena's red eyes and sad expression.

"I'm sorry for just coming by like this…Wait, I didn't even knock… how did you…?"

Gloria waved her off. "Oh nonsense. Come on in here. Sit and rest your tired bones for a spell. Looks like you could use some of my pralines and an iced chamomile tea."

"Oh, no thank you. I don't have much of an appetite right now." Alena sat on the sofa next to Gloria. "Really, I didn't even knock," she repeated.

"Oh…" Gloria smiled. "Motherly instincts. I've learned to listen to them over the years. Having a devil of a day, aren't you?"

Alena exhaled in a slow whistle. "Am I? The worst actually. I don't understand what's happening with my life. This time last year I was living a picture-perfect life on the Upper East Side with the husband of my dreams…well…with my husband. My daughter had everything she wanted—two great parents, friends, enrolled in the most prestigious school in New York City."

She couldn't hold back the tears any longer. As she cried, Gloria hugged her shoulders.

"Now I have five hundred dollars to my name, my husband left me for another woman and won't give me a penny, and if that wasn't enough, he's trying to take my baby away from me," she sobbed.

"That's good." Gloria smiled, her face taking on a bit of light.

"That's *good?*" Alena sputtered, looking sharply at Gloria. *Why the hell did I come over here? She's nice but this lady is batshit crazy.* "Good? Is it good that my entire world has fallen to pieces and I'm going through hell? Is it good that I'm going to lose my daughter?" Alena felt anger creeping up and begin to overtake her.

"Good is relative, my dear. Sometimes pain can shock you awake when nothing else can," Gloria said, her eyes focused on Alena, as if remembering her own journey.

Alena shook her head in disbelief. "I have nothing left, Gloria. Nothing. He took everything. He *has* everything. Don't you understand that?"

"Yes, believe me, I do. But anything outside of yourself that you believe you need in order to prove yourself worthy, you should be rid of! You are worthy now. Just as you are, Alena, *you* are worthy."

"He has what Maya deserves," Alena said. "A good life. Buckets of money. A nice home."

"Give her to him then," Gloria said flatly.

"What?" Alena whimpered, her eyes wide in disbelief.

"If that's what you really believe, then give Maya to her father," Gloria repeated.

The weight of mounting anguish finally caved in on Alena like a boulder, and she couldn't take it any longer. She collapsed right onto the linoleum and wept from the depths of her broken heart, her body weary from loss and defeat.

"Get up! Come on, baby, get up now!" Gloria yelled, pulling Alena up off of her knees. She took Alena's hands and dug her thumbs so deeply into them it hurt. "You are her mother! You're the only one she is ever going to have. You can *never* lose her! Now do *you* understand *me?* If God didn't want it that way, then you would not have been chosen."

Alena could only stare in response.

"Honey, there is nothing for you to be ashamed of. You're doing the very best you can, and your baby knows that. Best believe she can see that, and she can sense that. That girl's got a *powerful* spirit and she loves you, Alena." Gloria pressed her finger into Alena's chest.

"She doesn't need a big fancy house, or big fancy school, or whatever else it is you've been hiding behind. What she needs is her mama's heart. She needs her mama's love. She needs her mama to love herself. She needs you to see yourself clearly, through your own eyes. Through God's eyes."

Mama, Alena thought. Oh how she wished she'd been truly mothered.

Gloria wiped the tears from Alena's face with the crook of her finger and hugged her tightly.

"You've got to find your heart, baby. Call your spirit back home. You've got to wade through all this misery and muck and find the purpose for it. Let all this guilt you have go. Guilt requires punishment to survive, and as long as you've got it, you're going to go right on punishing yourself. Long as you believe you're a victim of life and you've got no choice in the matter, well then, you never will.

Alena frowned and shook her head slowly with defeat. "And what if I'm not strong enough? Strong as you?"

"Now I've had my troubles, too, a lifetime of them. I've been lonely as sin since my husband passed, and my girls have gone off to their own lives. But I know that I have to choose to keep moving past the trouble. We both have a life to live and work to do," Gloria declared, her hands now on her hips.

"Let it all go! Give it up, baby! Let it go or you will go down with it!" Gloria said, taking Alena into her arms.

It was the permission she'd needed so badly: to cry, be heard, and maybe even held. She let her body soften against Gloria's and started weeping like she never had before. The light fragrance of rosewater soap on Gloria's skin comforted her, along with the strength of her hands rubbing Alena's back. She spoke gently into her ears, her voice filled with love. An avalanche of hurt and despair sucked the air from

Alena's lungs. The sensation of breaking loose overcame her and for an instant, her lungs felt like they'd closed altogether. Time stilled, and Alena stopped breathing.

"Breathe, baby, breathe!" Gloria yelled. Alena was choking.

"Breathe life!" Gloria screamed, invoking and urging.

Still Alena struggled, suffocating under her pain.

"Girl, fight for your life!" Gloria commanded.

With that Alena breathed deeply, taking in an urgent gulp of air, and then cried again. This time she cried from the depths of her heart and soul, deeper than she ever remembered in her life. Warm, salty, purifying tears. She cried for every wound, every shattered piece of herself she had lost. She even cried for her daddy and his broken dreams. She cried for the little girl inside of her who he'd hurt so badly.

She cried for the woman she'd become, who still couldn't accept that she would never get what she wanted from her father. Or her mother for that matter. She even cried for *her*. She cried for Maya, for all the ways she felt she had failed her daughter. She cried for her broken marriage and all the ways it left her broken when she had hoped it would have made her whole.

Gloria cupped the smooth brown oval of Alena's face in her hands. With her brow furrowed and eyes blazing, she looked into the younger woman's soul and spoke to the hurt that she knew all too well.

"This is your road. God gave it to you, and you agreed to walk it. Remember this. It may be a long road, it may be a rough road, but it's the only one that leads to the glory."

Alena's cries made a sudden stop at Gloria's words. She looked deeply into her eyes. Gloria touched two fingers to the spot between Alena's eyebrows.

"Know the truth."

She touched those same fingers to Alena's tear-soaked lips. "Speak the truth."

She pressed those fingers into Alena's chest, over her heart. "Be the truth."

41

Those were the last words that Alena heard Gloria say before a sudden weariness settled down on her body, lulling her to sleep below the curious painting of Mary and Jesus. As her breaths lengthened, another voice reached her mind as if it had come from a very long distance. It was beckoning and comforting her all at once. Alena strained to hear what the voice was saying, but exhaustion rocked her to sleep with only one word in her ears. "Peace."

The ground rumbled, and distant sounds drew closer. The vibrations tickled the bare soles of her feet. Alena looked down at them to discover that she was standing on the cracking surface of a great frozen lake. Within seconds, the crack beneath her became a widening fault that swallowed her up, and she was suddenly falling into nothingness.

"Call on us lest you be swallowed up forever!" a chorus of mystical voices exclaimed from the darkness. In the next moment, she was surrounded by a brilliant, warm yellow light, and she heard only one voice this time, a woman's, slow and honeyed.

"I am that I am. I am Mary of Magdalene. Alena, we are here. Hold on, Dear One. Hold on. We are here. " And then it was over.

With her eyes closed, Alena sat in stillness, trying to weave the pieces of her strange dream together. But the harder she tried the faster the images flittered away from her memory. Only that sweetly reassuring voice remained. "Alena, we are here."

Gloria's rosewater scent wafted into Alena's nose as she gently nudged her awake.

"You'd better wake up and go get your girl, honey."

"We, the maidens, are messengers of light. Our tasks are more than the work at hand. Though we may look small, each fills our role, and thus bee, hive, kingdom and all the world move forward together."

SONG OF INCREASE

CHAPTER 6

Below her window, Alena heard angry voices raging in the stillness of dawn. They grew louder and louder until they filled up the courtyard. She pushed open a sliver in the blinds to see Takeah arguing with a man. It was one of those rude men that had cat-called her when she had first moved in—the one called Bengy. A young boy, about the same age as Maya, stood with her as she bickered with him.

"You ain't shit, Bengy. You leavin' again? You ain't seen your son in five—"

A swift blow across her face sent Takeah and the child tumbling onto the patch of grass. Alena forgot she was trying to be quiet and let out a shout. She watched Takeah push herself to her feet as the boy darted toward Bengy to defend his mother. Takeah grabbed the child by the wrist and ran inside the apartment as Bengy shouted curses after her. Alena could tell this was a familiar scene for her.

When the thought to go to Takeah's apartment and check on her first came to her mind, she was hesitant. She decided to mind her own business and fell back asleep. But even after she'd gotten Maya off to day camp, Alena still couldn't get Takeah and the nasty scene in the courtyard out of her head. She knocked on the door of apartment 2C.

Takeah threw open the door, a defiant look on her face. Alena stumbled over her words, not knowing quite what to say.

"Hi. I just… uh… wanted to say hello," Alena offered.

Takeah gave Alena a curious look.

"Okay, yeah. Hi, Rich Girl," she said coolly, frowning. The patch of skin under her left eye was bruised eggplant purple and her bottom lip was split.

"I know this is a little weird, me stopping by like this," Alena said.

"Whatchu need?" Takeah tapped her foot impatiently. The swelling in her lip gave her a lisp. A sheen of sweat covered her face and beaded along her hairline, plastering stray hairs against it.

"Do you mind if I come in?"

She stared at Alena without speaking. After a few moments, she shrugged and stepped aside, motioning with her head for Alena to enter. Takeah sat on a lumpy orange sofa. She twirled her fingers around her long burgundy-dyed braids. The boy sat at her feet playing a video game. The apartment was sweltering. The fan whirling in the background was no match for the heat.

"AC busted," Takeah grunted.

"So this is your son. Isn't he handsome?" Alena gushed at the child.

"Yeah this is my boy, Benjamin Jr. We call him BJ."

BJ smiled shyly at Alena.

"My name is Miss Alena. You are one brave boy, Benjamin. How old are you?"

"Nine and two quarters," he said.

"He smart, too. He gonna get out this 'hood and change the game for all of us," Takeah chimed in.

"I have a daughter about your age. What are you playing?"

"*Minecraft.*"

"Oh, I've heard about that game. You can build your own world or something like that. Cool. So what do you want to be when you grow up?"

"I'm going to be an aerospace engineer, making aircrafts," he answered, his eyes back on the game.

"That's great, BJ!" Alena said.

"So, what exactly you here for?" Takeah interrupted.

Alena took a seat next to her and cleared her throat.

"I know this is none of my business and believe me, I'm not trying to be nosy… but, for what it's worth, I just wanted to say that I saw what he did to you. And I'm sorry."

"Oh. You came to tell me that you sorry for me. Ain't that nice of you? Well thanks, Miss Alena, but I don't need no pity, 'specially not yours. And the next time you go spyin' on me, you'd do good to just keep that shit to yourself. Now is there anything else you needed?"

"Takeah, I wasn't trying to spy. I swear. I just wanted to reach out and make sure you were okay. It isn't right. He has no right putting his hands on you like that. I guess I just wanted you to know that you're not alone."

Takeah shook her head and snorted, an irritated look on her face. "Bitch ass nigga, my son's father. He always doin' this shit." She shot Alena a hard, exasperated look.

"You social services or something, Rich Girl? You Oprah?" What you know about my life? No, that shit ain't right, but what the hell else am I gonna do? Put that nigga in jail so my baby don't never see him and I don't never see no money? Who gonna take care of us then? Who gonna be a daddy to my boy? Shit, he barely around as it is. His ass is crazy anyway. He'll just get out and beat me up all over again."

Alena sensed the fear beneath her tough demeanor. Each time movement rustled in the hallway, Takeah cut her eyes anxiously toward the door.

"You're right, I don't know you, and I don't know your life. But I do know what it feels like to be afraid, to be treated like shit by the person you wish would love you. I can tell you this much, you don't have to put up with being hit," Alena said.

"Well, maybe one day I won't. It don't matter much now. I probably won't be seeing him for a while anyway. That's how it goes with Bengy. He put a few dollars in my pocket, find a reason to beat on me and BJ, then he gone for months."

"I hope you won't see him, Tacky. He's no good for you. You don't know me, I don't know you, but for some reason I was led to tell you that. Oh, and I have something for you."

Alena slid a thick gold toned bracelet off her wrist and handed it to Takeah. It had a clamp made of two crystal lion heads. She had no idea what had come over her to make her want to gift it, but she did.

"What this for?"

"It's swag. Rich girl swag. For you."

Takeah furrowed her brows suspiciously, but seeing Alena's sincere look, she smiled and took the gift.

"I'll go now. Again, sorry for barging in." Alena patted Takeah on her shoulder, waved to Benjamin, and headed back up to her own apartment.

Inside, she went to her bathroom to douse her face with cold water and rinse the sweat away. She felt glad, proud even, that she had gone by to check on Takeah. It gave her a warmth in her chest that usually only came from Maya or Gloria.

But as she turned the corner into her living room, she felt a gust of air and saw a black figure scuttle past her. All that warmth from a moment ago was now ice-cold.

"Who's there?" she demanded. She stood motionless.

The old sense of dread filled her again as she tried to fight the nausea rising in her throat. Alena ran to the kitchenette and grabbed a knife, wielding it in her quivering hand as she searched the apartment. Nothing. The front door was still bolted shut, and there was no sign of an intruder. She tried to reassure herself, push away the old fears again. Maybe it was a mouse darting for cover. No, it was too big to deny. This time she knew. She saw it, whatever it was, and there was no mistaking that smell. Alena decided that the best course of action was to leave.

She rushed to Gloria's apartment, pausing at the door to slow her breathing. She'd decided that she wouldn't mention it to Gloria. Gloria came quickly to the door and smiled a greeting. Once inside, Alena saw that she had set out plump tea cakes and chai, seemingly in expectation of her.

"So how are you making out, Alena? I hope you aren't still shutting yourself in when you're not visiting me," Gloria said.

Alena tried hard to put the vision in her apartment out of her mind. She smiled wanly. "Funny you should ask. I just went to visit one of the neighbors today. Takeah."

"Ah yes, Miss Tacky. Sweet girl."

"Are we talking about the same person here?"

"Don't get me wrong, she can be a little sassy. But she really is a sweet young woman. She's got a good heart, that one."

"Well her boyfriend just about knocked her teeth in this morning. I saw it with my own eyes. I don't know what came over me, but I went to her apartment and gave her some encouraging words. It's sad. I just wish these people would get it together, you know? Do better. Her son is so bright! I mean this kid is really smart, Gloria. She needs to get him out of here and give him half a chance not to be a statistic."

"These people?" Gloria asked, her eyes narrowing. She sat her glass down on the table and leaned forward. "Now honey, you know I don't mean any harm, but Lord you sure have some learning and some growing to do yet. Use some of that worldly sense you have and open up your eyes. These people are your people, girl. No matter how different their lives may have been from yours. Alena, be very clear that division is a dark creation that has no place in this community or in this world. Division of the races and division among blacks in particular is a key part of a very sinister master plan, you hear? The haves versus the have-nots, the talented tenth versus all of the 'others.'

Alena crossed her legs and flexed her feet in her high heels. It was all she could do not to run away.

"That silly mess is nothing but a diversion that'll keep all of us bound up no matter where you might think you stand on the totem pole. Any judgement we project is judgment heaped right back onto ourselves. None of us are any better than another, Alena, not one person, not one race." Gloria's words were gentle, yet the truth of them still stung.

"I see," Alena looked away, embarrassed. She felt suddenly foolish and ashamed of her arrogance. Once again, she was on the verge of tears. She hid her shame with another taste of tea and let her eyes wander away from Gloria's, then over the apartment until they rested again on the Black Madonna painting.

In hopes of changing the subject, she said, "I absolutely adore your painting, Gloria," and stared longingly at it. "I don't know what it is; it seems to draw me in every time I see it."

Gloria's expression softened. "And for good reason." She grinned and motioned for Alena to relax. "Get comfortable, honey, I want to tell you just what this painting means."

She eased back into her chair.

"Do you know why Jesus and Mother Mary's skin is painted brown?"

Alena gave Gloria a blank look. "Diversity?"

Gloria smiled and shook her head gently. Then in a calm and measured voice, she spoke. "This image reflects how Mother Mary and Jesus truly appeared in their earthly bodies." She paused and stared at their faces lovingly. "They were of African descent, people of color. It's a well-known yet much hidden fact, but it goes far deeper than that. If you looked in almost every corner of Europe and in the Catholic Church, you would see either the painting or the statue of the Black Madonna. Some say that it's soot or dust darkening her skin, but that's all nonsense that they use to try and cover up a very inconvenient truth. The mother of us all is a black woman, the Great Dark Mother of the Universe."

Engulfed in Gloria's words, Alena forgot her quickly cooling tea on the table.

"The entire human race began on the continent of Africa, born from the womb of a black woman. Within her is the mitochondrial DNA of every race in the human family. This means that every being on earth is a descendant of The Great Dark Mother, our Black Madonna, and she lives in you. It's that truth that keeps drawing you in when you see this painting. It's helping you. You're awakening to who you truly are, remembering yourself, Alena. All the parts of you that have been lost or forgotten are being pulled back into wholeness, now. They are here."

Alena nodded, though she didn't fully understand. She was even ready to dismiss Gloria's words until suddenly she remembered the dream she'd had on her sofa, and the strange, sweet voice telling her that 'they' were 'here.'

"Well I certainly feel…different when I'm around it," Alena said. She decided to probe deeper. "Who or what is here? What are these parts you're talking about, and what is it that I'm supposed to be remembering?"

Gloria smiled her usual patient smile. "In due time. You see this spot here at your forehead, between your eyebrows? That's called your third eye. It's where your soul's vision is. It's your third eye that's leading you to ask new questions, questions you might not have considered before. Unlike your two physical eyes, you can believe what you see here. It is *true* sight. You can start by practicing stillness, Alena. Set your feet steady on the earth, and while you're at it, bring your head along. Close your eyes and concentrate on seeing through your third eye, that's a good start to find what you're looking for."

A few days after her visit to Takeah's, Alena ventured outside of the apartment, this time without the intention of rushing by her neighbors as she usually did. The courtyard was full of tenants noisily reveling in the remnants of the fleeting summer. She spotted Takeah and made her way to her in a few quick steps, still a bit surprised at her urge to reach out. Takeah was sitting on the stoop, drinking a grape soda and eating corn chips with a packet of cigarettes on her lap. Alena sat down beside her.

"Ain't expect you to come out with us common folk," Takeah teased. "Why you out here with us, Rich Girl? Thought you was scared of niggas."

"Very funny," Alena answered with a smirk. "I could use the sun and fresh air, that's all. Clear my mind a little."

Hmmph, Takeah grunted, lighting a cigarette. She took a drag then released it through her pursed pink lips.

"Who watchin' your baby girl? Surprised she ain't out here with you. Even though it ain't like you let her play with the neighborhood kids no way."

Alena tensed and didn't answer.

"Chill. You know I'm just playin' witchu," Takeah said, giving Alena a warm smile.

"She's with my neighbor, Miss Gloria," Alena answered. "They're over there baking a cake, so I've got a little mommy time off."

"That's cool, she in good hands then. We call Gloria 'The Teacher' 'round here. She's always looking out for the kids, letting these young girls know how to be little ladies."

"Yeah. She told me she had a school at one point."

"Oh yeah, that's right. Hey, you wanna know somethin'?" Takeah asked.

"What?"

"So I told Bengy what you said the other day and that I think you was right."

"You told him what exactly?"

"That he ain't got no right to be hitting me and if that's all he offerin' he can walk. I told him I ain't stuck like he think I am. I got friends in high places now," Takeah said, grinning at Alena.

Alena blew out a breath and shook her head. "I didn't mean for you to tell him what I said."

"Hey, it wasn't all *you*," Takeah continued. "I been thinkin' 'bout my situation for a while now. Bengy ain't a good influence on BJ, and my baby BJ is special. You seen him. He smart as hell in school and he love to learn. This country ain't like Guyana. You got the world at your feet if you work like a mule and use your brain.

"I ain't got much to give him, but I'm gonna make sure he get his fair chance. My mama left me with nothin' to hold on to but her tears. She ain't had no green card, no money, no school, no nothin' but my step daddy. He ended up killin' her 'cause she ain't had no choice but to stay with him and take his shit. Well anyway, I ain't her. You reminded me that I ain't my mama. I ain't gotta stay with a no-good man. I ain't leaving my boy to these streets or to his daddy when he come around with all that nonsense."

A proud smile broke across Alena's face.

"No, you don't. You're a beautiful girl with a good head on your shoulders, Tacky."

"Hey BJ, come over here," Takeah yelled to her son. He was perched on an old railing across the street with his friends.

"My baby won an award in that special program of his today," Takeah announced as BJ approached, beaming his gap-toothed grin. "Best science project in his grade. You see what I told you? This boy right here is gonna make it on his brain alone."

Takeah folded a clump of wrinkled bills into BJ's hand. "Go to the corner and get some ice cream from the bodega for you and your friend." He grinned, and the boys took off running for their treats.

"Oh look, here come Big Rome. Good, I need some more oils," Takeah said, nudging Alena.

"Who?" Alena craned her head to see a large black man approaching them. He seemed to be as wide as he was tall and wore all black with strands of braided leather necklaces around his neck. Each necklace had a large green, red and black pendant in the shape of the African continent hanging from it.

"Big Rome, but he like to be called Brotha Rome," Takeah answered under her breath as he came closer. "He a Muslim, one of them New Black Panthers."

Alena glanced at him before he reached them.

"Hotep. Peace, beautiful sistahs. Y'all need some oils? I got that Black Woman, Jamaican Rum Punch, Juicy Couture, the new Coco Chanel. I got everything for y'all, new shipment. I got incense and burners, too. Oh and Sistah Tacky, I got that Money incense you like back in rotation," he said.

"You know it! Let me get that, Brotha Rome. Matter fact, gimme two packs. God knows I could use some cash quick, fast, and in a hurry. I'll take a five dollar vial of that Black Woman, too," Takeah said, handing him a crumpled ten-dollar bill.

"And what about you, Sistah Queen?" he said, turning to Alena. "Anything for today? You look like a Nile Jewel-type classy lady. I got the oil and the incense today, two for five just for you."

"No thanks," Alena gave him and his inventory a look of disdain.

"All right, next time then, Sistah. Enjoy the day, ladies. Stay blessed."

As soon as the man sauntered off to his next customers, Takeah turned to Alena and cut her eyes.

"Ugh. You so uppity, damn! Brotha Rome is cool. Why you actin' like that?"

"It's not that. It's just… this is part of the problem— the oils, the beads, the dashiki, the back-to-Africa necklaces. I know his type, the so-called conscious ones. I bet he doesn't even know the first thing about Africa. People need to start getting behind something that's actually useful. You can't feed your children with all that Pan-African nonsense. Teach them how to fish. Teach them how to get out there in the real cold world and invest, buy low and sell high, own some real assets. Now that's real black power. Green power."

"The *problem*? Yeah, okay." Takeah said and rolled her eyes. She took another long drag of her cigarette, then let it go. "You know what, Rich Girl? You really need to chill the hell out. You soundin' real reckless right about now. You soundin' like one of them, like you a straight up Oreo. Just 'cause you got a baby by one of them don't mean yo' shit don't stink. Shit, they ain't no better than us anyway."

Alena started to feel the same embarrassment she'd felt back at Gloria's.

"Brotha Rome and his people help plenty of these kids out here 'fish' as you sayin'. He even gave li'l BJ some of his product to sell one time when I was low on food and ain't had no back to school clothes. He had our back. They might not be on Wall Street, but they businessmen, and they hustle. They get out here slangin' oils or whatever they got to sell and earn they livin' in a honest way when they could be slangin' drugs. They do what they gotta do. They do they best for the community, which is much more than I can say for them bum-ass, snake-ass whitey bankers that's robbin' everybody blind and gettin' off scot free."

Alena considered what Takeah was saying and realized how she must have sounded. "I'm sorry, Takeah. I take it back, all right? I just got worked for up for nothing I guess."

"*Girl.* You got me heated over here, like for real. You lucky I like you." Takeah took a breath and flicked the ashes from her cigarette onto the concrete. "So what's your deal anyway, huh? I know you ain't from no 'hood like this. Why you here? I tease you with the name, but you really do look like you rich. Shit, you sure act like you rich."

Alena frowned, then looked down at her shoes.

"I'm not rich, far from it. To be honest, you're probably doing better than I am right now. Before I came here, I used to live in the city— a beautiful place on Fifth Avenue. It was lavish, like in the magazines. But now, my husband and I are getting a divorce. It's a long story, but I didn't have the cash to stay, so I moved here." Alena smiled wryly. "I used to have a doorman and a maid, now I barely have enough to pay rent and put food on the table."

Alena expected to hear the same dissociating judgment and pity that she had heaped on Takeah, but when she looked in her eyes, she saw understanding.

"We all been there. Don't nobody plan on doin' bad in life, sometime bad just follow close, you know?" Takeah crushed out her half-smoked Marlboro, dug into her purse, and offered Alena a twenty-dollar bill.

"Takeah, I can't take your money. Thank you though."

"Girl! They ain't teach you no common sense uptown? My mama always told me don't be no fool when you see help comin'. You believe in God don't you?"

"I do. At least I think I do." Alena said.

"Well God come in all ways. God came to me through you, so let me take my turn. Besides, we single mothas gotta stick together." She gave Alena another smile and a light jab, prodding her to take the bill.

Alena took the money and stood up. Her eyes were shining with tears she felt too proud to shed. "Thank you, Takeah."

Before leaving for her apartment, she glanced at Takeah and all of the others she had judged to be an embarrassment to 'good black people' like her. Just like her, they were surviving the best way they knew how. She knew in that moment that she was no different from any of them, and that was one of her biggest fears. They too were brilliant, proud, and beautiful. They too were irreducible.

Alena had prided herself on being a 'different' kind of black woman, but most of all, on not being an *angry* black woman. Her problem was not anger. It was a latent, private fury that made her constantly aware of her dutiful blackness. It reared its head in everyday moments: like when store employees at high-end shops making far less than her would look down their noses or just ignore her completely while she had plenty of money waiting in her designer purse to prove herself a good and fit human. To this, she would say nothing. She'd simply clear her throat loudly and offer up an I-am-harmless smile. It was a part of her armor, too.

Alena thought that she could maneuver herself into what she deemed a safe, proper place in life. But marrying Gabriel thrust her into a world for which she had no template. It wasn't the hiding place she'd hoped for. Although she was poised, brilliant, and beautiful, there was not one day in all eight of their years together that she didn't feel like an impostor.

She jutted out like a lone black fraudulent dahlia in the midst of lily-white lunching ladies with old money who drank like fish while they argued over which were the best nursery schools to set their toddlers on the fast track to Yale. She knew they only spoke to her because they had to, or because they were curious. They were fascinated, really, at how she, with her brown skin and voluptuous curves, had even caught Gabriel Ford's eye, let alone snagged the key to the kingdom.

In the early days, their snide nickname for her was "that Black lady Gabriel married." She had first overheard it at a black-tie fundraiser in the sentence 'Oh no, she's not a nanny; she's that Black lady Gabriel married.' Gabriel immediately brushed it off and suggested she do the same. That night, Alena drank a tray full of champagne, feigned a stomach illness, then went home alone and cried.

Eventually, Alena pretended not to notice racial injustice at all, hers or anyone else's. It was more than she wanted to bear. She decided that it was easier to go on proving her respectability. She just needed to work harder at it, and then she could avoid the pain. If she shut her eyes to enough inconvenient truths like the police shootings, then somehow she'd get immunity from bias and bigotry. But what she saw in Takeah that day, and in all black people that had not 'made it', was a truth that she feared the most— that it didn't matter. They were already all that they needed to be, and it still would not be enough to prove them worthy to an eye that refused to see them.

"A swarm creates enough commotion to achieve one immediate mission: to conceal the beautiful queen as she flies in the midst of them and keep her safe from harm. Yet out of this chaos, order gradually emerges."

SONG OF INCREASE

CHAPTER 7

"Happy birthday to you! Happy birthday to you! Happy birthday, dear Alena! Happy birthday to you!" Michael sang as Alena opened her apartment door to him.

"Ha! You remembered! Thanks Mike." Alena said.

"Of course I remembered, Leen. And these are for you," he said, offering her a bunch of white lilies.

"Very sweet. Thanks Mike."

So what's on your agenda for your special day?"

Alena gave a halfhearted chuckle. "What agenda? I'll probably just grab another bottle of wine from the liquor store and toast myself some more after Maya goes to bed. As you can see, I've already gotten the party started," She gestured to the bottle of half-drunk wine awaiting her on the table top.

"Drinking alone on your birthday, Leen? You know I can't let you go out like that."

"It's just another year, not a big deal."

"Don't forget who you're talking to. I know you, and I know that your birthday is a *very* big deal to you."

"Look, I have no man, no money, and I don't have shit to celebrate. Why would I want to remind myself that on top of all that, I'm just getting older? Besides, you'll be with your wife tonight so what do you care?"

"Damn, Leen. First off, when did you become the Birthday Grinch? And second, that's where you're wrong. Lola and the kids are in Jersey. She's moving in with her parents soon."

"Soon? So you're separating?"

Michael nodded. "Looks that way. We agreed the only hope we've got to work this thing out is to get some space between us."

Tension was brewing in Alena's body. She took a sip from her wine.

"Well you're a good looking, gainfully employed black man. If it doesn't work out, you know you'll find another great woman to marry you in no time. If that's what you want."

Michael laughed. "So it's that easy, huh? And what if those great women aren't checking for a black man? *You* left the brothas alone for your husband, remember?"

"Well the '*brothas*' weren't exactly beating down my door if you recall."

"Please, there were plenty of us checking for you back in school."

"Hardly." Alena said, trying to end it there. She poured more wine into her glass, hoping the growing buzz would take her to a happier, more aloof place. But the pain inside of her wouldn't be subdued. It kept scratching and clawing to be heard, witnessed.

"You don't know what it's like to be a dark-skinned woman out here," she blurted. "I was teased all through school about my color. But women love your dark chocolate looks. You've been a white girl, light-skinned girl magnet since you were in junior high! Just look at Lola. Bright yellow with fine hair, just like every other girlfriend

you've ever had. Maybe if I was a red-bone I'd get some respect, too."
She regretted those last words as soon as they left her mouth.

"What I meant was, the popular, pretty girls, they never looked like me. All I ever heard was, 'You're so pretty for a dark-skinned girl,' or 'If you were only two shades lighter, you'd be so fine." Her eyes started to prick with tears. How had the conversation ended up here so quickly?

Michael searched her face with a crease of worry wrinkling his brow. "Okay, what's really going on?" He leaned forward, eased her wineglass from her hand, and put it on the table. Then he took one of Alena's hands in his own.

She said nothing.

"Leen, I don't get where all of this is coming from. You're acting like you were some hideous beast that no man would touch. Are you crazy? Woman, you are a beautiful, strong, brilliant black woman. You're gorgeous! And your skin tone is one of the most beautiful I've ever seen. You know that. I adore it, and I know for sure most of these men out here do, too." He tried without success to get a smile out of her.

"Right."

"And for the record, my marrying Lola had nothing to do with her complexion," he added.

Alena took another slow sip from her glass.

"I'm sorry. I know I shouldn't have said that, I'm just feeling...off. Very off. I feel like a damn volcano today."

"It's cool, no harm done. Yeah, something definitely is going on with you. This isn't the confident, cool and collected Leen I remember. What's up?"

"All right. Here it is." Alena breathed in and swallowed hard. By the time I met my husband, my self-esteem was almost non-existent. It didn't matter that I was smart, I was still a poor black girl from PG County. Gabe was silver-spoon white, powerful with a powerful family, fine as hell, and he wanted *me*. Shit, he adored me. I felt like Cinderella. I'd been shamed my whole life by my own people for the skin that he loved. I could finally show all those 'brothas' and the world that I was worthy."

Alena sighed and slid her hand out of Michael's. "Gabe was my trophy, and then some. His last name was my protection, his white skin…redeemed me. "

"Didn't expect that. Leen, I never thought you felt that way about yourself. Or about being black. I gotta say, it hurts me to hear it."

"I guess I hid it well," she shrugged. "Then came his parade of whores. The ones he wanted in the first place, his own women. I was just his rebellious streak. Just like that, Gabe turned me back to nothing."

"Okay, come on, don't let this guy or any of that other bullshit get into your head. He might've dogged you out, but that doesn't say anything about you, or have anything to do with you being a fine chocolate woman. And if my memory serves, there were droves of dudes trying to get with you, of every color. How don't you remember any of that?"

"I don't. The question is, what makes me different now? What the hell makes me special? I'm stuck here just like I was back then, the poor quiet nobody black girl."

Michael sighed.

"Why don't you let me take you out tonight? You can bring Maya. Just get a nice change of scenery for your birthday. "

Alena wiped her face and managed a smile.

"You know what? I'll take you up on that. You always did know how to cheer me up."

"It would be my pleasure. So I'll pick you up at seven then?"

"Yes, seven's good."

That evening at the restaurant, Alena watched the smiling lovers surrounding her and Michael, and longed to be one of them. The sommelier brought a bottle of aged Merlot to the table and poured them each a glass.

"Your favorite, right?" Michael said, smiling. "Thirty-three sure looks good on you, Leen."

"Why, thank you," she answered with a smile, trying to perk up for the occasion. "Not too shabby for an old lady, huh?"

"Stop that. You are ab-so-lutely gorgeous." He looked adoringly at her. "You always will be."

"Thank you for this, Mike," she said, her eyes darting around the opulent décor of the restaurant. "It was very kind of you to do this." Alena smiled nervously.

"What are you talking about? Of course. You're my friend. I'm glad I could make you smile on your birthday."

"So I mean to ask you, who'd you get to watch Maya?"

"My next-door neighbor is watching her."

Michael looked surprised. "A neighbor? I didn't expect you to trust anyone over there, let alone trust them with Maya. Things must be going pretty well."

"Gloria's good people. Great people, actually. I do trust her, absolutely. She's good with Maya and she's got grandchildren of her own and all of that. To tell you the truth, I don't know where I'd be without her. She's been more of a mother to me in these few weeks than my own mother has. Besides, I sure can't afford a real babysitter, and I don't have any family to watch her. I would've kept her myself, but tonight was urgent. I needed to get out of that apartment, bad. I needed to put this dress on. I needed to feel like an adult woman again."

"Well, you are most definitely all woman; you don't ever have to worry about that." He shot her a sexy smile, and Alena basked in his adoration.

"Leen, can I ask you a question?"

"Hmm, is it question time already?" she teased. "Yeah, sure Mike, go ahead."

"Why don't you call your family? At least your mother?"

"And say what? 'Hi Mama, this is the daughter you haven't spoken to in years and practically disowned. How's life and oh, by the way, can you spot me a little cash?' No. My mother's made it very clear how she feels about what happened and where her loyalties lie. She chose him. They all did."

"Leen, I get it, you know I do. And I'm so sorry for everything you went through. But the truth is that you need help. I know your dad is completely off limits, but can you at least try to let your mother back in? A little? You need your family, if not for yourself then for your daughter."

"It's not an option, Mike," Alena said sternly. "Can we drop it please?"

"Cool." He sat back in his chair. "Fine by me."

Alena let out a long sigh. "I know you're trying to help, but it's hard. It's complicated. You could never understand what it was like, or how it still feels. Trust me, even in this mess that me and Maya are in, we're still probably better off without her help, or any of theirs, for that matter."

"You don't have to explain yourself, Alena. You've been through a lot. I just want you to be okay."

"I know you do, Mike. Thank you." Alena listened to the Opera music playing overhead in silence for a moment. Then she looked at Mike. "You know, Gloria's always talking about God. Where the hell is He when you need Him? I know this is supposed to be my road, or my journey or whatever, but I'm getting tired of waiting on Him to stop turning a blind eye to my pain."

"You have to be strong, Leen. It'll all change for you. I know it will."

"I'm glad you're so confident."

"I am. This is all happening for a good reason, you'll see."

"I know I must sound like a whiny brat but, on top of all this, sometimes I really think I might be losing it. Something strange is happening." Alena looked around and then lowered her voice. "Look, don't think I'm crazy, okay?"

"I already *know* you're crazy, Leen." Alena swatted Mike across the table.

"Kidding! Just jokes! Go on."

"This is serious, Mike. I've been seeing these…" She searched for the right words, "Shadows… slinking around me. Kind of like… shadow people. At first, I thought I was imagining things, but the other day I saw one again. I know I did. I checked the apartment, but I didn't find anything. What do you think?"

She glanced up at him, bracing herself for the worst.

Michael chose his words carefully. "Well, I think anything is possible. But I also think you have a lot going on right now. You're under a lot of stress, Leen. You probably just need some rest."

"Yeah, you're probably right," Alena said, her eyes fixed on the pink lipstick stain on her wineglass. "Rest."

"Hey, come on, it's your birthday. We're here to celebrate! Let's make a toast," he said, raising his glass of wine. "Here's to you—the gorgeous, the brilliant, Miss Alena Ford. I know that things aren't exactly going as you planned right now, so here's to a life even better than what you planned."

"Cheers! Now I'll drink to that!" she said. They clinked glasses and sipped their wine, watching each other over the candlelight on the table.

After dinner, Michael drove Alena home and then walked her to the stoop her apartment. At the door, he folded two crisp hundred-dollar bills into her hand.

"Happy birthday," he whispered in her ear.

Alena looked down at the money, and her eyes welled with grateful tears. In that moment, she wasn't sure if it was the alcohol diluting her good sense, or if she was drunk with awakening desire, but she pressed her mouth against the warm softness of Michael's full lips.

Parting hers, she let her tongue slide gently over them, tantalizing him. She felt him harden against her. His hands rested in the groove between her waist and hips, eager fingers pulling her closer.

"Why don't you come upstairs for a little bit?" she purred. "I think I have a few more minutes before I turn into a pumpkin."

She let her palms slide over the solid curve of his chest and kissed him again. His skin was warm beneath his cotton shirt. She heard him swallow hard.

"Leen, I can't." He dropped his arms and took a half-step back. Alena frowned.

"Why? Do you still love her, Mike?"

He was silent as he looked everywhere but at her.

"Why can't you love me? Just for tonight, love *me*."

As usual, she regretted the words as soon as she uttered them. The shame of her desperation sobered her and she spread her palm over her face.

"Oh my God, I am so, so sorry, Mike. I'm so embarrassed. I shouldn't have kissed you. I just…Ugh. I'm messed up right now. I don't know what's going on with me."

"It's okay. Really, it's okay. Don't stress it," he soothed.

"No, I crossed the line. If you want to take another break from me, I understand. I didn't mean to disrespect your wife or you or your kids. I guess I'm just feeling lonely."

"I liked it, Alena."

Michael held Alena's face in his hand, his thumb grazing her cheekbone. The glow of the street lamp softly lit his face.

"Yes. I still love Lola." He kissed her forehead softly. "And I love you, too." He planted a kiss on her cheek. "I should get going. I hope you had a good birthday. Kiss Maya for me, okay Leen?"

Alena watched him walk to his car and waited for it to drive slowly away. Her mind raced, trying to piece together what had just happened. She was sure that underneath her brown skin her face was red with shame.

She closed her eyes and pressed her forehead against the cold steel of the apartment door.

What the hell just happened? Why did I kiss him? Wine, I need more wine. I need to forget every bit of this. She looked at her phone. 10:47 PM. Still a few minutes to buy a birthday bottle to enjoy while Maya slept. She headed for the liquor store at the end of the block.

Alena felt an eerie stillness in the sweltering heat of the night as a male figure walked toward her. For a fleeting moment, she recognized the jagged scar above his brow. It was Bengy, Takeah's boyfriend. Their eyes met. He glared at her as he bumped straight into her, using his two hundred and five pounds to push her into the alley a few feet away.

"So you wanna get all in my fucking business, bitch? You tell my girl to leave me?" he demanded.

"Oh God, please just let me go," Alena begged. She felt it coming.

Bengy pulled a gun from underneath his sweatshirt and shoved the muzzle into her temple.

"Gimme your shit, bitch! Gimme your fucking money! You gon' learn not to stick your fucking nose in my business."

Alena plunged a quivering hand into her bag and fished wildly for the bills Michael had given her. In her panic, she couldn't find where she had stuffed them.

"Oh you wanna play games?" He yelled, and then he punched her in the stomach with all of his force.

Alena's breath went out of her, and she doubled over. He struck her again, this time against her head with the butt of the gun. Warm blood drizzled down her face, staining her white dress. She collapsed onto the concrete. Blackness blotted her vision as she slipped out of consciousness.

"Alena," a woman's voice whispered gently from above her. It was sweet and faint. A peace that she had never known before enveloped her.

"Alena," the voice repeated, almost singing.

Something about the voice was deeply familiar to Alena. It nourished every cell of her body. Effervescent joy bubbled through her and she felt lighter than a feather. Actually what she felt was the unmistakable presence of pure, unconditional love.

Gradually, she opened her eyes. A sunburst of glorious golden light now filled the once dark alley. A beautiful woman stood smiling calmly at the center of it, a sphere of light surrounding her. Her rich ebony skin glittered as if it were imbued with gold.

A crown of light encircled her head. The extraordinary garment she wore was like nothing Alena had ever seen before. It was made of spun diamonds and pulsated with such radiance that it appeared to have a life of its own. The intoxicating beauty of the woman sent Alena into an even deeper trance.

All awareness of her body left her, and she felt weightless now, as if she were floating in air. The woman rested her light filled palm on Alena's head, covering her wound. Alena had almost forgotten she was hurt. As the woman gently pressed, a sensation like warm wax poured in through Alena's temple, down her vertebrae, and dripped through every cell of her body. She smiled blissfully.

"We have been waiting for you to awaken," the woman said. "You are finally able to see us, Dear One."

Bound in deep enchantment, Alena didn't even try to comprehend her words.

"I must leave you now, but know that all is well. I will return to you soon."

"Who are you?" Alena managed.

The woman smiled. "I am Mary. Mary of Magdalene." It was the name she'd heard in her dream, but Alena still didn't know what it meant. Then in a flash, the woman was gone, and Alena woke to red and blue lights flashing against the alley walls and paramedics running toward her.

"The song of the maiden tells the bees what they will do once they are born; the song of the drone tells them why they will do that. The wise drones are the only bees who sing the Song of Ancestral Knowledge. They carry the genetic line of the hive's queen."

SONG OF INCREASE

CHAPTER 8

Alena woke up in a hospital bed in Brooklyn. The room was a groggy swirl of sterile white walls and beeping machines. "Well good morning, Mrs. Ford," the nurse chimed.

"Where am I?" Alena tried to remember what happened.

"You're at Methodist, ma'am, been here for two days. You were hit pretty hard on the head but you're very lucky—no fractures or brain damage."

Wide-eyed, Alena touched the bandage on her head. A sharp pain sliced her above the ear. Another surge of pain pounded under her rib cage. She looked down. Needles were stuck in her arm, and a clunky apparatus towered over her bed.

"Here, take these. You'll need them." The nurse handed her a tiny paper cup with two white pills inside. "You're going to be just

67

fine. In fact, you may even be discharged tomorrow. They're calling you a miracle around here," she said, giving Alena a smile. "Dr. Brent will be in shortly to discuss everything with you. And once he's finished, there's a police detective who's been waiting to speak with you. Your husband was here, but he had to leave on business, he said. Your friend will probably be taking you home," the nurse finished. A sudden chill shot up Alena's spine.

"Husband? But my husband and I…" She tried to sit up, but the pain pulsing in her head urged her back down onto the bed. "Oh my God, Maya! My baby! Where's my baby?"

Gloria walked to the bed and stroked her hand.

"Easy, honey. Easy. He took Maya with him, Alena."

"Gloria! How could you let him take her?" Alena wailed.

"He's her father, Alena. There was no way for me to stop him."

"No! Oh God!"

"Calm down, Alena, please. Look around, honey. You're in the hospital. You've been hurt. How on earth do you expect to care for Maya in this condition? You're safe and Maya is safe. It's better this way for now, and it's just until you get back on your feet. Everything will work out, you'll see. Maya will be right back with you as soon as you get well."

"Gloria you don't know Gabriel! This is just what he needs to—"

"It's okay, everything will be right as rain, you'll see. Let's get you home so you can heal, and when Maya comes back, you'll be strong again." There was a knowing promise in Gloria's voice as she gave Alena a reassuring nod. Alena bit back a cry and forced a deep breath, remembering the woman in the alley and her words. Her panic melted.

"Okay. You're right. I'll get myself together and Maya will be right back with me."

Once the hospital released Alena, she took a taxi back to the apartment with Gloria. There was a large package waiting for her when they returned, leaned up against her door.

"What's this?" she asked aloud. "I didn't order anything." Gloria grinned and shrugged.

"Hmm, well open it and see."

She helped Alena take the package inside where they unwrapped it carefully. It was the Black Madonna painting.

"What! Oh Gloria, you shouldn't have! I can't take this away from you."

"Yes, you can. You must. I want you to have it. She's yours now, my dear. Enjoy her as much as I have."

Alena hugged Gloria tightly, grateful for whatever miracle had brought the woman into her life. "Thank you so much, Gloria. You don't know what this… what you… have meant to me."

"Oh that's what I'm here for, honey. It's my pleasure. You're like one of my own girls." She smiled and gently squeezed Alena's hand. "I'll let you get settled in, and then I'll check on you in a bit, okay? Do you need anything?"

"I'm all set. I'll be just fine. Thanks again." She smiled as Gloria turned to her apartment.

Just minutes after the door closed, the phone rang.

"Hi Mom! Are you okay?" Maya chirped. Her voice was high and anxious.

"I'm all better now, baby, just getting in the door. Oh my sweet, sweet baby, I miss you. How are you?"

"I'm fine, Mom. I miss you, too! *Sooo* much. Dad said you got a bump on your head. I was so scared, but he said you were okay, just resting."

Alena bit her lip to keep from blurting out what she really wanted to say, which was '*Oh that's funny because I haven't even heard from your father. He didn't have the decency to wait around long enough to make sure I was really okay.*'

"Yes, baby, that's right," she said. "Mommy is all better and ready to see her Maya Bear!"

"Oh Mom and guess what? Oh wait, Miss Brittany wants to talk to you."

"Brittany?" Alena said. She could hear Maya passing the phone.

"Hello, Alena?"

Her tone already held a tinge of condescension. Alena said nothing in reply.

"Hi there. Well I just wanted to say that I hope you get well soon. It really is dangerous out there in those ghettos, I hear."

"You listen to me, Brittany. Don't you ever, and I mean *ever*, interrupt my daughter when she's speaking to me. You don't matter. You're just another one of my husband's women, one of many, I'm sure."

"Ex-husband," Brittany hissed. "Well, I was just trying to be nice, Alena, but I guess I shouldn't have bothered."

"Keep your hands away from my child and put her back on the phone *now!*"

"Mom?" Alena heard the pained confusion in Maya's voice. "Yes, baby. I'm here. Listen to me, okay? No matter what happens, *I* am your mother and I love you... I'm coming to get you. You don't have to listen to anyone but me."

"And Dad?"

Alena sighed and rolled her eyes.

"Yes. And your father. If that woman so much as lays a finger on you or is mean to you in any way, you call me, okay?"

"Yes, Mommy."

"Put your dad on the phone, baby. Listen to me, Maya. Things will get better soon. I love you so very much. Always remember that."

"I love you, too, Mommy. Hold on please."

"Yes, Alena," Gabriel answered tersely.

"What the hell was that? That's how you're playing it now? What the hell did I ever do to you to make you hate me this much? I'm barely out of the hospital and you put your cheap whore on the phone? For what? I thought you would at least have some decency left. Keep that filthy bitch away from Maya. I want my daughter back immediately, and I'm coming to get her."

"To do what? To bring her back to that crime-ridden rat hole you call an apartment? Not happening. My lawyer filed for an emergency custody hearing. I'm sure you'll hear from the court soon.

You want Maya? Prove that you can provide a better home than I can and stop being such an irresponsible mother."

"She's all I have, Gabriel! How can you do this to me after everything you've put me through already?"

"Alena, look. I'm not heartless. I just want what's best for Maya, and clearly that's not you right now. Don't worry, you'll get visitation."

"Fuck you, Gabe!" she yelled. The phone clicked as Gabriel hung up. Alena hurled it across the room and then dropped to her knees, cradling them to her chest. "Where are you, God?" she cried out. "If you exist, then show yourself for once! If you're real, then do something! Do *something*, God! Tell me what I'm supposed to do, and I'll do whatever you ask. Anything! Please. Don't leave me alone in this horrible silence."

Several minutes later, Alena finally collected herself and dried her tears. Her head ached, and she was exhausted. The next best thing she could think of was to go to Gloria's, so she did. As Alena stood at Gloria's door about to knock, Gloria opened it.

"How did you know I was coming?"

Gloria gave her a warm grin. "Well, it's about time that you know." "Time I know what?"

Gloria opened the door wider and gestured for Alena to come in. "Come in, honey. Are you hungry?"

"Famished. But I couldn't eat a thing if I tried." She looked at Gloria despondently. "Gloria, Gabe's trying to take Maya away from me just like I told you," she sniffled. "I don't think I can take anymore. I really don't."

Gloria squeezed her shoulder and motioned for her to take a seat on the crimson sofa. She went to the kitchenette and returned with a plate of cheese and crackers. After placing it on the table, she sat next to Alena and paused briefly before speaking.

"I was born with a veil, the doctors call it a caul. My people down south call it 'the gift of vision.' It means I can see things before they happen sometimes. My mother had the vision also, and her mama before her, my Grandma Olivia."

"Oh great, so you're psychic," Alena said dryly, half as an accusation. "That's wonderful. Then you'll definitely be able to tell me what's going on with my life right now."

Gloria nodded. "Yes, I can," she said matter-of-factly.

Alena rolled her eyes. "No offense, Gloria, but I should've told you, I'm not into all this voodoo hoodoo, airy fairy stuff. I'm a Christian."

"Ha! What do you know about Voodoo? And what, pray tell, do you think you know about Christianity?" Gloria asked, her tone turning serious.

"I know enough not to tinker with psychics or third eyes or any other kind of that New Age mess. I'm going back to my apartment. I'll sort out my disaster of a life myself."

Gloria raised her hand, halting her.

"When she came to you, was she wearing this?" Gloria held up the deep purple stone necklace she wore.

Stunned, Alena rocked back on her heels and almost fell back onto the sofa.

"How did you know about what I saw that night?" Gloria was silent. Alena closed her eyes and strained to concentrate. She thought back to the vision of the woman. The fine short hairs on the back of her neck bristled as she remembered. "Yes! Yes, she was!" Fear gripped her. "What's happening to me, Gloria? What does all of this mean?"

Gloria unclasped her necklace. "Give me your hand," she ordered. She placed the necklace into Alena's palm and closed her fingers over it. "Hold it. What do you feel?"

She felt its power instantly. A great wave of energy raced through her hand and up the length of her arm. The stone was vibrating so powerfully that it slipped from her grasp. Alena dropped the necklace.

"What is this? What the hell is going on, Gloria?" she yelped.

"This amulet marks a High Priestess of the Tribe of Isis," Gloria said, picking up the necklace.

"A tribe of what? You told me your husband gave you that necklace!"

"Forgive me. I had to be sure that it was truly you. To be wrong would put everything and everyone in peril.

Gloria gazed at Alena intently.

"Alena, what I have to tell you may sound quite strange, but I assure you it is very real. It is more real than anything you have ever experienced in this lifetime. You must listen closely and take heed of my words. Do you understand?"

"Okay," Alena nodded slowly as Gloria settled back into her chair.

"We, Alena, you and I, are Bridgers. We are the human bridges sent to connect the holy realm of spirit to this third dimensional planet Earth. This amulet is bestowed to an initiated Bridger from the ancient Tribe of Isis, the Greek's renaming of our beloved mother, Auset. Auset is her name in our original tongue. The amulet's stone is a spirit crystal, a powerful generator of energy from that holy realm, cut from the Crystal of Isis itself. It amplifies the power of its wearer and can help protect her against a psychic attack, as long as she remains pure of heart."

Gloria paused, leaned back in the sofa, and closed her eyes before continuing. Alena sat with her clasped hands resting against her thighs, eyes round and wide as she took in Gloria's words carefully.

"There are factions of us Bridgers all over the world and within each of us, there is a code, a set of Heavenly instructions from the Black Madonna Herself. The Black Madonna isn't just some painting concept, Alena. She is the universal Great Dark Mother, the feminine aspect of God. She's been missing from earth for many years and we're here to bring her back. These instructions we hold are healing codes for all of humanity, codes the earth is in dire need of."

Gloria stretched open Alena's palm and traced her finger down the middle, over the dark brown crease in it.

"Honey, you have come from a legacy of Bridgers. It is your supreme destiny. All of your pain from this and from many lifetimes you have had before this one has helped you to awaken and steady your feet on this road, Alena."

Gloria peered at Alena intensely, whose lips remained parted in shock.

"To release the codes that you've been given, you must do what you have agreed to do. It was an agreement that I'm sure you don't consciously remember, yet. But I assure you, what you have come to do has been ordained by God thousands, if not millions, of years ago. You are reaching the completion of a spiritual mission that began for you at the dawn of time. Alena, you've come a very long way and worked for many, many lifetimes for such a time as this. Through the Sirius star, ancient Egypt, Kemet, the land of the Dogon, the Yoruba lands and now across the waters to the Americas you have come as the beautiful young woman I see before me."

Alena took another glance at Gloria's necklace, closed her eyes, and contemplated the truth in Gloria's words.

"Alena, this a great, great honor. We are the mothers of freedom, the keepers of truth. We are the keys that the world has been waiting for." Gloria's expression then darkened.

"But, I must tell you that this sacred path does come with a heavy price. Alena, you are in grave danger," Gloria said.

"Danger?" Alena sat up.

"Yes. Your daughter is protected, for now. It's you they want the most."

Alena felt a flutter of panic strangle her breath.

"And who are *they?*"

"The Dark Ones. The Shetani. They're here. I can smell them on your heels."

Smell!

"The shadow people," Alena whispered, recognition filling her thoughts. Finally, someone understood. She could always smell dark spirits right before seeing them. It was an ability her mother told her to forget about and never speak of, and so she'd shut it off completely. But in that moment, Alena knew without a doubt, they had been haunting her throughout her whole life.

"Yes," Gloria said gravely. "The Shetani are the origin of all evil in the Universe. It was the Shetani who created the Fallen Ones, the dark angels. Their creations birthed evil and chaos on the earth. Their mission now is the same as it ever was from the beginning of time— to destroy humanity and to destroy all members of the Tribe before we can fulfill the Divine Plan.

"What divine plan?"

"Let me explain. The Shetani despise human life. They thrive on our darkness of any kind—our hatred, envy, and our insistence on separation from one another. Well, they are getting quite close to finally destroying us once and for all."

Alena leaned forward with a horrified look on her face.

"Every forty-nine years, the level of mass violence on the earth has become increasingly more intense. More wars, more murders, more intolerance, more hatred, you see? It is a dark cycle that the Shetani have always manipulated humanity to continue." Her eyes were gleaming with truth.

"Our violence against each other and against the earth has intensified to such a degree that humanity has finally come to a grim tipping point. A great door in the cosmos will open very soon, opening to only two possible fates. If the Light prevails and we stop the Shetani, then the doors of the cosmos will open to a New Heaven, and we will bring in the New Earth. This is the Divine Plan.

"If the Shetani are not stopped, then the final wave of mass human violence will initiate the beginning of a Dark Age. It will be a treacherous time, one that humanity has not suffered since the Great Flood. If the Shetani gain entry through those doors, the great Cosmic Door... then Hell will be loosed on earth." Alena adjusted herself on the sofa with deepening dread, trying to imagine the end of the world. Gloria continued, the gravity of her words adding a sadness to her voice.

"The Tribe of Isis is a living defense against the Shetani and their plans. The only way we will survive is for each priestess to claim her rightful place and fulfill her own divine mission. It is not an easy feat. Those vicious minions will try anything to suppress us. They force

75

us into poverty, hurt us, and—the worst—either hurt or work to infect those we love to do their will."

"Like my husband, Gabriel?"

"Yes, it is quite possible that they are working through him. The Shetani took my Adeyini trying to scare me away from the Plan." Gloria paused, and there was silence as emotion welled in her. She breathed deeply and then she spoke again.

"Fear not, Alena," she said, her voice now holding only traces of grief. "I've come to help you. This is my assignment at this time. You will also have divine help, from the Beings of Light. The Beings of Light are beings of the heavenly realm that give us strength and wisdom. If you accept their call to initiate into the Tribe, and that of the Great Mother, then you will not only save yours and your daughter's life, but all of humanity.

"Time is dwindling. On the night of the Spring Equinox, the planets will align into something called the Grand Cross of Initiation. This formation will mark the convergence point in the sky at which the doors to the New Heaven will open once again—the Cosmic Door. It is this door that will change everything."

A knot of fear was forming in Alena's throat, and she wrung her hands together.

"The Beings of Light are sending forth seven holy powers to help redeem us and seal the doors to darkness. Yet, because of the Law of Free Will, the divine realm cannot interfere directly. A human vessel must receive the holy powers and voluntarily anchor them into the earth—seven powers from the Great Dark Mother, and seven powers from the Great Dark Father.

"Humanity was freely gifted these powers long ago, but in our disobedience, we abandoned them and so they became lost to us. The reinstatement of these powers will give us mastery over this material world and all of its darkness, the Shetani."

Gloria took Alena's perspiring hand.

"Alena, the Great Dark Mother has chosen you to anchor Her powers, the force of the Divine Feminine. During your initiation, a Being of Light will unveil a key learning for you, and with it, a power that will assist you and humanity in overcoming the Shetani. Restore your connection to Her. If you are diligent in your journey, they will be yours to receive.

"Among our Tribe is a great Oracle, the one who will set the final order once we Bridgers have all completed our missions. There is much for you to learn. For now, you rest and wait. The Beings of Light will surely let you know what your next step is, so listen for them. I know that this is a lot to hear, but you do believe what I've told you, don't you?"

"I do." Alena nodded numbly.

"So, what do you say to it all?"

Alena paused for a moment. "I'm scared. Why me, Gloria? I'm a complete mess, probably the most unholy person I know. These Beings of Light, are you sure it's me they want? And what if the Shetani try to hurt me, or Maya?"

"As I said, do not be afraid. The Shetani can only harm you if you are not pure of heart. Otherwise, they are nothing. Your emotions and beliefs are the only things that can give them power. The danger is real, but you are greater than even it is. You're purposed for this. Alena, the only question you need to answer is this: are you willing to follow your great destiny?"

Alena thought about Maya, and what her safety meant to her. It meant everything.

"Yes. I am," she answered. Her words sounded strong even though she was trembling inside.

That evening, Alena sat in her living room for what seemed like hours trying to process what Gloria had told her. Though it didn't make any sense, she knew it was all completely true. She felt it. Right before she finally decided to go to bed and sleep on it, she heard a voice call her name. Alena started to breathe heavily. Whoever it was called in the same sweet voice from the night of her birthday, soft and mystical. She looked around the room. Nothing. The voice called her name again. It seemed to be coming from the corner of her living room where she'd propped up the Black Madonna painting.

She stood up and walked slowly towards it. The voice grew louder and clearer with each step. When Alena stopped in front of the painting, the voice spoke again, this time sounding as if someone was standing right in front of her.

"Alena, close your eyes and see from within. Breathe deeply. Allow your heart to open. Come to me, Dear One. Touch me," it said.

The urge to obey lulled her into trance and her weightless body felt as if it wasn't her own, as if it were adrift on a rhythmic sea. Alena reached her fingertips to Mother Mary's brown painted face. In the instant that she touched the canvas, it trembled and gave way to an opening of sparkling light. The room filled with brilliance. In that breathless moment, she was pulled through the swirling vortex of light, squeezed between two worlds and then transported to another realm.

In the next instant, she was standing at an enormous gilded door encrusted with glittering emeralds, rubies, and sapphires. Alena gasped as she beheld the magnificent vision. Before her, Mary Magdalene appeared in all her glory.

"It's you!" Alena beamed, her face lighting up with joy. "You came back for me!"

"It is you who has returned to us. Welcome, Dear One," Mary said, smiling warmly.

The huge door swung open at their approach. Beyond it awaited a dismal and decaying palace, despite its splendid entrance. Alena cringed. There was barely enough light to make out its crumbling columns and floors, or its massive soaring gray walls shrouded in cobwebs. Mary turned to Alena who peered back at her with questioning eyes.

"You must trust," she said, already sensing Alena's fear. She held Alena's hand in hers and led her through the opening. "Let us explore, shall we?" The love and mercy that Alena felt emanating from Mary gave her the courage to step into the grim unknown world.

"Where are we? What is this place?" Alena asked, her anxious voice echoing off the vast emptiness inside.

"This is your divine Queendom. My Dear One, we are inside of your heart."

"The sun's light reaches into the queen bee, initiating a process that unlocks and vitalizes."

SONG OF INCREASE

CHAPTER 9

Alena struggled to grasp what Mary had just told her. "We're inside my heart?" she asked in amazement.

"Yes. This is your heart, and this is where the first lesson of your initiation begins."

"But—" Alena began to mutter.

"You will understand more clearly as we proceed," Mary assured her before she could continue. "Let us walk further."

Alena decided that it would be wise to follow Mary's lead in silence. Her stride was graceful and majestic as they went on, over the filthy stone floors and through the immense breadth of Alena's heart. Alena wondered how a being as glorious and pure as Mary Magdalene could stand a place like this one.

As they walked, Alena saw that the dark palace was a labyrinth of great halls and staircases that opened up to five separate grand chambers. They were nearing the first chamber when suddenly Mary halted in her tracks.

"Careful!" she warned. They came upon a crevasse in the surface of the floor. Embedded into it was a hardened, brownish-gray substance that had corroded into the stone. Mary helped Alena jump over it.

"Dear One, do you see here?" Mary said pointing to the brown matter embedded into the fissure. "Old hurt you have refused to recognize. This is the decay of false promises, those made to you and those you have made to yourself."

Alena could only nod as Mary motioned for them to continue. As they walked, the light grew even dimmer until the hall they were traveling became almost completely dark. Alena advanced cautiously and reached her hand out toward the wall for guidance. An acrid smelling sludge oozed down the stone walls. It glowed a sickening yellow-green in the wan light. She drew her hand back in disgust. Her stomach began knotting as a telltale stench snaked into her nose. The Shetani. Alena shot Mary a pleading glance. She again sensed her trepidation, yet nodded at her to forge ahead despite it.

With every step into the darkness, Alena knew there was no going back. She swallowed and pushed on, spreading her hand across her chest to press down against her terror. In the distance, growls and snarls sounded from the shadows. Something was approaching. The sounds drew closer and closer, and the ground rumbled. The rising odor made her want to vomit.

The hall opened into a hollow stone clearing. As soon as they stepped into its dim light, a tremendous beast vaulted at her. Its slimy skin was the color of soot, and it hissed like a viper. It was so close to Alena that she could feel its hot breath sweeping over her face.

"Heel! Get thee behind us!" Mary commanded the beast. Mary's voice thundered and echoed, no longer holding the sweetness it had minutes before. The beast's lips peeled back, baring a row of dagger-sharp fangs and snarled at Alena. A second beast darted at her, its bulging eyes glowing red.

"Demons, heel in the name of Christ!" Mary commanded once more. The power of her words sheared through the darkness, and the beasts relented and fled. Alena crumbled onto the cold floor, her chest heaving. Tremors of icy terror wracked her body as she screamed.

"Peace," Mary said to her calmly. "Peace be still, Dear One. You are safe. You must remember your words hold power. The beasts must submit to your belief in the light."

"Why? Why did you lead me here if you knew I'd be killed?" Alena cried breathlessly. Mary only smiled and helped her to her feet.

"Dear One, those beasts cannot kill you unless you give into them." Mary placed a hand on Alena's shoulder. "That was Heaviness and Rage, two of many demon servants to the Shetani."

"How did they get into my heart? Who put them here?"

"My dear, it was you who allowed them entry. You let them in with your own rage, bitterness, and self-loathing."

Alena's brows furrowed. "I don't understand."

"Come and see."

Unbeknownst to Alena, they had finally reached the door of the first chamber. Mary approached the door, and it burst open for them to an enchanting sight. The bright chamber held a massive emerald table flanked by seven golden sconces, each about four feet in height, with violet colored fires roaring atop them.

"Alena, your heart is your power source. Your heart also gives either permission or denial to the realm of darkness. It is the doorway between heaven and earth, where the spirit realm and the physical world meet. It is an epicenter of infinite divine power and gives you the ability to create any and everything. This is the Power of the Heart."

Mary placed a hand over Alena's still thumping chest. "Creation is manifested with belief and feeling. In the grand design of the human heart, your emotions are the rulers. They are the doorways that either shield and fortify your heart or give beasts of darkness, such as those, the right to invade it. This is the Law of Free Will that the Divine has granted man. Do you understand?"

Unable to speak, Alena nodded.

"The beasts of the Shetani have no power in or of themselves; however, emotions like bitterness, guilt, shame, resentment, anger, and fear open up heart wounds. They give these demon servants authority to infiltrate your heart, what we call your Queendom. The door that we entered your heart through today was an open wound, a breech in your heart that remains because you have not yet healed. You have not yet forgiven. Dark emotions are the Shetani's food."

Alena looked down at her hands. They were still trembling. "How do I get rid of them? Alena asked.

"That is what I have come to teach you. First, we will look at the walls of your heart, Alena. Tell me what it is you see."

Mary raised her hand to one of the enormous stone walls, and at her gesture, it shone like fine crystal. Alena recognized her own face in its reflection. Her life was playing like a movie upon the walls, memory by memory.

In the first frame, Alena saw herself being born.

"My God, that's me!" she clapped her hand over her mouth.

"Wow, I was so tiny. Three weeks early. My mother always loved to tell me how I had no patience from day one.

"And there's Mama. God she looks so young. Pretty." Alena pursed her lips and let out a heavy sigh.

"They'd tried to get to the hospital, but I wouldn't stop pushing through. I came out so fast that there was barely enough time to call the ambulance. Mama ended up giving birth right there in the house. My father had to deliver me. The ambulance showed up just as he was cutting the cord." She smiled nostalgically as a tear slid down her face.

"And there he is." She stood silent for a short while after her father's face entered the scene. "He looks so happy here, so…nice. No one would ever believe that there was something so broken in him," Alena sighed again.

Another scene flashed on the wall. Alena's four-year-old self sat on her father's lap.

"Me and Daddy." A grimace formed on her face. "Like always, or at least in those early days, I was trying to impress him. Here I'm trying to convince him that I know Spanish." Alena gave an empty chuckle.

"Uno, Dos, Three-cka, Four-cka. Thought it would make me special and smart. Back then, I would say and do about anything to make him proud of me, no matter how afraid I was of that man."

The next frame appeared on the wall.

Alena stood in silence for a while again, her lips quivering as tears tumbled over them.

"I'm seven here." She gritted her teeth. "Just seven damn years old. That's my favorite dress I have on. I'd put on my favorite dress for him." Alena bit her lip. Her hands knotted into fists.

"He'd come into my room after everyone went to sleep. Drunk, but smiling, being so nice to me. He told me to get dressed real pretty and meet him downstairs in the little room by the kitchen. He had a secret surprise just for me, he said." Alena swallowed hard. "I was so excited. I felt like finally, just maybe, my daddy did love me after all." She shook her head angrily and cupped her hand over her eyes. *This is too much for me.* "No! I can't do this. Stop it. Please, stop the wall, Mary."

Mary waved a hand and the scene quickly changed on the wall.

"I know it is difficult, Dear One, but there is a reason for all of this. Please, take courage and finish telling me your story. Release it completely."

After several long moments Alena finally continued.

"The thing I remember the most was that smell on him. He smelled like *them*, the Shetani. After it happened that first time, that's when I started to see them. I lost my voice, too. Literally at first. I could barely speak, not to anyone, for almost a month. And then, it happened again. And again. By then, I didn't even have the voice to talk to God anymore." Alena lowered her eyes.

"Daddy told me that what 'we' had done was our secret. He said that if I told, if he didn't kill me first, then folks would call me a 'dirty girl'. He would keep asking me if I wanted to be that girl. He said I would ruin everyone's life and we would both go to Hell. It took me years to tell Mama, and then my little sister Syreeta. I only told because I would die, anyway, if I didn't."

"All is well now, Dear One. I assure you that you have always been under our protection and most certainly, our love."

Alena felt a burst of anger, and her eyes darted from the scene on the wall back to Mary's.

"How can I believe that?" she blurted. "If I've always been under your protection, then how was my father allowed to hurt me? How was any of this allowed to happen?"

"Alena, I understand your need for answers. They are threaded into the tapestry of spiritual beings living in human experiences on the earthly plane. The answers are here for you. For now, I ask you to trust that what I say is true. Please, continue."

Alena sighed despairingly and lifted her eyes back up to the wall to the next scene.

"This is us getting evicted. The first time of many. That's my older sister Agatha. We were silly little girls trying to save the day. She's ten and I'm eight. My parents had left us home alone that day, and we almost got taken away after the landlord and the sheriff came to evict us. We thought if we could be defiant enough, then we could save ourselves, and our parents. So we wouldn't listen to a thing they were telling us to do or answer their questions, as if that would do anything. They're hauling our life onto the lawn, while my parents are still nowhere to be found. We knew what that meant—big trouble." Alena huffed.

"But the landlord and sheriff were the bad people according to my father. They were part of the collective bad people who were always lurking, waiting to split our family up, waiting to send us kids to foster care. He was good at playing with our minds like that, making a boogeyman out of everyone but him." Alena sucked her teeth in exasperation, ready for the scene to finish.

"He taught us that the world was a very, very dangerous place, especially if you were a black man like him. It was part of the black curse that all black people had hovering over us, he said. The bad people were the ones that made our family so poor, and made Daddy so sad and mean that he did those terrible things to me.

"Anyway, by the grace of God I guess, Child Protective Services didn't charge my parents with neglect or keep us in the state's custody that day. We were free. And we were homeless. It would be like that for years, in and out. We'd be in a home for about a good year, get evicted the next, and then end up in a shelter or in a cheap motel. Start the whole cycle up again."

Mary nodded knowingly as the next frame began to play on the wall.

"I'm eleven here, in the sixth grade. Everybody knew me as the poor, quiet girl at school. I didn't want anyone to get too close, so I kept to myself. My saving grace was my mind. I was smart, we all were, smart as whips. I may have been poor, but I was in gifted and talented all through school."

The images shifted and changed again.

"Here I am at sixteen. The beginning of the end. That's TK, Thomas Khalil, my first boyfriend. He saved me from my dad, from everything really. But it didn't last long. CPS finally caught up to us. The police came to our trailer while I was at TK's house. My brother Randy had gone to school one morning in my father's shoes, begging his teacher for food. My parents had left us home alone for weeks, and the neighbors tipped the police off that we were being neglected. TK's little brother had seen them taking my little brother Randy and my little sister Syreeta away into state custody and raced to tell me the news. By then, Aggie had already gone off to college. No one was there to stop them. Eventually Reeta and Randy were returned to my parents, but I hated myself for not being there to save them." The scene changed once more.

"That's me in college. All of those smarts landed me a scholarship to Columbia, and it changed the course of my life. I finally had a solid place to stay and do my work in peace. That dorm room was my haven. By the end of my first semester, I almost had straight A's.

"I thought my life was finally changing for the better. But in that same year, I made a poor choice to trust a co-worker at a temp job I'd gotten. He brought me to his house under the guise of a date, and I had consensual sex with him. Ugh. But just moments later, he let me know that his friend had been watching us the whole time and now it was 'his turn.' When I refused, they both held me down.

"I tried to talk them out of it. I fought. I cried. I begged. My begging turned to babbling. He yelled at me and slapped my face." Alena paused and pressed her lips together. Her grief was blocking her words. She could feel it pressing hard against her throat.

"'Shut the fuck up, my own mama don't tell me no,' he's saying. Then he pried my thighs apart, and he raped me." Alena stopped again. Hot tears of shame flooded over her cheeks. "I can't, Mary." She dropped her eyes from the screen. "I'm done."

"You are free from judgment, Dear One. Speak your story freely, Alena. Release it."

Alena swallowed hard and folded her arms around herself.

"They took turns raping me for hours. The next morning when they finally slept, I snuck out the back door. I ran and ran until I got to the subway station at five in the morning. My body was just throbbing in pain and my soul shut down. I never spoke about the rape, just like I never told anyone except Mama and Syreeta about Daddy. Just like then, I was so embarrassed and ashamed. I was sure that this was my fault too."

"It was not." Mary assured.

Alena shrugged, unconvinced, and continued. "After that, I went numb. I put everything I had into school and I vowed that no matter what, I was going to become someone so big and important that I would eclipse everything I had ever gone through. I would create a new me, and my life wouldn't have an ounce of resemblance to my childhood. I decided to go into law, and at twenty-three, I graduated from Columbia Law Magna Cum Laude."

A younger version of Gabriel had entered the scene.

"I'd met Gabriel three months after my law school graduation. Of course, he wasn't a hotshot attorney or the president of his father's company then. He was tall, handsome, and white. There was no hint of that poor black curse my father always told us about.

"On our good days, I basked in his adoration. On the bad ones, I was crying over one of his affairs, or something vile he'd said to me." Alena frowned. "But I couldn't keep up the image of a new me without having a man like Gabriel Ford, so I held on until he let me go."

Mary took Alena into her arms and spoke.

"All of these memories are keeping your heart open to darkness. Your memories have become wounds, open doors. It is not enough to forgive your father, your husband, or anyone else. To close these opened doorways, you must forgive yourself.

"What we have seen playing upon these walls are merely facts. They are experiences that you have had in your lifetime. It is your judgement of these memories that causes you pain and keeps you imprisoned by negative emotions. You must become aware of what you made these memories mean to you, what beliefs you created, and then heal the wounding with the truth."

Mary gestured for Alena to continue with her down another hall in the labyrinth, but halfway through, an invisible barrier stopped them from entering. They tried another, and then another. Each of the halls blocked them, except for the fifth and final hall. Yet when they finally came to its chamber door, it was locked shut.

"Alena, your dark emotions are blocking almost every hall of your heart," Mary said. "You must find their source and release them, Dear One, so that you can be free to put the infinite power of your heart to great use. You must rid yourself of the Shetani's beasts. Cast Heaviness, Rage, and all the others out in the name of Christ. Give them free range of your Queendom no longer!"

Mary walked Alena back to the first chamber's grand emerald table surrounded by the violet fires.

"These fires that burn, they are the seven spirits of good, of God. Take a good look at this emerald table. This is not simply a stone table, Dear One. This is the Emerald Tablet of your heart. As is true of all humans, the Divine, God the Almighty, placed it inside of you. All of your emotions, thoughts, and beliefs are inscribed onto it. Together, they become the instructions for your life's manifestation."

Just then, four beings— eight feet in height—appeared before Mary and Alena, surrounding the table. Dazzling white celestial light radiated from them.

"These are the Herald Angels. They are God's Heavenly Messengers. Their work in the Kingdom of Heaven is to manifest the spiritual realm into the physical world, which they are doing here. Whatever you inscribe on your heart's Emerald Tablet, whether it be in light or in darkness, is read daily by these Angels. The Heralds read what you have written on your Tablet and then go to manifest it in your human world.

"If you want to end the suffering that you have been experiencing, write your vision consciously with joy and expectancy, and make it plain on your Tablet so that the Heralds may read it and manifest a new life for you. This is what the words 'write the vision and make it plain' are referring to. As you believe in your heart, Alena, so are you, and so have you."

Alena hung her head down, the weight and truth of Mary's words spread through her. She had witnessed and experienced so much hurt in her life, she wasn't certain if she knew how to believe again.

"You want to know how to cast all servants of the Shetani out." Mary said, speaking the question before Alena could express it. "If you want to cleanse your heart of these beasts and reclaim your power, you must first believe in your ability to summon the light in the first place. Then you must do the work, your heart work.

"Each time you forgive yourself, or another, and release the beliefs and trauma that you have created around your memories, you are healing your wounds and sealing the door to your Queendom. You are releasing the darkness and embracing your own divine light for your own use. I will return here with you when your work has been completed. Until next time, Dear One."

In a dizzying flash, before Alena could respond, she was back in her apartment standing before the painting, breathless. It had begun.

"We wake up to the understanding that we are all one, all the time. Human beings exist connected each to each, but believe they are not. Honeybees dwell in the full realization of that connection and have done so for eons."

SONG OF INCREASE

CHAPTER 10

Alena had wrung her clammy hands together for almost an hour rehearsing the words she would say to her mother, Dinah. She couldn't believe it had been so many years since she had spoken to her. Finally, she dialed her number.

"Hello," Dinah answered. Alena closed her eyes and took a deep breath

"Mama, this is Lena Jae," she said while she drummed her shaking fingers against the kitchen counter. There was silence on the other end for several moments.

"Lena Jae?"

The shock of her mother's voice tightened Alena's chest. It was familiar, yet more aged and weary than she remembered.

"Ma, I know it's been a long time."

There was another pause. Alena stiffened her grip on the phone.

"Well yes it has, Lena. You've stayed away quite a while now. Too long. How are you? Your family?"

There was no warmth of a familial bond, only a frigid gulf between them. Tears welled in Alena's eyes and slid down her face. She took another deep breath.

"I'm okay. Could be much better," she breathed out. She wondered if her mother could heard the pain in her voice.

"I want to see you, Ma. I want you to meet Maya, your granddaughter," Alena said.

There was another long silence and then Dinah's voice was barely audible. "I would like that, Alena…"

Alena felt a sudden sense of urgency.

"Mama, I'm coming to see you then, okay? Alone. I'll bring Maya next time."

"All right."

Alena met Michael for lunch the next day. When they had both finished their meals, she shared her news. "I spoke to my mother today," she said.

Michael's eyes widened. "Whoa, that's great, Leen," he said. "I'm proud of you. So, what happened? What did she say?"

"Not much. I decided to go visit her, by myself. I'm going to Maryland in a few days."

"Really?" Michael's eyes widened. "Where did that come from?"

"Didn't a wise man tell me not too long ago that I needed my family? Well, you were right. But more than anything, I need to get these wounds out of my heart, and these bad dreams out of my head. I can't live like this for the rest of my life. I'm going to see her, and I'm going to confront her one last time."

"I don't know, Leen. You know what happened the last time you confronted her. What good do you think that's going to do this time around? I'm just asking. You're still angry. It's so raw. What if you heal a little more, chat by phone a little longer before you go out there?"

"I don't have any more time to waste. I have to say what I need to say if I really want healing. Of course I'm still angry. That's exactly why I have to try. I need to know why my mother took my father's side. To move on with my life, I need to hear her say, 'Yes, it happened. I knew and I'm sorry.' That's what I'm praying for. Even if she can't explain to me why she didn't protect me, I just need to hear her say it.

"Before I can even think about letting her back in, I need closure on that time in my life. That's the only way I think I'll be able to forgive; I have to confront them both. That's the only way to get rid of all this darkness." She searched Michael's face for a reaction and took a sip from her water glass.

"Once I do this, maybe there'll finally be chance for a real relationship with them, whatever that looks like."

"If that's what you need to do to get there, you know I'm behind you," Michael replied. "I just don't want you hurt all over again. Are you sure about this?"

"Yes. I'm sure. It's either I take the chance and go all in or I keep dying of rage, Mike. So, you feel up to a road trip?" She gave a hopeful smirk.

"Whoa, you really want me to go with you."

"I do. You inspired it after all. Besides, I could really use your support. Is it too heavy for you?"

"No, I'm honored. Let me take a look at my calendar." Michael peered at his cell phone and tapped around on the screen. After a few moments, their trip was set.

"For you, Leen, of course."

"Thank you! This means a lot. I'll go ahead and rent a car then."

"You don't have to do that. I'll drive," Mike said.

"Look, I can't ask you to drive too. Coming with me is huge already in addition to everything else you've done for us. Plus, I have a little cash coming in. A few pairs of my shoes sold at the consignment shop."

"You and that pride, Alena," he said, shaking his head. "Always have to be the superwoman, huh? Save your money. I'll be happy to drive us there, okay?"

"All right, all right. I'll take your ride," Alena flashed a grin. "Thanks again. By the way, I might stay for the whole weekend depending on how things go so…"

"So a hotel?"

"Yeah. But we can definitely do separate rooms."

"I think we're adult enough to bunk in one room, Leen. That is unless you plan to get frisky again," he chuckled.

She slapped him on the shoulder.

"Please, don't remind me. I hoped this could be one of those things that we never ever talk about again. I'm still so embarrassed. But just so we're clear, you do know that was the wine talking, right?"

"Right. The wine." Michael laughed again. "You worry too much. Actually, I've been thinking about something. Seeing as though I'm kind of… on the outs right now with Lola, and Maya's not living with you at the moment, I thought it would probably be safer if you had some company until they catch this guy…."

"Are you talking about moving in?"

"Not permanently or anything like that. Just until we both get on our feet."

"Mmm I don't know, Mike. Gabe's got eyes everywhere. For all I know he's having me watched. It's probably how he found my address. I know you want to help but I can hear him now, 'Your Honor, she's living in sin with a big black man.'"

"Who cares what he thinks, Leen? Doesn't he already have a girlfriend himself, who he cheated on you with while you were married? Anyway, there's no need to get all complicated. If you're not comfortable, we can drop it. No biggie."

"Step into my shoes before you judge, Mike. Yes, I definitely still care what he thinks. Believe me, it matters. Gabriel Ford does not fight fair, I should know. But, I think you may be on to something here, it could be good for both of us. I do get scared sometimes that

Bengy might come back to finish the job he started. Of course, you'll go back home before Maya gets back. Deal?"

"Deal," Michael said, looking pleased.

As Michael's car passed the 'Maryland Welcomes You' sign on the highway, he glanced at Alena. She was nibbling her top lip the way she did when she was worried. Michael reached over and gave her hand a squeeze.

"Try to relax. You're doing the right thing, Leen. Just hang tight. I got your back, remember?"

"Thanks. I'll try." She dredged up a smile. "I hope you don't mind; I need to do this first part alone."

"Of course. I get it. I'll meet you at the hotel when you're done."

An hour later, Alena rapped on the door of the little yellow house. It was flanked on both sides by two cheerful looking azalea bushes. Dinah answered the door and greeted Alena with cautious affection.

She had the same natural grace as Alena. She'd lopped off her long graying hair and styled it into a tapered bob, and she wore a dignified pink pearl earring and necklace set.

"Come in, Lena Jae," she said and offered Alena a stiff embrace before leading her to the table in the dining room. After years of homelessness, that little house was the first and only home her family had managed to keep. It looked just like Alena had left it. Pictures of Alena and her sisters as girls were still lined up on the old piano.

"I forgot to buy the Jiffy so there's no cornbread," Dinah said.

"It's fine, Mama. There's plenty here. Everything looks great. Like always."

They sat awkwardly at first, watching each other while barely seeing.

"It really is good to see you, Lena," Dinah said finally, breaking the silence. "I mean that. You look well."

"It's good to see you too, Ma. Where's everybody?"

"Your guess is as good as mine. I hardly get any visits unless I cook. They're around. I should hear from Reeta here shortly."

"And where's Daddy?" The sound of his name leaving her mouth made her stomach turn. She hadn't expected it so early in their conversation.

"Oh," Dinah hesitated. "He isn't, um, here right now." Then she changed the topic. "So how have you been? I know that fancy rich New York high life is treating you *real* good."

Alena gave a wry chuckle. "I wouldn't say that."

"No?"

"Well, let's see. For starters, everything is all messed up. All of it."

"What do you mean messed up?"

"My child is gone. My husband is gone. Job, everything. Gone."

"Your child is gone? Where is my grandbaby?"

"She's at her father's. Look, Ma, it's a long story. We can talk about all that later."

"Tsk. Tsk. Tsk. I told you about marrying that white boy. There's nothing loyal about them. I could smell he was trouble a mile off. Just as slick as a weasel with all them fancy suits and that smug way about him."

Alena resented the sting of judgment in her mother's tone, and that clucking noise she made with her tongue was like fingernails trailing down a chalkboard.

"Yeah, Ma. I know what you said. Please, don't give me any of your I-told-you-so's. I really don't need them right now."

"Put your faith in the Lord and He'll see you through. Trouble don't last always, Lena Jae," Dinah said hollowly.

Alena scoffed, "That's it? Now how did I know you'd say that at some point today? The Lord. That's still your answer to everything, I see."

"Indeed, He is, and you might want to take that sass out of your voice and start looking to Him for once. You been going to church up there, I hope."

Alena tried to subdue the anger roiling up with a deep inhale.

"Anyway. How is everybody? What are Randy, Aggie, and Reeta up to?"

"Oh, they're doing all right. Randall said he talked to you a few years ago."

"Yeah. He was in New York for a convention or something like that. He brought some girl with him."

"That's his wife now, Sheila."

"Wow, Randy got married? I guess my invite got lost in the mail."

"Well you know how that boy is. Impulsive, just like his father. It was a quick wedding anyway if you get my drift. She just had the babies a few months ago. There's a picture of his girls right over here." Dinah pointed to a photograph on the piano. "Aren't they just precious? They're identical twins. Must be on her side 'cause we sure don't have twins anywhere in the family."

"They're beautiful." Alena answered. "They look just like Randy. What are their names?"

"Ava and Marie." Dinah beamed. "Isn't that perfect? Sounds like two angels. Oh, and they're good babies, too. They slept right on through the night since day one. Well, let Randall tell it. Not even a year yet and it already looks like they'll be talking soon."

"Impressive." Alena said flatly.

"Yeah, Randy's done pretty good for himself. We're proud of him. They just bought a house down by the old pavilion in Waldorf. And Sheila, she's a nice girl—a nurse. Always offering to help me out around the house when they come around with the twins."

"And what about Aggie and Reeta?" Alena asked.

"Agatha's doing well. She moved out to Virginia, working for a technology company over there. A manager at that. She lives in a fancy little condominium and drives a fast little red car, although it rarely makes it to this side of town these days. And Reeta," she let out a noisy sigh, "well, Reeta's getting her footing again. I hope. She had some bumps and stumbles over the years, a few bad bouts with the blues. She was living with us up until a few months ago. Still single as a dollar bill just like Aggie. Neither one of them will settle down with a husband and give us any grandkids."

Dinah looked at Alena with an odd expression. "She's missed you. They all do. You know, to tell you the truth they're hurt, Lena. You went and got all highfalutin and left your family like you never had one. It hurt me too, if I'm being honest."

Alena's anger broiled into a familiar rage.

"Wait. Did I just hear you correctly? *They're* hurt? *You're* hurt? Because of *me*? Am I in the *Twilight Zone*? Did everyone get amnesia and pretend that I just left for the sake of it?"

"Alena, please. This isn't the time or the place. We just missed you is all I'm saying. Your father, too."

"Right. Daddy missed me," Alena said flatly.

"He does. We do. You know I love you, Lena Jae. Your Dad does too, he just…"

"He just what Ma? Huh? Say it." The rage was starting to overcome her.

"He just was never good with things like that, tender things like showing feelings."

"Oh, he sure as hell was good at showing feelings, that's where you're wrong, Ma."

"Now you watch your mouth! We're not doing this again, Alena, hear?"

"Doing what, Ma? Telling the damn truth for once? Mama, what about me?" The rising pitch in Alena's voice unnerved her mother. Dinah shot her an exasperated look.

"Alena, I don't want to go there, okay? My goodness, you just got in the door! You said you wanted to meet so let's meet and have a nice, peaceful meal like a normal family." She said with her fork poised above her plate, gesturing for Alena to follow suit.

"Ma, how do you still not get it? How the hell do none of you get it? I didn't leave because I wanted to be highfalutin. I left because your damned husband, my father, raped me, and every last one of you turned your back on me when I confronted him."

Dinah gripped her fork in midair, shame clouding her eyes.

"He hurt me, Mama, and you didn't do a thing about it! Even now, you're still sticking to your act like nothing ever happened. Like some country ass Stepford wife. And your precious Reeta? Ever wonder where her blues came from? He raped her, too, Mama. But I'm sure you already knew that. You had to have fucking known! And you chose him anyway! You told me, 'Family business stays in the family.' Remember that? I was eight years old and that's all you gave me. Protecting his ass above all else!"

Speechless, Dinah shook her head, the fork trembling in her shaking hands.

"And y'all were hurt because I left?" she continued. "Funny, not one of you, not one damn soul from this family, came looking for me except for Randy. And after all I've done to hold this family up."

Alena fumed, remembering the day she vowed to cut them all out of her life.

"Reeta wouldn't even open her mouth and vouch for me. She just let everyone think I was lying on Daddy. How could anyone sane have stayed here another minute?"

Alena pushed her plate away, her eyes blinking back hot tears. Dinah slammed her fork down on the dinner plate, huffing and puffing.

"I done had about enough of that temper of yours, Lena Jae. I am still your mother, you hear me? Don't be vulgar. You save those foul words for the streets. You ain't seen your family in years and you come all this way to ruin what could be a perfectly good time. What you even doing all this digging around in the past for, huh? Again? You want to break my heart a little more then leave us behind again, that it? Hmm? Let the past stay buried in the past!"

"Enough!" Alena screamed.

In one swift movement, she swept all the dishes off the table, sending macaroni curls and mashed potatoes crashing to the ground as she stood up.

"I've had enough of this shit, Mama! You know what? Forget it. Don't even stress yourself, Ma. You want to act like it never happened? Fine. But I'm not carrying this shame a day longer. Not one day. *I shouldn't have come here. I was so stupid for coming here. Even after all this time, what was I thinking?* You'll never change.

Whether you take responsibility or not is between you and your Lord. I'm sure your Jesus has a special place for you for what you let him do to us, and it ain't the Promised Land. I'm out of here," she said and turned to the door.

Dinah stood up. "Please don't leave," she said with a sense of desperation. "Please."

For the first time since Alena had arrived, Dinah looked at her directly and went to her. There was the hard glint of anguish in her eyes. Alena noticed her mother's jaw muscles clench under her smooth skin. Her lips started to tremble. Then, for the first time in years, Dinah held her daughter as tenderly as she knew how to for what felt too long to Alena.

"You're right, Lena Jae. You are right. I did know," she confessed.

Alena had to hold herself up against the shock.

"I knew he did it soon as you told me when you were a little girl. I did a terrible thing. I was a shameful woman, pitiful, and I'm sorry. I'm so sorry for what you went through." She held Alena closer to her. It was a strange feeling, hollow, even so, Alena tried to welcome it.

"I can't change anything, but I, I am sorry. I swear before God I am. You were too young to understand. You still might not. I was weak... too weak."

Her voice was heavy and regretful, her face wet with tears.

"And scared. Lena, I was so scared. Our family would have been broken up. He would've been marked a monster and sent to jail for a very long time. What could I do? We were already living hand to mouth. But I swear, I didn't choose him over you. Baby, please believe me. I swear it on my own life."

She pulled back and stared into Alena's eyes, pleading.

"I was too weak to stand alone, to stand up to him, and too weak to stand by you and Reeta, my baby girls. I hate myself every day for what he did to you. It haunts me every single day of my life. My mind and my spirit weren't right. I thought I needed to sacrifice. I thought if we never spoke about that—despicable thing—that your pain would go away and we could stay a family."

Alena pulled away, a steady stream of tears down her face, mascara stinging her eyes.

"All of these years," she whispered, disillusioned. "You let us suffer for all of these years to save your own ass. You didn't want to break the family up so you broke me instead. What did I do, Mama? What did I ever do to become the sacrifice? I just wanted to matter. I just wanted to be worth your protection and your love, his love," Alena wailed, grasping her head in her hands.

"Lena Jae, I told him I would put him under the jail. That I would kill him myself if he ever touched you or your sister again. I told him he had to get that sickness out of him or I would cut it out. For some reason, God put mercy for that man in me."

Alena's feet wanted to pace right out of the front door, but she knew the only way to complete this heart and soul surgery was to stay. At least until all the words she'd waited for were heaved up into the atmosphere.

"He's the father of my children. I know this doesn't make any sense and it definitely don't make it right, but your father was the very first man that loved me, and the first and only one who asked me for marriage. I thought that he was the only man who would ever love me, and I held onto that fiercely. I held on so tight that I lost myself. I lost you. Lena, I know you don't love me, but I'm asking that you try to find it in your heart to forgive me."

Alena let out a breath and looked at her mother. She took in the frailty of the woman she had once entrusted her life with, and for the first time, it did not completely disgust her. Oddly, a seedling of compassion blossomed in her.

"You *were* a pitiful woman. And none of this will ever make any sense, not to me, and not to my sister. But I didn't come all this way to condemn you, I came to understand."

Alena released a frustrated sigh.

"Thank you Ma, for finally telling the truth. And if that's all you have for me, I'm going to get on my way now."

Dinah rested her trembling hand on top of Alena's.

"Before you go, you should know something, Lena Jae. Linny is ill. He's not doing well. Doctors say he has no more than six months left."

"Daddy? What's wrong with him?"

"Cancer in his blood. Leukemia."

Alena felt her knees quiver as the words found their way to her ears.

"Where is he now?"

"General. They transferred him back from Hopkins a few days ago."

"Well, I'll have to go see him then," was all Alena answered. She hugged her mother goodbye and whispered "And I do love you," a declaration that took her by surprise. Dinah waved at her as she drove off in Michael's car.

"How did it go?" Michael asked after Alena plopped down at the little table in the hotel suite. She leaned over to set down her purse.

"I talked, she talked. Yelled, rather. It got ugly. I still can't believe I cursed at my mother like I did. I'd bet money she's in there clutching her glass pearls with that Bible peeled open, rebuking the heathen out of me. But it was good. I guess I got what I came for.

"She told me that she's sorry and that she believed that he did it." Alena gave a resigned shrug. "Sorry. That's what she told me. She's finally sorry." She let out an airy sigh. "Well, it's over. Prayer answered. I won't get back my childhood, but after all these years, she witnessed me."

"It was a long time coming," Michael said. "You came, you saw, you did it, Leen. So how you feel?"

Alena paused and felt a faint smile widen across her face.

"You know what? I feel… a little better. Lighter.'

"Well you know I'm proud of you. I think this deserves a celebratory dessert before we head back, don't you? How does red velvet from Cupcake Love sound? They're supposed to be the best in town."

Alena looked away, biting her lip.

"There's more…My dad is in the hospital. He's dying." Michael reached for her. "Alena. I'm so sorry. Are you all right?"

"It's all coming so fast," she said. "I don't even know how I feel yet. I'm sad, of course. Shell-shocked. But then there's so much other stuff mixed in. That's why I'm going to go see him tonight, before my mind can catch up and stop me."

"Are you sure you're ready to do that? Your mom alone was some pretty heavy emotional lifting."

Alena's eyes flashed with indignation.

"Mike, don't worry I can handle it. Of course I'm going to visit the man. I have to, ready or not, that's all I know. My dad is dying. If I'm going to close these doors and clear my heart, I have to tell him what I need to say before he's gone. It's time for me to get my peace. And in spite of everything, he's still the only father I have."

That evening, Alena drew in a deep breath and walked through the hospital doors, down the stark white corridors, and into her father's room. She never imagined she would ever be this close to him again. Linwood Johnson. Three feet away. Just the two of them.

The sight of him sent a barb of pain through her. A face that was terrifyingly familiar, once strong and muscular, was now gaunt and hollow. Chemotherapy had burned his already dark skin, singeing it blue-black in some places. He lay unmoving, a white blanket pulled to his chin. A felled giant.

She stood by his bedside listening to the slow rasp of his breath. In her hands was a cup of hot coffee to soothe her, thick with cream and sugar. Despite the freshly mopped floors, Alena could smell the stench of death creeping over him.

Old memories and thoughts simmered up from their hiding places. She thought of how many nights she had wished him dead. She thought of his betrayal, his lustful treason strangling her innocence. No matter how hard she tried to push those vivid memories away, they broke through into her consciousness like thieves in the night, filling her nightmares even as a grown woman. Sensing a presence, her father opened his eyelids slowly.

Those once soul-piercing eyes were now half-mast and took on an empty greyish haze. Alena's heart pounded. Was she really there? Yes, those were her fingers wrapped tightly around the bar of the hospital bed, which was lending her its strength to stand.

"Di?" He mumbled in a labored breath, staring with bewilderment at her.

"No, Daddy. It's me. Alena." Addressing him felt awkward on her tongue.

"Lena Jae?"

She had not touched him, voluntarily, since she was a little girl, but the moment gave her courage to hold his large skeletal hand in hers. "Yes."

Alena felt her father's tension and discomfort as he pulled his hand out from hers. She drew in a long deep breath and all the courage she could summon with it.

"How are you feeling?" she asked.

"I'm comfortable. It's been a long time. I didn't expect to see you again. Where's your mother?"

He spoke so slowly and in a voice so low, that she could barely hear it. She leaned in closer to him to hear his words.

"Yeah, it has been, Daddy. Ma's not here. I came by myself. So, how are you feeling? She said you were at Johns Hopkins before."

"They say they can't do anything for what I have anymore. It's eating through my lymph nodes now. Hospice next. I'm ready to go, I suppose."

"Daddy, I have something to say to you, and I just ask that you listen. I came here fully expecting to hate you for what you did to me and to be relieved that you finally get to rot in hell for how you treated us. But I don't feel that way anymore. In this moment, I just need to say this to you."

He stared at her listlessly, his eyes void of emotion. Alena took a long inhale before speaking.

"I need to know why. Why? You were my daddy. I looked up to you. I loved you so much. Why did you hurt me? Why did you tell them I was lying? You ruined so much of my life, Daddy."

Alena searched those empty eyes for any hint of guilt, remorse, regret, love. Perhaps sensing so, he turned his languid gaze away from hers and trained it on the opposite blank wall instead, shifting away from her. No matter what his reaction, she was determined that he wouldn't stop her from saying what had welled inside for all of those years.

"Every single day I had to live with all that pain and anger you put in me. I've been out here trying to find love with half of a heart. I have nightmares all the time. I'm a grown woman and I still cry at night over what you did. I still wake up afraid for my life. You were a monster to me, Daddy. You were the boogeyman that I couldn't get out of my head. But the crazy thing is—the thing I really hate — I still love you. After everything you have been and done, I still love you." She stood there for what felt like hours, waiting for her father to meet her on the cliff she'd brought them both to, and plunge into the depths with her, into her healing. Once again, he threatened to leave her stranded.

"You're not going to say anything?" she asked finally.

After another long break of silence, and with his back still turned to her, he answered.

"That was a long time ago," he said weakly. After a long pause, he continued. "Only God can judge me, and I know He will, sooner now than later. What else do you want from me, Lena?"

"I'm not asking for anything from you, Daddy. Not one thing. I'm taking everything back. I'm taking my life back with me. My heart. What I came for is my freedom. You have no idea what it's like to hate every part of yourself, to wake up disgusted by your own husband's touch, to live in constant fear because your father swore he'd kill you. But I won't let what you did and how you were keep me captive anymore. Today I can finally see you just as you've always been. You ain't no Big Bad Wolf. You're a coward! And a liar! You're just a scared little sheep in wolf's clothes."

To Alena's surprise, a tear trickled down his cheek. His lips balled up into a grimace, as if he was disgusted with himself for allowing it. He was silent as Alena gave his bony hand a soft pat.

"Bye, Daddy."

Her fingers were quivering and numb now from gripping the bedrail so tightly. She snatched up her purse and coffee and turned to leave. His weak voice called from behind her.

"Lena Jae, what I did to you girls was done to me. And not by no woman, either. I am what I am, but I always loved you girls. You're right, I ain't no wolf. No, I ain't no wolf. I'm a sinner, that's what I am."

Love. She wished just a kernel of her heart could believe his words for its own sake. *I love you too, Daddy* was what she wanted to say, but disgust constricted her throat, closing it tight. Again, her heels clacked against the tiled floors, now going out of the hospital room and back through the corridors, leaving all of her raging ghosts behind on his dark altar.

"The Queen is the mother of every bee born until the end of her reign.

Queenright hives remain joyous, steady, and filled with purposeful action."

SONG OF INCREASE

CHAPTER 11

"Well, the preemptive strike has arrived," Alena announced to Michael and sighed, tapping the envelope from the New York City Family Court against the palm of her hand. She plunked down on her sofa and tore the seal open.

Michael watched and waited as she read silently.

"Court papers for the custody hearing. September 9th. How does this bastard just get to decide to snatch up my baby and tell me when I get to see her again?"

"That's what I've been trying to tell you," Michael said. "He has no right to jerk you around like that and lay down the law according to him. You're the girl's mother. Where I come from, that shit's called kidnapping."

"You sound like Gloria. I told you, I called the police, but they said they don't get involved in civil matters when there's no court order to enforce. What can I do? I have to wait for my day in court."

"You can steal her right back from him. Give him the same bowl of shit he served you, and let him be the one waiting on the court before he gets to see his daughter."

"And what will that do? He'll come over here to get her back, take her again, and then I'll go wherever the hell he is to get her back, and we'll just have this nasty tug of war with Maya in the middle. No. I wish I could be as cold-blooded as he is, but I can't do that to my child. I can't put Maya through that kind of drama."

"It's your choice, Leen. Have you thought about what you're going to say? I mean, you still don't have a lawyer, and since you're representing yourself, you're going to have to be flawless in front of the judge."

Alena rolled her eyes.

"I'm well aware, thank you. No, still no lawyer and you know what they say about the man, or woman, who represents herself. She's got a fool for a client. I'm sure Gabe will come in there with both guns loaded, particularly that smug bottom feeder lawyer who made sure I didn't get to touch a dime of my money while he turned my life upside down. I've researched every single program I could find for low-income folks."

"And you checked for public defenders again?" Michael asked.

"Over and over. There's no public defender for family court unless you can prove that you're unequivocally destitute, only a joke of a legal clinic that gave me a few basic pointers I already knew from law school. My hands are tied. I'm just going to go in there and tell the truth, in my most elegant, Columbia Law-educated way, of course. And the truth is that I'm a good mother and what Maya needs."

"A great mother," Michael added.

Alena flashed him a grateful smile. "Not to mention I'm doing everything in my power to get back on my feet, which reminds me, I have good news! I had an interview to do some clerking with a temp company and they asked me back for a second one. If all goes well, I'll have a job. And get this, I spoke to one of my old co-workers, Karen. Looks like K&K isn't doing too well. She told me now would be a great time to file a wrongful termination suit and win. Who knows, after this custody nightmare is over, I just might sue their sorry old asses."

Alena looked up to catch Michael staring at her with a smirk on his face.

"What?"

"I'm liking the new you. You sound really good, Leen. Stronger."

"The new me, huh?" Alena echoed.

"Yeah. Ever since you reconnected with your parents, you've been different, in a good way. I like seeing you smile again. I missed this, Alena."

"Hmm. Well good, I think she's here to stay. Now that you mention it, you're right. I do feel kind of... new."

"Well, I'm going to take a nap," Michael said, standing up. "I have a client tonight, so I should get some shut eye. Wake me up at five, will you please?"

"Will do," Alena promised. She stretched out on the empty sofa and let herself relax. With a clear mind, a scrap of Mary's words came to her. "Write the vision and make it plain." She closed her eyes and envisioned exactly what she wanted to happen in court and in her and Maya's lives. Fueled with love for Maya, she saw them living happily in a new house, even a harmonious co-parenting relationship with Gabriel. As she pictured her new life, something else was happening.

"Alena," someone called and broke her out of her vision.

She knew this time exactly what that something was when she felt and heard the beckoning coming from the Black Madonna painting, only this time it was not Mary Magdalene's voice that called.

"Alena, come now." She opened her eyes and walked toward the voice. As she got closer, the painting's portal swirled open up in front of her. In the next moment, she was no longer in her apartment. Alena staggered back, dumbfounded. She clamped her eyes tight, then opened them again, looking around in disbelief at the strange space she'd been transported to.

Where am I? With a grimace, she took in every detail.

She was in a small house, a cabin. Rain beat ferociously against its roof. She felt soft dirt underfoot and looked down to find herself dressed in a tattered brown flannel dress that hung down to her bare feet. The stench of pine tar and herbs burning filled the cabin along with the oily smell of two grease lanterns. The thick black soot that unfurled from them made her cough. A scream tore through the cabin. Before her was an old woman tending to a young pregnant woman in labor.

"Push, Sarah, hear?" she commanded. The young woman let out a long guttural bellow through gnashed teeth.

Oh my God, this can't really be happening. Alena's heartbeat raced in her chest as she backed up against the oak plank wall behind her, causing a thud that irritated the old woman. "Come on, gal, get the molasses outcha! I said fetch me that Mugwort tea and get me some more hot water from out the fire!" she spat the words at Alena.

Alena had to listen hard through the woman's sharp southern Gullah twang.

"Who are you?" she asked the old woman.

"Child, what done got into you? Are you sick? You know I'm Granny Pearl, gal, and you best straighten yourself out quick! If you think actin' crazy gon' get you a rest, then you got a whole 'nother thing comin'. It'll get your hide skinned off by Massa John is what."

"What year is it? Where am I?" she asked desperately.

"Gal, I swear to you I ain't got the patience for no foolishness."

"Please, just tell me."

"You in Georgia. It's 1814. What that got to do with anything?"

Alena looked through the cabin window and onto flat swaths of rice fields. A realization shuddered through her. She was a slave girl on a Georgia rice plantation.

"Get me out of here please! I want this to stop!" She was panting, her breaths short and quick.

Alena frantically scanned the room for a way back to Brooklyn. There was no Black Madonna painting in sight, or much of anything else for that matter.

Another long, strained bellow filled the cabin as the pregnant woman labored.

"Now I done had it! Effie, you been swillin' moonshine? You ain't got a bit more sense than a June bug. Cain't you see we over here birthin' a baby? Looka here", she snapped, pointing a knotty finger at Alena. "I ain't gon' tell you again. You stop this here fool nonsense or else!" Granny Pearl shook her head in disappointment. "And you call yourself apprenticing under me."

Her ruddy brown skin shone like wet red clay in the lantern's light, giving away her Congolese and Chickasaw bloodline. A life toiling over rice fields had bowed her back like a cat's arch. She walked with a limp, and her weak foot trailed the dirt floor as she shuffled about the cabin. One long gray plait peeked from under her headscarf. She had placed an ax under Sarah's birthing bed in her efforts to cut the pain, but from the sound of the woman's screams, the remedy had failed her.

Alena, still plastered against the cabin wall, breathed deeply and tried to calm down. Surely, she would be out of this dimension soon, she hoped.

"It take a special kind of evil to put a pregnant woman under the lash and whip her nearly dead like this. Especially when the child is by the buckra himself," Granny Pearl muttered angrily as she pressed her medicine against the wounds lining Sarah's back.

Sarah heaved one final push with Granny Pearl in position to receive the baby with swaddling cloth. The pale child slid forward but lay still between Sarah's blood-soaked thighs. Granny Pearl rushed to cut the child's cord and held her by the feet, slapping her backside. Still, there was no movement. She moved the baby's tawny limbs and sent her breath into the lungs trying to resurrect life in her body. But when she held her ear to the infant's nose and mouth, no breath stirred. The child remained lifeless and silent, her tiny palms and soles tinged blue.

Granny Pearl ordered Sarah to push again, releasing the afterbirth.

"What's the matter? Why aint't it crying? What's wrong with my baby, Pearl? Give me my baby! Please. Let me see my child!" Sarah demanded.

Granny Pearl frowned and lowered her head, "Lawd, Sarah, I'm sorry. Your baby gone. The child passed in the womb."

Sarah wailed loudly. Her cries filled the cabin, clung to the rafters, and up to the heavens they rose. Granny Pearl placed the baby in her arms. Sarah's tears splashed over the girl's eyelids. She held her daughter's hands and kissed them. She ran her fingers over her thatch of jet black hair and then kissed her rosebud pink mouth. She pressed the child against her swollen, sweat-drenched bosom, as if to breathe in the last of the warmth left in her little body. With sorrow, she held her girl for as long as she could before the child's body was taken away. There would be little time for bereavement.

In the dark of the early morning, Alena awoke to the sound of the old cabin door creaking open, then banging shut. She hadn't even remembered falling asleep. *Oh God, how am I still here? What if I've gotten stuck here?* She poked her head up slowly and strained for a glimpse, listening intently through her panic. There stood Granny Pearl and another figure.

"Mornin', Miss Pearl. I come for some more herbs for Noah. That foot of his ain't looking good." It was a young woman wearing a blue smock and the same dull brown shift dress Alena wore.

"Mornin,' Tilly. You keep an eye on your boy's foot today, don't want to lose it."

Granny Pearl was the slave's doctor and midwife, or Bush Woman as some of them called her. Sickness was common on the plantation. Most came to her for some ailment they had caught in the squalid rice waters.

"Thank you, Miss Pearl." The woman gave Granny Pearl a sympathetic look.

"I heard about Sarah last night. Poor gal. This the fifth child she done lost. And the word is that dirty buckra fixing to sell off Hayden and Aaron to some of his kin up St. Helena Island. Them her last boys. How can Massa sell off the last of her boys knowing they all she got left? Can there be any darker evil than that there, Miss Pearl?"

"Yes sir, they can sell every last one of her babies off just as easy as pie 'cause that's what they is; they pure evil," Granny Pearl answered.

"I's an old woman and Lawd knows I seen a lot on this plantation. I come to know they cain't help to be no other way but evil. They don't stop 'til they strip everything from us. They ain't got no problem spoilin' the wife right in front of her husband like they done with sweet Sarah and her husband Roy Lee, then snatch the children up right from under our arms and sell 'em right off.

"Or they leave the children be and then carry the Ma this way, and the Pa the other way. Make us dizzy in the mind 'til we forget all that we is and all we ever was 'fore we come here. Damn devils work us to the very death to boot."

"Ain't that the truth?" Tilly said a scowl. "After this you suppose they take her out the field? She was a good house woman before the missus got wind of Massa John's rascal ways."

Granny Pearl tilted her head and put her hand on her hip. "Now Tilly, you know better'n I do that if Missus Ashby got anything to do with it, poor Sarah'll be back puttin' down rice in one week's time. Hell, you know she won't even give the gal time to stop her bleeding. If the child's pappy get any heart he may give her ten days to heal up. But Massa'll likely be tryin' to calm that 'ole mean missus down with anything she ask for, now that Sarah come up with another one of his babies. So ten days probably ain't got no hope of happenin'. That missus got the evil eye on Sarah, and she ain't gon' let it up 'til the poor gal either get sold off herself, or she six feet under."

Tilly clutched at her heart and both women shook their heads sadly.

"Well, at least this one was took by the good Lawd Himself and won't be sold away by no buckra." Tilly offered.

Granny Pearl nodded in agreement.

"Well, Roy Lee gone preach up a nice sermon tonight. He'll give a good one when they bury the child, too. A little shoutin and praisin' will sure help Sarah get her spirit strength back up. That's if she even strong enough to get out to the praise house.

"Heart and spirit strength is what she needing now. Anyhow, I got to wake this 'ole crazy gal and get this day started. You bring your boy by after supper tonight if the foot get any worse and I'll see what more I can do for it. Good day, Tilly."

The dawn's light pierced through the cabin window. Alena's rustling caught Granny Pearl's ear.

"Get on up now, Effie. It almost day-clean. I hope you slept off whatever it was making you act up like a plum fool last night. It's time for you to get to them fields and don't you be late, hear?"

"Miss Pearl? Gr-Granny Pearl, is it?" Alena stammered.

"What is it now, Effie?" she said sharply, giving Alena an irritated scowl.

"I'm not Effie. Please, you have to listen to me. I am not Effie. My name is Alena. Alena Ford. I'm a free woman and I live in the 2000s, okay? The 21st century! The painting….it brought me here, but there must have been some kind of a mistake, a huge mistake. Please, help me get out of here," she pleaded.

It was clearly in vain. Finding no empathy in Granny Pearl's eyes, she shouted into the atmosphere. "Mary! Mary Magdalene?" she begged desperately, turning in all directions. "Please. Mary, help me! I'm not ready for this," she groaned.

Granny Pearl grabbed Alena's chin, tilted it up, and examined her face carefully.

"Mmmhmm," she grunted, then shook her head solemnly. "Just like I thought. Mania. Confusion of the mind," she pronounced after a long pause.

"This here ain't the work of no poison, and I know you ain't fool enough to get into no liquor," she explained. "This here ain't nothin' but the devil's work. Somebody done put a root on you, child. They set a root on my very own grandbaby. Lawdy!" she exclaimed, slapping her palms down on her apron.

"This some bad juju that's got ahold of you right here. Lawd, I should've known it from the way you was jabbering on last night. But don't fret, Effie. We gone bring you to Old Mother tonight."

Granny Pearl went to a row of mason jars lining the cabin wall. They were brimming with dried herbs. She scooped a handful out and sifted them through her slender fingers.

"I got herbs for everything from swamp rot to snake bites, but Old Mother is the one who know all about them roots, charms and them conjures. She know how to get 'em off you, and she can turn 'em right back on the folk that sent them to you, too. She'll know what need to be done," she assured.

Alena shook her head slowly in disbelief. She wondered how much good it would do to try to set the woman straight again.

"Yes sir," Granny Pearl continued, "Old Mother is a for real African, she know 'bout these kind of arts like the back of her hand. In the meanwhile, you stick close to me li'l gal, you hear me? Now it's too late for us to tell Massa's peoples that you too sick to work. It wouldn't work no way. So you got to go on and work through whatever this is on you today.

"That rain gone and turned them fields to mush, so the soil will be nice and loose for sowing. Listen to me good, Effie. Mind yourself as best as you can while you out there unless you want to get yourself whipped."

"Granny Pearl, you have to believe me! I'm not cursed. There is no root—" Alena tried.

"Hush now! Heed to what I'm sayin'! Now, you do just what they tell you and you stick to your work. You don't breathe a word of this crazy talk to no one, hear?"

Granny Pearl's hooded eyes glared at her, a warning that filled Alena with more fear.

"Keep quiet as you can, then come on straight back home so we can carry you to Old Mother and get you fixed up."

With little choice left, Alena walked half a mile down the sodden dirt road with the other slaves to work the field. As she stooped low to sow rice saplings into long neat rows, her bare feet squelched through the muddy earth, and thick black water rose up to her shins. Alena hadn't farmed a day in her life and could barely keep a cactus alive. She stole glances at the other slave women crouched in the fields, studying their techniques.

Young and old, their brown faces were woeful yet determined, shining with sweat in the blaring sun. A hum of grunts rose from all of them as deft and calloused fingers worked the rice.

As the day wore on, Alena felt faint and weak. Her back ached terribly, and her fingers chafed and had started to bleed. She stood up to relieve her back and rub the sunburned skin on the nape of her neck. Suddenly an excruciating pain cut across her shoulder blades and then down her back.

"Lazy nigger wench!" An overseer had thrashed her with his bullwhip. His eyes raged with a wicked glare, pink face twisted with hatred.

Stunned by the cold, searing burn of the lash, Alena screamed and collapsed in the black water. The blow had confirmed an immediate truth. Here, she was defenseless subhuman chattel in grave danger. It hit her with crushing darkness.

"You stand up, nigger, before I give you another!" The words clanked out of his mouth with vile loathing and disgust. "I won't hesitate to turn your flesh through the hog press if I catch you lazing off again, girl."

Terror raked through her body, and her legs trembled violently, but with all of the strength she had left, she stood. She knew if she fell again, the beastly man would surely make good on his promise.

"I'm sorry, sir," she managed hoarsely, averting her tear-filled eyes from her captor's impatient gaze, holding both of her palms up to her face.

"What you say, nigger?" He lurched forward as if to strike her again, but at that moment, his attention was captured by a scream. Another slave had been bitten by a snake.

Pain peppered through her body and urine ran down her legs. Alena toiled away in horror, until at last, the reddening dusk sky ended the working day. Supper was lima beans, pigtails, and a palm-sized piece of hominy bread. She ate quietly but quickly. Hunched over her meal, Alena gobbled the food down in four forkfuls.

Back at Granny Pearl's cabin, Alena nearly collapsed from exhaustion, and pain that set her back ablaze. She stunk of urine and her feet were caked in dried mud. The humiliation and rage she felt would be forever emblazoned in her memory. She lay on a small makeshift cot on the floor, wincing in pain and weeping, as Granny Pearl dabbed a salve over the long, thick welts on her back.

"Oh li'l Effie, why couldn't you just listen!" Granny Pearl moaned. "I done told you, do what they tell you! There ain't no break 'til they tell you there is. Thank the Lawd all he gave you was one lash, you mighty lucky for that. Ain't too much skin broken back here neither." She wrapped a strip of damp cotton cloth gently over Alena's wound.

"You sleep on your belly tonight. This'll heal you up some by morning."

Strangely, Alena felt the breadth of Granny Pearl's love as if she were truly connected to her. It was tinged with the same helplessness that had plagued all slave mothers and caretakers. Granny Pearl knew that she would never be able to truly protect her grandchild.

"I got something for you." She handed Alena a hunk of hominy bread wrapped in a blue handkerchief.

Almost as soon as Granny Pearl had handed her the morsel, she devoured it gratefully. Alena had never been so hungry in all her life.

"Thank you," she muttered as she chewed.

"Wash up in that pail and put on your church dress, Effie. It's time to see Old Mother, and then we'll be on our way to the praise house."

With a lantern in tow, Alena and Granny Pearl walked to Old Mother's cabin at the edge of the woods.

"Old Mother, something sinister has touched Effie." Granny Pearl explained. "I suspect it's a root. Somebody is sending black magic to this here youngin'. Outta the clear blue sky last night, she ain't know who she was or where she was. She was acting like she gone pure mad. She says she a free woman, and her name ain't Effie. She say she from the way far out future and she trying to get back out there," Granny Pearl whispered.

Old Mother was even more aged than Granny Pearl. She moved her wrinkled ebony face close to Alena's and studied her with her soft brown eyes, just as Granny Pearl had done in her cabin. She drew in from a clay pipe and blew its fragrant smoke over Alena, letting the wisps curl over her, as if to cleanse her with it. Old Mother muttered a prayer under her breath and after a few moments, her ancient eyes were riveted on Alena, filled with awe. A smile curled over her brown lips.

"There ain't no vengeful spirits on this gal. I can see just who she is. The gal ain't lyin', Pearl. These eyes of hers is from the other side indeed. They from the side of where there's freedom. They got magic in them, oh yes they do." Old Mother's smile widened even more.

"She right, this sure ain't Effie, but Effie'll be back. Don't you worry none, Pearl. This gal got a spirit that come with hope, from the Promised Land. She come here with the promise from the Lawd I known would be delivered on. Known it with all my heart. I know God ain't brought us all this way to leave us be."

Alena pleaded, "Old Mother, do you know how to get me out of here? How can I get back home, to the other side?"

Old Mother nodded. "When you get whatever you come here for, you'll go back. Every little thing, place, and person got a reason. When you find yours, you'll get back to wherever it is you come from. And you take us back with you." She tapped a finger at her chest. "Here. In your heart. Our memories, our suffering, they flow in your blood. But so do our goodness, child. You take our goodness back with you, hear? You must not forget."

Old Mother worked her gnarled fingers over her blouse buttons and opened it to reveal a ropey S-shaped scar branded above her left breast.

"Look here. You see this letter "S" them white people done burned in my chest? It been there since I was a wee gal, stolen and brought here to work the rice. I believes it stand for Sierra Leone, my home. Mother Africa, our home.

"They burnt it right in me like I ain't nothing but a cow. But I tell you, I'm grateful. They say 'Nigger, you ain't got no home, but the one we give you.' I look here and I know they is full of lies! They say 'Nigger, you ain't got no name but the one we give you.' I say no, my people already done named me, my Ma and my Pa. I sang my name in my head every day and every night since I was stole away from them. I am Fatimata. I won't ever forget. And you, gal, you must never forget."

"I have indeed seen the misery of my people in Egypt. I have heard them crying out because of their slave drivers, and I am concerned about their suffering. So I have come down to rescue them from the hand of the Egyptians and to bring them up out of that land into a good and spacious land, a land flowing with milk and honey

EXODUS 3:6-8

CHAPTER 12

The packed little praise house was jammed full with thirty other plantation slaves. Hallelujahs and handclaps poured from the windows and rang from the trees. When Granny Pearl, Old Mother, and Alena filed inside, they found Sarah hobbling slowly.

Sarah was tall and willowy. She was also very beautiful despite the grief in her face and vacant almond eyes, eyes that felt curiously familiar to Alena. Her glossy raven black hair was plaited into thick braids that hung down either side of her head to her shoulders.

After listening to Granny Pearl and the other women talking, Alena learned that Sarah had been carrying the child of the plantation owner, Master John Ashby. It was Sarah's beauty and natural charm that had first inspired Master Ashby's short-lived favor. Many years prior, he allowed her to have a few lessons and books. To her great misfortune, her radiance and resulting "pretty talk" had also inspired his lust. The master's wife, Mistress Jane Ashby, was maddeningly jealous of his affairs with his slave women and made it her duty to torment Sarah, even though it had not been voluntary on her end.

The vengeful mistress had ordered her to be whipped severely for the mild offense of breaking a dish in the kitchen. She called in her brother Peter to do the deed that her husband would not, and then lied to him and told him that she caught Sarah stealing a jar of jam from the cannery in the pantry. For this, he whipped her unconscious.

"Evenin', Miss Sarah," Granny Pearl greeted. "Now you know you should be restin' and healin' up. We glad you came, though. You gettin' some rest when you can, ain't you?" Granny Pearl asked her. Sarah stared blankly ahead.

"I'm done with resting. I've got something to say to God, and it can't wait," she answered, expressionless.

"Well how you feelin', honey child?"

Sarah still did not meet Granny Pearl's eyes. "They only have my body. They ain't never gonna have my mind. Tonight, I'm going to fly away home," she said. The moon glimmered in her dull eyes. They held an emptiness that made Alena's heart ache.

"Oh yes, Sarah. Tonight, we gon' be praisin' and dancin' and the Holy Ghost gon' fill us all!" Granny Pearl assured her.

For hours, Roy Lee preached and all but Sarah shouted, sang and danced. When the sermon was over, the congregation filed back outside into the forest behind the makeshift praise house, gathering in a ring around their dear Sarah. Soon they were shouting and singing with even more fervor than they had started with. The ones that got "touched by spirit" screamed out and fell to the ground.

"That's right! Lift her up, Church. Call on the Lord and give your praises to Him! The devil won't stop our praise tonight! Tell 'em thank ya! Thank ya, Lord, 'cause we know He gon' deliver us just like you did the children of Israel!" Roy Lee shouted, sweat dripping from his forehead.

"Lies! Lies!" Sarah's shrill voice stabbed through the reverie. All went quiet, and every eye fell on her. She stepped forward into a pool of moonlight underneath an old oak tree.

"You want us to talk to the Lord? Send up our praises?" she screamed at her husband. "For what, Roy? For stealing our children? Well, let me do the talking then."

"The Lord's ways are mysterious, Sarah," Roy Lee answered quietly, the mellowness in his voice deepening her rage.

Sarah stood with her arms spread out like an eagle and her face skyward.

"So much pain you have allowed and still allow!" she screamed up to the sky. "And still you sit, a dormant God, so cruel while your children suffer down here. We must be the bastards. We must be the cursed ones you hide away, the ones you never included in your promises! Either that or you ain't really God, or maybe you just don't care 'bout no Negro tears." Her face grew more and more wild; a storm brewed in her eyes.All of the women in the congregation turned their sweat-glossed faces to Sarah and glared in disbelief at such blatant blasphemy. Granny Pearl's mouth gaped open in shock. Old Mother closed her eyes, humming quietly to herself, and Alena stood, watching, entranced.

"I cry to you and you ain't answered yet, not once in my whole life! I cried through all the sowing, pounding, threshing, and tilling their damned rice all the day long, nursing my children through the night," she said as she gestured at her breasts.

"Only for them to sell them away whenever they damn well please. I cried to you when they stole away my body, then my children! I begged you on my *knees* to save them. Another gone, then another and another. Finally, I realize I was a damned foolish woman. You ain't never coming to save us. You ain't never coming to answer my prayer! So I tried to cover my heart up with mud and stone, so I don't feel anything no more. But I couldn't," she said, now turning her tortured face toward Alena.

"Can't kill a mama's heart, can't never close it. It ain't made that way." Sarah was panting and swaying on her feet, drunk with fury.

"It was you!" she continued. "You who I prayed to, you who I lifted my hands up in praise to. I've been a good woman, a faithful Christian woman! And what for it? You let my baby die!"

Roy Lee reached for her, trying to offer comfort, but Sarah pushed him away. Her face was twisted by anguish. "You get off me, Roy!" she warned. "You just stay away from me!" Then she turned her face back to the sky and broke into a despairing cry.

"You let these white men with their silver crosses dangling from their necks ravage my body with their stink and their hatred for me. You let all of this happen in your name. Why won't you release me in death, Lord? Let me go!" she pleaded. "You are a cruel, cruel God. You are nothing but cruel." She stopped to point at each member of the congregation, who stared back at her in silence.

"We're in bondage! We got the noose right around our necks! Chain at our ankles! We out here hoopin' and hollerin', runnin' around in circles like fools. Ain't nobody deliverin' us from nothin' or nowhere, and we gon' be forever in these circles of hell! Don't ya'll see?"

Old Mother stepped forward and rested her rough palm on Sarah's back.

"Peace be still, child. God *is* hearing you. He ain't forgotten you, Sarah. God ain't forgotten none of us." Her spoke tenderly yet sternly. She then moved her gaze over the rest of the congregation.

"God sees and hears every grievin' mother, and every cryin' father that cain't do nothin' when another child of his is sold away, or when the buckra get a hankerin' for his wife. God blesses every child even if they born with shackles on they feet and a muzzle at they mouth, no matter how it seem."

Old Mother's voice intensified. "He sees your heart. He knows you. Look at your skin," she said, drawing Sarah closer to her. "All of y'all, look at that purdy brown skin you got. Why you think you got it? We Spirit People. We Heart People. We God's people." The churchgoers clapped and stomped their feet in agreement.

"Well, God sure has a way of showing it, don't He, Old Mother?" Sarah spat, her wild eyes dilating into huge black orbs. "I ain't got no more spirit left in me. No heart neither. It was eaten all away while I was busy waiting on the Good Lord. These white devils won't take anything more from me. My life won't be bitter a day longer."

She turned calmly to her husband's achingly mild face.

"Roy Lee, would you have 'em bury me with my fists full of honey?"

Roy Lee gave her a puzzled look.

"So when my spirit goes over yonder, my life'll be sweet the next time. Roy, forgive me. I'm dying free," she said.

Without warning, Sarah drew a stolen blade from a small pocket in her petticoat and slashed its edge against her throat, slitting it.

"Alena! Alena? Are you okay?"

Michael was shaking her. "What is *wrong* with you?" Alena gulped frantic mouthfuls of air. Her eyes were wild.

She caught her breath and blinked as she looked around her apartment.

"You've been in la-la land for at least five minutes now, staring off into space like a zombie. I was about to call someone!"

She knitted her brows in confusion. "Minutes? But I've been gone for days."

"What? Alena, did you take something?"

Gradually, her consciousness began registering all that had happened, and she remembered all of the horrors she had seen. She fell weak into Michael's arms and unleashed a deep, ancient cry. Her soul ached.

"What? Alena, what is it? Tell me! What were you thinking about? Is this about Maya? Talk to me, Leen!" Michael pleaded.

"I can't. I have to go. I'll be okay, Mike, don't call anyone. I'll be back soon."

Michael watched her go, worry dimming his face.

"Eat of this honey, and your spirit shall be revived."

CHAPTER 13

Alena left her apartment and walked to Gloria's. She found her waiting, ready with a cup of jasmine tea.

When Alena's sobbing tapered off and she finally felt calm enough to speak clearly, Gloria listened patiently.

"It was awful, Gloria. Just…awful. The painting or the Beings of Light, whoever, took me to a slavery plantation! I was a slave! They treated us like animals. It was disgusting."

"Yes, those times were certainly horrific. The vile acts they inflicted on our people and the inhumanity that whites, especially those slave masters, showed us were heinous. The cruelty our ancestors endured…" Gloria shook her head, "almost unimaginable. But, as hard as it was, Alena, and as preposterous as this sounds, what you witnessed today was necessary. As I said, this path will not be easy."

Alena threw her hands up.

"Necessary? I watched a woman kill herself! She had all of her babies taken away, and then in front of all of us, she just…she just."

Alena buried her face in her hands. "It was horrible, worse than I had ever imagined slavery to be. And I was whipped! They worked me half to death and whipped me! What is the point of all of this? Is it to traumatize me? Well they succeeded. I just don't see why I needed to go through all of that."

Gloria sighed and took a sip of her tea.

"Alena, the time has come when you will need to sharpen your own sword. All that you need to know is already within you. Anything further, you are here to learn. You must trust the Divine Plan, honey, and the order of your initiation. You must trust the Divine who has sent you. Remember, this is your destiny."

"What happened to you assisting me?" Gloria smiled and patted Alena's hand.

"I still am. And I can tell you that all is well. You're much stronger than you know, Alena. And no, you won't be traumatized. Your soul knows much better this time. Initiation is a crisis that shatters the ego and the reality that you have clung to. This is the beginning of your journey into mastery. Honor all of those that gave their lives for the Divine Plan not with your sorrow, but with your joy and freedom. Turn those beloved ancestors' anguish into victory. Let what you've seen and what you've heard help you to steel your way through."

"Okay. I have another question though, and this one I need you to answer for real."

Gloria listened, sipping quietly from her teacup.

"Am I just going to be snatched up into wherever and whatever? I mean, can I control this thing, or do I need to get rid of that painting when it isn't, you know, a good time? I was with my friend when this happened, and he's over there waiting in my apartment pretty spooked."

"No, there's no controlling it, Alena. You are traveling inward. But as you hone your power and connect with the Queendom of your heart, you will easily break through the fragility of reality. You'll soon be more aware and deliberate when you bridge in and out of these dimensions, and you'll no longer need a wormhole."

"A wormhole?"

"The painting. It's a doorway between this world and *all* of the sacred realms, the dimensions of the spirit world. It's actually just like us, the Bridgers, in the way that we hold transformational codes from other dimensions and bring them into this one. I know it's difficult, but trust in me, you're finding your footing quite well, Alena. You are a natural Bridger. You'll find out soon enough."

Back at her apartment, Alena opened the door to find Michael on the sofa with the same worried look on his face.

"Alena, what's going on here? Are you all right?"

She sighed deeply and opened her mouth to tell him everything, but decided to swallow her words.

"I'm okay, Mike. Really, I'm fine. I just… had a little flashback." She gave him a reassuring smile that he immediately saw through.

"A flashback of what? Be straight up, Leen. You go catatonic on me then bust out in tears and leave the apartment. What aren't you telling me? What made you so upset?"

"All right," she said resignedly. "Remember when I told you that I was starting to see these… shadowy things?"

"Yeah," Michael said, raising a skeptical brow.

"You see? You didn't believe me then and you won't believe me now. Never mind, Mike. Shouldn't you be getting ready for work?"

"Alena, I'm listening. Just tell me."

"Look, I'm not crazy and it's not the stress. This is real, and I need you to take me seriously, okay?"

Michael nodded.

"I told you that I've been seeing things. Well, there's more. Much more is happening and it's as amazing as it is terrifying. What I experienced today was something like a vision, but it wasn't, it was real. I actually went to another time and space…" She hesitated again.

"Alena, tell me. Please." His eyes finally looked sincere and ready, so she did. She then told Michael about Mary, the painting, the Shetani, and her initiation.

"Wow," he said when she finished. He looked stunned.

"Wow? What does that mean? Do you think I'm nuts?"

"Of course not. I believe you. It's incredible, no doubt. But I'm with you. So what's next? What do these Beings of Light want from you?"

"That's what I don't know exactly. I just follow and listen and try to piece all of this together as it happens."

Michael walked over to the Black Madonna painting.

"All from here, huh?" he said, his eyes gliding curiously over the canvas.

"Yep. This is where the magic has been happening, although Gloria told me that soon I'll be able to tap in without it."

"So you could, like, at any moment get sucked into that thing and into, say, the fifties or Mars?"

"I'm pretty sure my body stays here in this world. But yeah, the painting takes me wherever and whenever they decide I need to go to get the lessons, my keys to the seven powers."

"They're not going to hurt you, are they?"

"No. They're trying to help me. The ones who do want to hurt me are these shadows I keep seeing. I don't know why or when they'll attack me. Gloria said that they killed her husband. I'm going through this whole initiation thing to defeat them, for everyone."

"Well," he started, clearing his throat and scratching the stubble on his chin, "I'll be straight up with you. This is blowing my mind a little bit, Leen. I'm kind of at a loss for words here."

"It's a lot to take in. Believe me, I know. I'm still taking it in." An awkward silence started to grow between them until Michael broke it.

"So, what's she like anyway?" he asked.

"Who?"

"Mary Magdalene. Wasn't she supposed to be this holy prostitute or something like that?"

Alena narrowed her eyes at him. "First of all, she was *never* a prostitute. She couldn't have been."

"Geez, sorry. I'm just going off of the Bible. She was the woman that Jesus sent the seven demons out of, right?"

Alena measured her words.

"Mary is glorious. She's got to at least be a saint or an angel or something up there on that level if not higher. Not some whore that had to be saved. How could she have been and still be Jesus' favored disciple? She's so loving and gentle and to call her beautiful would be an understatement. Just being in her presence changed me right away. She's divine, and I wish the world would respect her for it, at least in the same way they respect the other Apostles."

"Sorry, I didn't mean to—"

"Don't apologize. You didn't know. I certainly didn't. Almost none of us know the real deal about anything. Hell, who would have ever guessed that Mary was black with all of those stark white paintings of her? Just don't believe everything you've been taught. That's the biggest thing I'm learning with this. What we see and hear is about 10 percent truth and 90 percent control."

"Well, I've never heard or seen anything like this in my life," he said, almost whispering. Then after a deep breath, "But I support you. You know that."

"I know. You always do," she said with a warm grin. Michael looked at Alena as if he was seeing her for the first time. He eyed her silently for a long moment, searching her eyes and marveling at her beautiful brown face.

"What? Why are you looking at me all googley-eyed like that?"

"Because you're amazing, you know that?"

"Um, thanks, Mike. I guess."

He shook his head dreamily. "No really, Alena, you are. I've always loved you. I never stopped."

Alena's heartbeat quickened at his confession, and she swallowed hard, listening intently.

"When you called me after all that time, I was relieved. We went our separate ways, lived our separate lives, and went on to love other people. I thought I lost you, you know, to life. I thought you'd be with that Gabe dude forever, and I definitely thought I'd be with

Lola forever. But when I saw you, at your apartment, I thought to myself, 'Life made a way, man. You can be with her again, even if it's just to be her friend.' And just like that, here we are. Again."

Suddenly their desire for each other surged up, their passions taking them by surprise. Michael leaned in closer to Alena. He held the nape of her neck and pulled her into him for a deep, long-awaited kiss. Alena braced against the sofa as he slowly undressed her, and then himself.

Michael's naked body was even more glorious than she had imagined when she allowed her mind to go there. Slices of moonlight punctuated every well-defined muscle under his smooth, warm skin. His stomach contracted with pleasure as she gently slid her tongue over the taut ripples.

He ventured further down the curves of her quivering body, sending a shock of pleasure through her as his warm tongue swept between her thighs.

Michael lifted her from the sofa and carried her straddled around his waist to her bedroom, flinging her onto the bed, where he took her right then and there. Alena wrapped her sleek, satin legs around him, digging her fingers into his broad shoulders as he moved between them. She opened her entire being to him, allowing him to penetrate past her body and into the sweet and sacred space that had curled itself so deeply and tightly inside her like a rosebud waiting to bloom.

Michael healed and pleased her with every powerful thrust and every soft moan until she could take no more, reaching a height she never did with her Gabriel.

After a wave of shivers, their bodies sagged with blissful relief. She lay in complete surrender in his once forbidden arms. He stroked her hair and caught his breath, gearing up for a second round.

"I can't believe we finally did it after all these years. I just made love to my best friend."

"Who said it was over?" He grinned mischievously, closing his hand over the curve of her behind. Alena pulled the sheets over her naked breasts. Now that their passions were fed and their minds settled back into reality, a nagging fear eclipsed Alena's euphoria "I'm being serious, Mike. Everything is different now, right? Where does this leave us? What are we doing here?"

Michael raised his finger to Alena's lips and planted a soft kiss on the top of her forehead. "I told you, you worry too much. Relax. Let yourself just feel good for once." He pulled her close to him and gently stroked her back, then suddenly stiffened next to her.

"Hey, what happened to your back? Feels like you have a long welt here," Michael asked.

"What?" Alena scrambled from the bed and flipped on the light switch. Standing in the full-length mirror, she reached back and traced her fingers over raised skin. There it was—a puckered scar left behind from the overseer's bullwhip. She wheeled around.

"My God! It was real, Mike. I told you it was real!" She paused in front of the mirror silently for a few moments and then seemed to enter into a trance.

"I keep thinking of them and seeing her face, that woman who killed herself. Sarah. Those eyes. I knew that I knew those eyes, they were just like mine. They're in the faces of so many black women I see here. We've lost something that we can't remember anymore. Our eyes are beginning to stop even searching this world for beauty, for joy, for signs of real love.

"Just like me, Sarah was just longing so bad for what was hers. She was telling me something with her eyes, all of those women were telling me something. I feel like they're saying, 'No more pain, take the hope we held onto and do something real with it. You go on and live for us. You are free.' I understand it now. She took the night so that I could have the day, so that I could have the honey."

Alena's face held a far-off look, and she seemed to have forgotten that Michael was even in the room.

"I'm fighting because she couldn't, but now I can. I can create a completely new world. I have the power now. I can say yes or no to life. I have a choice. We all do. We've just forgotten. They're telling me to go back for what I thought I lost. It's still there. It's always there because, truly, nothing is ever lost in spirit. There are no more shackles, no more Massa Johns."

The next morning would put Alena to the test.

"Mom, I miss you so much! When are you coming to pick me up?" Maya squealed through the phone. She sounded as if she was on the verge of crying. Alena yearned so badly to be with Maya that she felt as if she could easily kill Gabriel with her bare hands for his arrogant cruelty. How could he not see that in hurting her, he was also wounding his daughter?

Ask your father why. Ask him why he stole you and used his connections to keep you out of my arms, was what she wanted to say. She was so sick and tired of being the diplomatic one who had to hold her tongue, the only one who thought of Maya's feelings and tried to protect her. She was done with being afraid of the fight.

"Maya Bear, I know it's hard to understand, but this is more adult stuff your dad and I have to work out. Honey, you know your dad decided that it was best that you live with him until a judge decides. What I need for you to do is tell him. Tell them all how you feel and what you want."

"But why, Mom? I just want both of my parents and for things to be normal again." Maya was crying now.

"Oh, Maya." Alena bit her lip and balled up her fist, holding the phone to her chest so Maya wouldn't hear her.

"Maya, please don't cry. You know I love you so, so much. I'm doing all I can, baby. Okay? Mom's doing all she can to get you back. Please, honey, put your dad on the phone."

When Gabriel took the phone, Alena had to take a deep breath to stay halfway in her right mind.

"Do you see her? She's hurting, Gabe. You're hurting Maya. Whatever this little crusade has been about for you, I want you to look at Maya right now. She needs me, she needs her mother. How can you look her in the eyes and continue with this bullshit?"

"We'll see you in court," he said before he hung up.

Alena stood there, her fists still clenched with rage and tears streaming down her face. Michael took her into his arms from behind and kissed her temple.

"Stay the course, love. You're almost there."

They had done little more than make love for two days straight, but this was the old platonic Mike holding her. She blotted her face with the sleeve of her robe.

"I'm getting my daughter back. No matter what."

Just then, across the room, a sudden movement caught her attention. Something twitched and then lunged from behind the drapes. Its black form made Alena gasp and step back. She stared at the point on the wall where it had disappeared just as quickly.

"What is it?" Michael asked.

"It's them. They're here. The Shetani…" Alena let herself be comforted by the strength of Michael's arms around her, but her eyes remained fixed on that spot.

"Nothing is going to keep me from my child. No matter what," she repeated.

"Even when a colony loses its Queen... the living bees she leaves behind still bear the knowledge unique to her clan."

SONG OF INCREASE

CHAPTER 14

"All rise!" barked the court bailiff. "The honorable Judge Francis W. Lathrop is presiding on the bench."

Alena stood up quickly without looking at the table where Gabriel and his lawyer were seated in the courtroom. Judge Lathrop settled into his chair, the legs creaking under his ponderous weight. A shock of white hair standing up in a crew cut gave the impression he was ex-military. Thick black glasses sat on the bridge of his nose, and his hands looked like those of a boxer, with twisted knuckles and bent fingers.

"This court is now in session," announced the bailiff.

God, please help me, Alena silently prayed. *Give my baby girl back to me... please...*

"I have read and reviewed the case for custody for minor child Maya Ford as it pertains to either joint custody with visitation, or sole custody with either Mrs. Alena Ford or Mr. Gabriel Ford," Judge Lathrop began.

Against her better judgment, Alena impulsively raised her hand.

Judge Lathrop looked up over the top of his papers, pulled his glasses down the bridge of his nose, and said, "What can I do for you, Mrs. Ford?"

Alena had enough courtroom time to know that she should tread lightly when it came to approaching a judge, but she felt desperate.

"Your Honor, I just want the court to know that the Plaintiff left me and my daughter in the precarious situation of homelessness when he decided to leave our marital home, knowing that it was on the tail end of a foreclosure. It was a fact he kept hidden from me. Even then it took him several days before he contacted me and expressed any interest in our daughter's welfare."

She felt Gabriel's white-hot gaze on her as she spoke as confidently as she could.

"He has kept our assets frozen from me and, yes, as a result I had to relocate to a much more affordable living arrangement. But all the while, I have kept my child safe, fed, and she has continued to attend one of the top private schools in Manhattan. Your Honor, please, I've done nothing wrong. I've given my child the absolute best I could. You've seen in the file that I've recently secured employment, which will soon lead to a new living arrangement," she pleaded.

"Mrs. Ford, you do know that I've heard your testimony already," the judge responded sternly. "You are an attorney by profession, are you not? Perhaps proper counsel could have advised you of the workings of this courtroom."

Gabriel and his attorney snickered loudly enough for Alena to hear.

"I understand that you've made your best and most earnest effort to provide for your daughter. I must remind you that the court must rule on what is best for the child, and at the present time you have no employment Mrs. Ford. In the circumstances presented to me today, that appears to be placing the child in the father's care.

"In the case for physical custody for minor child Maya Ford, it is the court's ruling to award temporary sole custody to the plaintiff, Mr. Gabriel Ford. The defendant Mrs. Alena Ford, shall be awarded visitation on weekends as outlined in the order. The court shall reconvene on the matter in three months. At such time, the presiding judge will review the Defendant's appeal for a change in custody order. Mrs. Ford, the court would advise that you retain counsel prior to that date. It is so ordered. This court is adjourned."

The thud of the gavel tore something loose from Alena. It pounded into her gut and slowed all of her senses. The scenes following Judge Lathrop's words passed like movie stills. One still showed Gabriel with a smug grin on his face, one hand in his Armani suit pocket, the other shaking his lawyer's hand. The next image was of Gabriel hulking over her wearing a black cloak. He was growling threats at her. His voice seemed unfamiliar, as if it was from another time, but it held his same menacing presence.

It was then that the revelation hit her, and she understood.

Gabriel was Master John Ashby.

Nigger wench must I remind you who you are? You ain't nothing, girl! You have nothing! You go on your way and give me this child or I will have you whipped again! And this time I will kill you!

She was Sarah. It was her own past lifetime that she had witnessed when she set foot on that plantation. The veil between dimensions was getting thinner. She had indeed been lashed again, this time through her heart and through her soul.

Don't you go forgetting that I own you! Now get, nigger! Get!

He had already taken her children then and here he was again, back for another. She gasped loudly. Suddenly her awareness returned to the courtroom, where all eyes were planted on her in stunned silence.

"Mrs. Ford! Mrs. Ford! Are you all right?" the bailiff asked, rushing to her side.

"Mom!" she heard Maya scream. She had slid from the chair and crumpled to the floor.

"Mrs. Ford, are you hurt?" The bailiff asked, helping her to her feet.

She glanced at Maya, who was dressed in her Sunday best, tears streaming down her cheeks. She hated that Maya had to witness any of this. Gathering herself, Alena glared back at Gabriel.

"I will never stop fighting," she said just above a whisper. "You will *not* steal this one from me."

A shadow slid across the judge's bench and perched itself over Maya. The Shetani were on the move.

"An ascended queen stores light like a holy sacrament within her."

SONG OF INCREASE

CHAPTER 15

As soon as Alena stepped inside the apartment, Michael sensed the air of defeat in her silence. Her face held no expression, as if all life had left it. She could only solemnly nod her head to his questions, struggling to find words.

"I didn't win," she managed finally. "I'm her mother, and I didn't win." Alena, going through the motions, managed to take a shower, change her clothes, and make it to her bed, where she spent the remainder of the evening.

That night, her body lay slack in his arms, she couldn't find solace in them anymore. Grief had sealed her into a daze and tears streamed down her face through the day into the next night. By the third evening, the numbness finally began to lift. She'd barely spoken more than a few words to Michael until finally she blurted, "Mike, you should go. I need to be by myself for a while."

"Okay. I understand. I'll be back in a few hours. What do you want to eat for dinner later?"

"No. I mean I don't think I can do this anymore, you staying here with me. It's time for you to go back to your own place."

"You want me out? Alena, I know that you need space right now and that you're very upset, and hurt, but I'm not leaving you alone. Not like this. You need someone, Leen. My heart is broken right along with yours, but it'll work out for you in the end, I can feel it."

She held his hand and met his eyes.

"It's not just about Maya and court. It's this pretending to be something we're not, Michael."

"Oh come on, Leen."

"Go back to Lola, Mike. Leave. Go to your kids. What you have in them is real. It's real love. And I know you still want her. More than you want me."

Michael's face darkened with guilt. He looked into her eyes for a long moment while Alena waited for him to deny it.

"You don't think I listen when you talk to her? She's the mother of your children, I get it. That's a bond that's never going to break. I know she wants you back. And I can feel your love for her even when we're together, I just don't say anything. I'm not even going to try to fool myself anymore. I know she's where you belong. You know it, too."

"But Leen—" Michael started.

She cut him off again. "I mean it," she said. "Go try to put your family back together. Don't worry about me, I'm a big girl. I'll be okay. Just like you always tell me. This is the leg of my battle I have to fight on my own. Michael, let me be a true friend to you for once. Go to them."

"But Leen, I do love you. I swear, I do."

Alena's silence was answer enough, her choice was made. Michael stuffed his belongings back into his leather duffle, crossed the living room and stopped at the door.

"You sure about this?" he asked, leaned against the doorjamb with his arms crossed.

Alena nodded.

"All right then. The last thing I want is to upset you. Call me if you need me. Take care of yourself, Alena." He kissed her cheek softly, and she watched as her best friend and lover walked away. She stood in that spot long after he'd disappeared down the steps, tears spilling from her eyes. Eventually, she turned back into her apartment to face her grief alone.

What had she done? When night fell, loneliness descended, too. Alena tried soaking her sadness away with a hot bath. She let the water run until it covered her breasts, her heart. In the silence Gloria's words threaded through her consciousness: "The time has come when you will need to sharpen your own sword."

She tried to keep her mind on all of the grand, divine promises made to her, but she felt nothing worth trusting in. Since meeting Mary Magdalene, she reasoned that her life had only gotten harder and hurt even more.

I've been sharpening my sword all my life! Where the hell is the reward? Where's the sweet nut beyond this hard-ass shell of a life? What the hell is it all worth if I'm miserable?

Her head ached with the unanswered questions, her heart felt heavy in her chest. She slammed her fists angrily into the water, sending it sloshing over the edge of the tub. After Alena dried herself and climbed into bed, she could find neither peace nor sleep. It was dark morning when Alena heard a low voice murmuring.

"End it. End it all. Just go ahead and kill yourself," the sinister voice urged.

It startled her at first, and she shot up in her bed, her knuckles gripping the edge of the mattress.

"No one cares about you, anyway," it continued. "Your little girl is with her rich, white father now. If she wanted you, she would be with you, and you would have won custody. She doesn't. Now all you've got are those measly weekends with her, and you know: out of sight, out of mind."

As it went on, it's dark, mesmeric voice became hypnotic to her.

"Maya will forget you soon, and if not, she'll probably grow to despise you. You lost because you're unworthy of her. You're an irresponsible mother just like Gabriel said. She has a new mother now, a white woman, who will be all that you are not. They're probably off right now having a beautiful family moment—without you."

Alena bowed her head and wept.

"So kill yourself and make everyone's life easier, especially your own. Michael doesn't even want you anymore. He's just been tolerating you because he pities you. Where is he now, Alena? He's back with his wife, where he's always wanted to be. He only used you as his tramp-in-waiting until she came back around."

A terrible pain took hold of Alena's insides.

"You'll never be good enough to be anyone's one and only. That's why your father did those things to you, Dirty Girl. You are just a lonely, bitter woman. Just look at you. You're still just as ugly as you were as a kid—dark and ugly like mud. Pathetic. No matter what you do, your life will never be any different, Alena. Just end it! You're alone and you always will be." It spoke her name as if it owned it.

Alena's eyes fell on the bottle of Merlot on the side table.

"That's it. You've got the right idea now," it said. "You won't feel a thing, and there will be no mess to clean up after you're gone."

Alena staggered to the bathroom and gathered all the pills she could find: prescription, over-the-counter painkillers, even vitamins. It didn't matter. She emptied the bottles into a pile on her bed, popped the first handful of poison into her mouth, then clutched the neck of the wine bottle and took a long swallow.

"There you go, Alena. Take more of the pills now. More, more! Take enough, Alena dear; don't fail at even your death! End all of your pain once and for all," the voice growled with grim satisfaction.

A vision of Maya flashed before her. She was crying and screaming for her dead mother and she couldn't be consoled.

"No! No! No!" Alena cried, flinging the bottle of wine across the room so hard it shattered against the wall. Her stomach felt like it was being twisted in half. "I want to live! I am going to live! Help me! Help me, God, wherever you are. Mary, help me now! Please! I can't leave my child alone in this world," she pleaded through pain with wire-thin hope.

"Do it, fool! Or we will!" the dark voice roared.

Suddenly Alena began to retch and choke violently as something wicked rose from her throat. She heaved forth a column of black smoke that unfurled from her mouth and swelled into a beastlike form. It drew itself up to full height, towering over her. There it was. The evil shadow thing lived. Alena stared at it, revolted. The being's skin had the texture of decaying wood covered in a slimy film. Its face was that of the beasts that had invaded her heart. It glared at her through the same fiery glowing eyes, pouring its fetid scent over her.

The creature reached down and wrapped her throat with long fingers topped with claw-like nails, pinning her down to the bed. Gagging, Alena railed against it with all her strength. Her blows were futile. Neither her fists nor her nails could begin to injure its slimy arms. She thrashed against the mattress in efforts to twist out of its deathly grip.

"*Heel! Heel in the name of Christ!*" She'd remembered Mary's words of power and screamed them at the top of her lungs with what breath she had left. The beast curled its fingers tighter.

"Heel in the name of Christ!" She bellowed even louder this time, and with all the belief she could find within.

A sudden brightness poured in from a floor mirror propped up against her bedroom wall. The shaft of light grew wider and more intense, until it drenched the bedroom completely. The dark being seemed to crumble to ash then vanished. Alena slowed her ragged breath and then walked cautiously to the mirror. She was unsure of what was happening, but whatever or whoever was responsible for the light she knew had come in peace.

Standing before the mirror, she searched for the source of its illumination. Looking into it, she was surprised to see that the reflection was not her own. She let out a gasp. It was a woman of startling beauty. Her iridescent black eyes looked back kindly at Alena as she beckoned her forward with an inviting grin. Alena stood frozen, mouth agape. *That is definitely not Mary.* But she was just as fascinating.

The mysterious woman let out a throaty laugh. "Well, are you coming or are you not?" she asked.

Alena reached out and pressed her palms flat against the mirror's cold surface. With a firm push, it yielded, and her hands sunk into it. The woman reached in and grasped Alena's hands, pulling her through until her entire body was firmly on the other side. From this new dimension, Alena could see the world she had left behind—her disheveled bedroom, the now bare mattress, the splattered Merlot on the walls.

Alena's mouth opened again in astonishment. Unable to stop herself, she drank in the woman's beauty. Her skin was smooth as glass, and mahogany brown just like her own. The jewels dripping from her golden headdress glowed with the same dazzling brilliance as Mary Magdalene's crown of light had. In her dainty hand, she clasped a fan of peacock feathers.

Golden combs swept up half of her thick lustrous hair. The other half of her long mane was draped over the firm swell of her naked breasts. She stepped forward and wrapped her arms lovingly around Alena. Bangles of pure gold climbed up her wrists and ankles, chiming with her every move.

"Who… who are you?" Alena said through a dreamy smile. "Welcome to my grove, Alena, my daughter. You will find that I have many names. I am Compassion, the Great Queen and the keeper of the honey and all things that make life sweet. Most know me as Oshun, the Yoruba Goddess of Love and Wealth. You may call me Yeye Oshun, meaning Mother Oshun."

"Wow, you are *beautiful*," Alena exclaimed quietly with a childlike wonder. "You saved my life back there. Thank you." Oshun's presence heartened Alena, and she felt a strange urge to bow.

"No, you've saved your own life, my child. You are fighting for it and, my love, and you are winning," Oshun assured with a bright smile.

"Your voice. Why does it sound so familiar to me?"

"Come, rest a while, and indeed I will tell you all."

Oshun led Alena through her magical grove. It was dense with flowers and fruit trees, and a pleasant warm breeze laced through it. The goddess' curvy hips flowed in an elegant, almost leonine gait, and from around them, a flowing golden yellow skirt hung and billowed in the breeze. They walked into a clearing where a table holding a splendid feast awaited them.

"Please sit. You're my honored guest." At that, the candles on the table lit, and a golden chair emerged as if waiting for Alena to take her seat upon it.

Once they were both seated, Oshun began to speak again.

"My voice is familiar because you have heard it many times. Your soul knows it. I speak to you through your intuition, the small voice within. I am the power that urges you to pleasure and joy, to help you live the life that your soul has chosen. I am your fiercest defender, She Who Heals, and I am your mother," Oshun said with her wide smile and a wink.

"Enjoy the food. It is a meal fit for a queen, fit for you, Alena."

Alena did just that, gorging as politely as she knew how to on Oshun's heavenly feast. Once she was finished, Alena met Oshun's eyes.

"Really, I want to thank you um…Yeye Oshun. That thing, that beast back there, it almost had me. I wouldn't have made it if you hadn't intervened.""Again, my love, I tell you the truth. You summoned me and I only answered the call. It was you who stood firm in the light, and when you do this, you cannot be defeated. At their core, they're nothing at all except the absence of that light. So when light appears, the Shetani cannot exist. Darkness cannot tread on holy ground.

"Well I guess I did save myself, then." Alena smiled wistfully.

"Indeed. You are so much stronger than you know. When the Shetani could not break you with their latest assault, the court's verdict, they used their greatest weapon against you, your own inner thoughts."

Alena heaved a defeated sigh.

"Then Yeye Oshun, why did I feel so weak? Alena said. "I swear that thing was definitely going to kill me, just like it almost convinced me to do!"

"You must remember that the Shetani are masters of illusion. It may have seemed real, but it has no power of its own to destroy you. But with access to your fears, it did have all it needed to manipulate you. That is how it took hold. It attacked you because they know that your belief is growing stronger. They think they know you, but they don't. And neither do you, not fully—not yet. This is why you have come to me. You've suffered long enough. It is time for you to be made anew!" she said with a laugh and an exuberant wave of her fan.

Oshun then gestured Alena to her feet and studied her from head to toe. Something she saw filled Oshun's sparkling eyes with tears.

"So many layers, my child. Surely I have my work cut out."
"Layers of what?"

"You soon will see. Why don't we begin with a nice dip? My river is better than any spa you'll ever find!"

With a snap of Oshun's fan, they stood at the mouth of her sacred river.

"Before we leave our old home, we who are departing fill our bellies with honey, enough to last through the journey. We make joy a celebration, the hive is filled with exhilaration."

SONG OF INCREASE

CHAPTER 16

On the bank of the sacred river, an altar awaited Oshun and Alena. On the altar sat a golden bowl filled to the brim with honey, a hollowed calabash, a golden hand mirror, and five cowrie shells.

Alena sensed that something much bigger than a swim in the river was in store for her.

"What is the meaning of all of this?" she asked.

Oshun perched her hands on her hips.

"There has been a running theme throughout your initiation, has there not?" she teased.

"What? Getting thrust into weird places and meeting strange and beautiful beings?" Alena answered.

"Trust!" Oshun proclaimed. "If you want to receive all that we have for you, then you must trust us."

149

Alena nodded agreement. Oshun waved her hand, indicating that she wanted Alena to take a seat next to the altar. She then handed Alena the mirror that laid on it.

"Now, look here and tell me if you recognize the real you," Oshun said.

Alena glanced at her reflection and almost dropped the mirror. She shrieked at the grotesque sight staring back at her.

"Ugh! What the hell is this? Where did this nasty stuff come from? This is disgusting!" she shouted.

Her face and body were covered in a webbing of a thick, ropey substance that resembled moss and dried mud.

"Wounds that aren't properly attended to tend to appear like this." Oshun gestured toward the mirror. "This, Alena, is my Mirror of Truth. What you see there is the filth of your subconscious mind. It is reflecting what you believe about yourself and about your world—until today. Somewhere along the way, you made it your law that you are not good enough."

Frustration began to overtake Alena, and she felt her emotions welling up.

"Well how can I help that? How am I supposed to feel good enough when no one else thinks I am?" she demanded, her voice cracking.

Oshun knelt beside her and held her like a child.

"You have so much rage, my daughter, so much fear. I do understand. Nevertheless, this is how the Shetani were able to infiltrate your defenses back in your bedroom, and throughout your life thus far. This is not the first time they've used your own rage against you to tempt you to destroy yourself. During your lifetime on the plantation, they used these very same manipulative forces."

"Yes, I know." Alena snapped. "I was the slave woman, Sarah, wasn't I? And that son-of-gun Gabriel, he was my slave master, right? Old Mother had to be Gloria, and she's the Oracle."

"Clever girl. You've got everything figured out, I see. Always in control," Oshun said with a sly smile. "You are correct, but only about yourself and the one you call Gabriel. Gloria is not the Oracle."

Alena shrugged. "Well, what does it matter anyway? I still lost my child! I didn't defeat the Shetani back then, and I only barely did this time. It's too damned much, Yeye Oshun. I'm done fighting. How can I even start to feel 'good enough'? The same pain that drove me to kill myself back then is still in me. I told you, I'm not strong enough for this. I've never felt weaker. I lost my baby all over again! I don't trust God anymore. I definitely don't trust myself. I can't trust anyone." Alena almost gagged on the bitterness she felt.

"You are not weak. Far from it," Oshun assured. "You are goddess, becoming. You have not lost your child, nor have you lost your power. You've only forgotten how to use it, the power of your honey," Oshun said.

From underneath her billowing yellow skirt, she drew a dagger from a sheath at her thigh. She then carefully sliced the tangled muck away from Alena.

"Undress and place these old clothes on the altar," Oshun commanded.

Alena complied.

"We've cut away what you could not see, and now we must cleanse what you can, the filth in your conscious mind."

Oshun walked Alena into the roaring water until they stood thigh deep in the river.

"When Yemaya, Goddess of the Great Mother's oceans, carried our human children to the Americas, we grieved for them, for what had to be done, and for what had to come to pass. It was from the ocean that all life began, and it was to her that many of our children returned in that terrible journey. Even though your journey was prophecy and vital to the Divine Plan, we grieved," Oshun lamented.

"We quaked the earth with our sobbing. Our anguish split its floor. We wept with floods and with hurricanes. Yet, we rejoice because your souls have grown deep and wide like our waters. There is immense value and purpose for your trials that you may not understand yet."

Oshun whispered into the mouths of the cowrie shells, and a solid mass of brilliant yellow light appeared in the palm of her hand.

She flung it into the river, quickening it. The churning waters rose eight feet high, spun into a whirlpool, and then settled back down. Once it calmed, the goddess dipped the calabash into the cool, swirling river. She poured the water over Alena's head while scrubbing her hair with a soap of consecrated herbs.

"No more trying to convince yourself that you are broken. You must let Sarah's pain go," she called out to Alena as her hands worked furiously. "Your heart still remembers the terror and the hopelessness of those dark, dark nights. It still remembers your husband's face, watching in vain while that slave owner raped you. You must let all of your past go—every role of every lifetime, every ancient and recent memory that no longer serves you. Keep only the good—the wisdom, the victory... the honey."

Alena erupted into deep, rolling sobs.

"I want to let it go! You think I don't want to let it go? Of course I do!" she spat at the top of her lungs. "I want out of all this duty! I don't want to be the chosen one, or whatever I'm supposed to be for some stupid divine plan. It's not fair! Why is my load so damned hard when so many people out there are having the time of their lives? They get to have their soul mates, their money, happy little nuclear families, and I've been cursed since childhood with all of this pain and poverty? I am thirty-three years old. For god sakes, I feel like an old woman!"

"Take heart, my daughter," Oshun said in a low voice, and draped her hands softly over Alena's shoulders. Consumed by her pain, it was a gesture she barely noticed.

"I should be enjoying my life," Alena continued, "Instead, I'm heartbroken, barely hanging on and barely living. Is this what God calls loving His children? Her children? Do any of you perched up in your lofty realms get that? What kind of God would let us suffer so deeply?"

Searing rage rippled through her, and she could barely breathe. All of the questions and frustrations she held about God came bursting through her mouth in that river.

"You have not been cheated out of a good life," Oshun promised. "Beyond appearances, you are living a grand one. You have not been forgotten. Only good is planned for you. Only good. You must trust and surrender into our arms, Alena."

"Good? Ha! I'm tired of the world treating me like trash because I was born a black girl. I'm tired of being told I'm too ugly to love, too strong to be protected. How long am I supposed to be ashamed of who I am? Haven't I given enough? How many lifetimes of struggle is enough? I didn't sign up to be anyone's martyr, Yeye, and if I did, I cancel the contract!" Alena choked out.

Her rampage sent her legs thrashing about in the water like an errant toddler. Nevertheless, Oshun continued cleansing with the greatest care and patient affection, listening intently. She dipped the calabash into the river and let a cool stream of its mystical water pour over Alena's head again. Oshun then held her close to her bosom until she calmed.

"My daughter, I know life on Earth is not easy. I understand how difficult life has been for you, and how broken your heart feels. I tell you the truth; the pain will not stop until you stop resisting. Accept what is, accept what has been, and then you will begin to heal."

"What about the people who've hurt me, Yeye?" she wept. "The ones who've taken everything I had inside and left me empty. What about the parents God was so kind to give me? Should I just accept that? A perverted ogre for a father, a coward for a mother! I was born into their shitty care, not to mention into the agony of slavery, and God knows what else I've had to endure over my lifetimes! Did any of you think about the cruelty of that?"

"Yes, this, too, you must accept. You chose these experiences, as a soul, long before you came into your human form. You chose them because you and Creator knew how great the reward would be. Every second of your life on Earth has equipped you for your purpose."

Alena rolled her eyes and listened quietly, still seething. "And," Oshun continued solemnly, "bless them. The ones who've hurt you, bless them all and give thanks for the strength they have forced you to cultivate in order to get you to this appointed time and place.

Difficult teachers are part of the divine path. They are the teachers that you chose."

"Is that right?" Alena grunted sarcastically.

"My daughter, might you consider that you have had an affinity for agony? It did not begin as a conscious choice of course; no one with sense would choose agony over joy. But little by little, you've learned that you can rely on despair, it was comfortable and predictable, and it became an expectation that you weaved into your existence. No more. To choose happiness and joy requires you to be courageous enough to be take responsibility for them; courageous enough to stand in who you are."

Oshun went on to scrub the length of Alena's arms and legs, this time adding a bit of her honey.

"My love, you must accept your power and stop pitying yourself. You have the power to end your agony once and for all. Alena, you must accept that which is required of you."

"And if I can't?" Alena asked with tear blurred eyes.

"Well, then you will remain in agony for a very, very long time. What you judge as defeat is victory. For instance, your very death on that plantation was a catalyst for the heinous practice of slavery to end." Oshun's words hung in the air.

Alena lowered her eyes apologetically and sobered. She was ashamed of how she had lost her self-control and lashed out at such a graceful presence.

"It's just so hard, Yeye. Two steps forward, four back. It feels so hopeless, like I'll never get it."

"I promise you, you are moving forward. Human existence unfurls in a spiral, not a straight line. On every ring awaits a new learning, a new level of awareness and mastery."

Alena's anguish wracked her body with another wave of sobs. "Yes, yes child, purge it all," Oshun soothed as she cascaded water over her for the final time. Together they walked back to the bank of the river, where Alena dried her body and Oshun lovingly dried her hair. She then wiped Alena's tears away with the back of her hand.

"Sit here."

Subdued with emotion, Alena sat as Oshun instructed, naked with her legs outstretched. The moment her skin met the soil, she felt the hum of the earth. It intensified into long waves of vibration pulsing from the ground and gently surging into her through the opening of her womb.

"You are communing with the Great Dark Mother," Oshun announced. "Let her heal you."

Alena managed something of a smile. She remembered that those had been Gloria's exact words.

"You hold so much power here, the power to both create and heal. Your womb was made for much more than sex and babies. It is a gift from the creator, a gift to mankind and to all creation."

Alena raised a questioning eyebrow.

"It is true", Oshun assured, smiling. "While your heart is your gateway to God, your womb is your second heart, another divine portal that bears humanity's life blood. It is a vessel that holds the same infinite void of creational power as the vast skies of the universe."

"Wait, so what does that mean? In layman's terms please."

"That means that by virtue of simply being a woman, you have a divine feminine power with which you can create anything and any possibility you want to, provided that you take responsibility for the temple that is your womb, Alena."

"Well I haven't always been in control of my own body, let alone my womb." Alena said as another tide of sadness began to swell in her.

"Yes my dear, we know. As you sit, feel the Great Mother's heartbeat join with your own. Let her pulse purge your womb of the violation your father inflicted, the rapes you have endured, and all of the heartbreak you have held in your sacred vessel."

Alena sat still with her eyes closed. The Great Dark Mother's healing love kindled new life in her. She felt lighter and more at peace with every passing moment.

"Are you beginning to understand now? Return to Mother. When you still yourself and attune with her, she will work with you, and your womb will begin to heal and purify itself. It can do the same for anything you bring to it. The wisdom of your womb can save your world."

Alena nodded slowly with her eyes still closed. A smile gradually formed on her face.

Oshun waited patiently as the Great Dark Mother continued to course through Alena and impart all of the healing that she needed. When she opened her eyes again, Oshun continued.

"What is it that you want, Alena?"

Alena looked back at the river before answering. "I want love," she said definitively."

"Ah yes, my favorite! Let's talk about love." Oshun's golden bangles jingled as she clasped her hands together in delight.

"The truth is that you *are* love. Since you already are love, what you are really wanting is to experience and express more of what you truly are."

"Hmmm. Well, if I'm love, then how does love seem to always elude me? I loved Gabe for eight years. He's the one who's been nothing but cruel and malicious. That's how he won the custody case," she said bitterly.

"Remember what you learned about difficult teachers. In his callousness, he has illuminated the dark places within you that need more of your own attention and tenderness. Through your experience with him, you also learned to reclaim your freedom and stop making yourself a slave."

Alena thought about it.

"When you put it that way, I can definitely see the good, but I still don't see the love."

"Tell me, have you been vulnerable and accessible to love, Alena? Or have you withheld it trying to assure that you would receive it first?"

"Maybe," Alena said sheepishly. "I might have been withholding… a little. Gabe doesn't even know me completely, he never did. I knew he wasn't strong enough to bear my pain and love me anyway."

"Daughter, you alone are responsible for the sweetness that you bring to the world. Your honey is your power. Be discerning, yet generous with it. You cannot use it to get what you believe you do not have."

"And what does that mean?"

"You cannot love until you learn to love without conditions. And you cannot fully love another person or even God until you've learned to love yourself without conditions first."

Alena bit her lip and nodded pensively as she took in Oshun's words.

"Until then, you will work desperately to fill a void within you. You will continue to manipulate love and bring even more difficult teachers into your life until you get this lesson and accept the truth of love. Now, I must ask, do you want your daughter back out of fear or out of love?"

Alena grimaced.

"Love, of course. I'm her mother for goodness sakes!" she exclaimed defensively.

"Yes that you are. The profound love between you and your daughter is clear to anyone. What I am asking you is this: do you want your child back because you fear that not having her will prove that you are indeed not enough?"

"Yeye, I want Maya back because she is mine, because I love her. But if you're asking me if I'm afraid, yes, I am. I'm terrified of not being worthy of my own daughter, that Gabe is better than me and Maya knows it. That she loves him more because of it."

Oshun squeezed Alena's shoulder.

"Rubbish. Torment yourself no longer with thoughts of what you must be or what you must do to have love—Maya's or anyone else's. You must give these outworn thoughts away in exchange for your glory. This is what true forgiveness is. You must give away the old to receive the love that gives. If you want to experience more love, simply choose it and then allow it to rise up to meet you through whatever channels it returns to you."

"Thank you, Yeye," Alena smiled. "I've got it."

"All that appears in your life reflects that which you called into being at some point or another. It is the answer. You just have to remember the question."

Alena thought about the statement for a long moment.

"I do remember the question. I asked to be healed," she responded.

"Very good. So go forward and bless your healing path. It is true that abundance, joy, and love are your birthright, but you must claim them. When you get back to your world, get out there and claim what is yours!" Oshun smiled broadly.

"That includes claiming love and complete acceptance for yourself," Oshun added as she took Alena's hand in hers. "My daughter, you are such a beautiful woman, a beautiful *black* woman. Black like me. Still, you rail against this skin. You betray this lovely dark skin with your rejection, why?"

Alena felt her face flush with shame, speechless.

"You've been hiding from your blackness, hiding from who you think a black woman is and what a black woman can be. And that's why it was so easy for you to give all of yourself away."

"Yes, it's all true." Alena confessed quietly.

"Then you also know that you've been creating your life with a paintbrush of lack and inferiority."

"You're right, again." Alena lowered her eyes. "I guess I'd never had the courage to think of it like that." Oshun held Alena's face in her hands and looked intently into her eyes.

"Hear me now," she said emphatically. Her expression took on a fierce intensity. "Your self-hate was a planned result, daughter. From your birth, you have felt an unrelenting resistance against you. You have been feeling the Shetani's forces enacted through those fallen humans who are empowered by them. They're aimed at you so brutally because you are the key. The dark beings and those that serve them work diligently to convince you that there is a well-defined place for you, and it is not a seat at the table of life. You've been deceived, my daughter. They depend on this deception to keep themselves alive."

Alena held Oshun's heavy gaze.

"If you and your people discover who you are and act in your royal nature, they know their reign will be over. So, you must honor and cherish your black skin and, most importantly, your mighty spirit contained in it. It is a sacred blessing, a calling from the highest crest of Heaven."

Oshun presented the Mirror of Truth to her again. "Now, look here and tell me if you recognize the real you."

Alena glanced into the hand mirror and saw that the woman of startling beauty was indeed her. Her face was now pristine and glowing. She had never thought of her black skin, not to mention herself, as sacred. But in that moment, the truth of it filled her along with an exhilarating sense of pride.

"Your face is God's face. Your breath is God's breath." Oshun said. "It is not enough to simply know these truths; you must know thyself if you are to defeat the Shetani and their allies. Their might lies solely in the depth of your fears and beliefs. You must receive the truth and then feed it to the world's children. This is a legacy of true power."

Oshun then anointed Alena with her sweet perfumes and oils and clothed her in a regal white and gold dress she had prepared for her. "Garments for a bright new day," she said to Alena.

"The Black race is not a minority. There is nothing minor about you. You are the seeds and the tree. What need have you for an oppressor, for those that fear and envy you? Free woman, you do not need to beg a gatekeeper to deem you worthy enough to enjoy the abundance of life. You alone are the gatekeeper. The beacon, not the victim. Nothing on the earth can bind you now, you are liberated."

Alena felt light and giddy.

"Are you willing to step into the wonder of life and live with all of the joy your heart can hold?" Oshun asked.

"Yes, I'm ready, Yeye," Alena promised.

She gestured for Alena to dip her finger into the golden bowl and taste her blessed honey.

"Be lifted up so high and so wide that whatsoever touches you is glorified by the light of God," Oshun said with a deep, effusive laugh.

Alena savored the earthy sweetness of the honey melting over her tongue. Its aroma conjured a memory.

"That poor slave woman Sarah—well, me—I asked to be buried with my hands clutching honey."

"Yes, of course. My honey is the kind that sweetens the soul, the kind that heals and restores—in life and in death. Sarah passed it on to you and now you must fulfill the destiny that only you can. As the daughter and heir of the Great Dark Mother, you are chosen and ordained. Mother's reemergence is humanity's only hope for balance and restoration, fulfillment of the Divine Plan. This is why we need you and all women awakened. My daughter, a woman must lead them!" Oshun looked at Alena and grinned.

"It is time for you to go back to your world. You are cleansed anew. Remain this way. A warning: do not reclaim the ills that you have purged. Wear the truth. Put on your garment of truth and sweetness each day with faith, praise, and joy. The vision you have written upon your heart is coming to pass, all in the timing of the Divine Plan."

Oshun drew close to Alena and whispered in her ear. "We are always with you, guiding and helping you. Joy is your name, my darling daughter." Oshun smiled and her beautiful headdress bowed gracefully before she was gone. Alena smiled, too, deeply fulfilled.

"I am joy," she repeated. Within moments, she was back in her bedroom. It was there that she discovered it, waiting for her on her still bare mattress—the golden Mirror of Truth.

"Some have said that honeybees are messengers sent by the gods to show us how we ought to live: in sweetness and in beauty and in peacefulness."

HONEYBEE DEMOCRACY

CHAPTER 17

Alena pulled her coat closed against the crisp October air. Though she still felt the emptiness and hurt of not having Maya with her, life felt new. As Oshun had promised, fresh joy had sprung alive in her, and her radiance was captivating.

That morning, she savored every moment of preparing for her first day at the new firm. She slid on a curve hugging satin dress, painted her lips bright cherry red, and gathered her curls into a neat ponytail. All of her senses had heightened since her visit with Oshun. She had never felt so feminine, whole and sensual. Alena could not stop beaming as she hurried to the train.

"Hey slow up, Rich Girl," Tacky called from behind her, drawing on a fresh cigarette.

"Hey, Tacky. I'm kind of in a rush. How are you and BJ?"

"We good, girl. Sorry I ain't come by," she said, her eyes downcast. "I thought you was mad at me, you know, for what Bengy done to you."

"I was never angry with you. It wasn't your fault. I was a little disappointed you didn't come to see about me, though. But we're cool now."

"Cool. You know, you real decent. That shit should have never went down on you like that. I'm mad sick about it. They got 'em though. The cops nabbed that crazy nigga."

"I know, the investigator called me. So how are you managing now that he's gone? You okay?"

"Like I said, we good." Alena could see that Takeah was still sad. "A little bit of money ain't enough to get slapped up all the time anyway, right? Plus I found out he got at least four other chicks out here with babies by him. He wasn't shit of a father to BJ no way.

Anyway, what about you? I hardly see your baby girl no more. Where she at?"

"It's complicated, Tacky," she said, feeling her longing tug at her. "She'll be back soon enough. Look, I'm glad to see you're doing well. I'll catch up with you later." Alena then hurried to the train station and off to her new job.

"Allison Casowitz. Welcome," the chubby plain-faced woman said with a tight smile that didn't quite reach her eyes. She wore black-rimmed spectacles with long pearl chains against her ivory skin and a shapeless matronly dress.

She started Alena off with a tour of the office.

"Coffee's in the break room along with an almost endless supply of donuts thanks to Heidi. Her husband owns a bakery. So this is your new home at Lesser and Piesel," she said, showing Alena to her cubicle.

"Things move pretty fast around here, but I heard you're a quick learner with a good track record," she said, raising her penciled eyebrows. "We'll start you off with the Cayuga Wetlands briefs. We have our staff meetings every Thursday in the atrium, so I suggest you get caught up with them by then, all right?"

"Thanks, I'll definitely be ready," Alena assured with a polite smile.

"Great," Allison said, giving another weak, nicotine-stained smile as she walked away.

Alena exhaled with relief and flipped open one of the briefs. The weight of the bulky document in her hands filled her with gratitude. She had work, she had hope, and she was coming back to life. The thought of all of the new possibilities that could turn her dreams into reality made her smile.

She chided herself, but strangely, even back at her desk she still couldn't get Michael's face out of her mind.

"How're we doing? Ready for the meeting?"

Allison's voice broke her out of her thoughts as she poked her head into the cubicle. Her spectacles now hung at her bosom like a lanyard.

Alena looked up from the thick brief. "Yes, ma'am," Alena answered confidently. "I've just finished up my notes and I'll make sure Heidi has a copy for everyone." When Allison smiled and left her cubicle, it occurred to Alena that she really did feel confident, like she was in control. It was something she hadn't felt in a long time. Everything was going to be okay. She knew it, she just didn't quite know why. So she decided to take everything one day at a time, one moment at a time.

At home, Alena was ever vigilant in clearing any lingering darkness still slithering through her heart. When despair crept up over her thoughts, she refocused on what thrilled her heart. That was getting easier to do since she would be seeing Maya soon. She had planned every moment, determined to make the very best of their visits. Now she had the money to treat her girl to a fun day out, and even buy herself flowers on her way home from work. Her talks and tea with Gloria always lifted her spirits, as did the love she was finally giving to herself.

At night as she lay in bed, Alena told herself that what she felt was not loneliness, but stillness. She was on an extended journey of stillness with God and all of the Beings of Light. Her resistance to life and all that it had to offer had ripped her spirit to shreds. The judgment she held against it, of how it should be different, held her prisoner. Alena decided to flow like Yeye Oshun's river and press forward into the new waters before her.

"And praise Him who leads those from famine to where there is honey in the wilderness."

WILLIAM B. TAPPAN

CHAPTER 18

Alena still had her hand on the doorknob to leave when her cell phone buzzed in her purse. It was a number she didn't recognize. She swallowed down the last of her breakfast and answered.

"Hello, may I speak to Alena Ford please?"

"This is she."

"Mrs. Ford this is Samantha Harper from the Custody Crisis Project, how are you? I'm calling to inform you that your application for assistance has been selected."

"My application? Can you please refresh my memory, ma'am?"

"Yes, of course. CCP is an organization that grants aid to low income mothers in a custody or visitation crisis due to lack of financial resources. You submitted an application on... let's see... August 21st. Are you no longer in need, Mrs. Ford?

"I am. I am! Oh, my God, thank you for the news, Ms. Harper!"

"Oh you're quite welcome. Congratulations. You will be receiving a grant for your legal expenses up to but not exceeding twenty-five thousand dollars. A CCP sponsored attorney will be in touch within the week for your intake interview. Have a great day, Ms. Ford. Goodbye." Alena hung up, then wiped tears of gratitude from her eyes and danced like she had won the lottery.

She tried to scurry off so she wouldn't be late, but her phone rang again, this time it was Michael. "Hey Mike," she answered cheerfully.

"Hi, Leen. How are you? Thanks for finally picking up my call. I just wanted to reach out to make sure you're all right."

"I'm doing okay, thanks for checking on me. Taking it a day at a time, you know. I had my visitation with Maya again. It was so good to be with her."

"That's great. Enjoy her and keep your hope up. It's going to get better from here."

"Yeah, I'm finally starting to believe that."

"Well you sound really good. I'm happy for you, Alena. Look, I know you're probably busy, so I'll make this quick. I want to say something to you. I wanted to say this earlier, but when you told me about your dad I knew it would have to wait for a while. I still want to tread lightly, but can I be honest with you?"

"Go ahead, Mike. I can take it."

"I get that you needed your space to process but shutting me out like that? After all I've been through with you, it really got to me. I'm not going to lie, it hurt."

Alena sighed.

"Mike, I told you, I have to fight my battle by myself now. I had to let you go. I don't know how else to explain it. Look, I can tell that you've really got to get some things off your chest about whatever that was between us, and so do I. I would love to hear everything you have to say but now is just not a good time. I'm in a rush to get to work. Besides, I think this is definitely a talk that we need to have face to face. We should meet later. Can we continue this conversation over a drink or something? Why don't we go to Arrindale's? My co-workers rave about the place.

"Sure, Leen. we can do that."

"Can you meet me in the city after work, say about six? I won't keep you out long, I promise."

"You got it. "

"Arrindale's at six then. I look forward to seeing you, Mike. Thanks again for checking on me."

At a quarter to six, Alena was sure to be seated at a table where she could see Michael the moment he walked in. She scanned the restaurant anxiously as she waited for him. While it was packed with droves of well-heeled mid-towners, it was still cozy with an antiqued ambiance. Tiffany pendant lamps hung from the ceilings.

The walls were lined with seemingly hundreds of photos flaunting the many celebrities who frequented it. It seemed like every A-lister had eaten there at some point. Alena was smoothing her hands over the linen tablecloth when she spotted Michael finally emerge through the doors. He sauntered over with a grateful smile and hugged her tightly before taking a seat across from her at the table.

"It's good to see you again," Alena said, keeping her composure mild yet sweet.

"It's good to see you, too, Leen." His smile spread even wider.

"You look well, Leen, happier." Michael reached out and rested his hand on her shoulder. "I'm glad to see you like this. I haven't stopped worrying about you."

"Thank you, so do you." She floundered. "Look happy, I mean... Well, things are looking up. I'm finally getting to spend time with my daughter again, I'm working. You were right, slowly but surely things are changing." She picked up the menu to place an order. "Well I'm starving. I think I'll go with the caprese salad and some house wine. What are you having? It's my treat by the way."

"Woman, please, you know I'm not going to let you pay."

"Mike, I'm gainfully employed now. Let me repay at least some of your kindness."

"Well if you insist, but I'm not even that hungry. And I can't drink either. I've got a client at eight. I really just came to talk to you."

"Alrighty then. Let's get to it. But before we get all heavy, I've got a question for you." Alena said. "So by some incredible miracle, *someone* put in an application for me to this low income mothers grant for legal aid. It's called the Custody Crisis Project. And well…I got it! Did you have something to do with this?" she asked, smiling coyly.

"I would love to take the credit, Leen, but no, I had no idea something like that even existed. Congratulations though! So this means you've got an attorney then?"

Alena shook her head. "That's so strange. If it wasn't you then who could it have possibly been? Anyway, yes, I'm all lawyered up now." She smiled anxiously. "And now that that's out of the way, what's up? What do you want to tell me?"

Michael cleared his throat and paused for a few moments. "Okay, well I'll just put it out there. You're not gonna like what I have to say, but it's real, Leen. I've been thinking about things for a long time after you put me out of your place, and I figured that part of your problem is that everyone, except for Maya, is disposable to you. You feel some pain and then you cut us off just like that, like it never mattered.

Alena grimaced, and folded her arms.

"Don't get me wrong. I know you've been hurt—a lot. But even before your ex came around, I've seen dudes, good dudes, try to love you. I was one of them, Leen. I just want to know why you can't stand to be loved. I mean, other than Maya, have you ever *really* loved anyone? Have you ever opened yourself all the way up and loved somebody for real? If your soul mate was staring you in the face, would you even recognize him?"

Alena raised an incredulous eyebrow and leaned hard in his direction.

"Really? How dare you! Oh no, you don't get to do this, Michael. You're the one who came over to my apartment shacking up with me like you were ready to go all the way. Like you were ready for something real between us. You didn't even tell me your heart wasn't in it, that it was just passion."

Alena's voice was rising, and people at nearby tables were starting to stare. Michael gestured toward them with a look and she took notice. She bit back her emotions and lowered her voice to a fierce whisper.

"Just where do you get off telling me that I shut you out? I let you in. You of all people should know how hard that was for me, and like everyone else, I trusted you and what did you do with it? You made a different choice, and I made one for myself." Alena's voice was ripe with indignation.

Mike looked down at the table, then he slowly brought his eyes up to meet Alena's.

"I… I don't know what else to say to that except you're right and I'm sorry. I was wrong about a lot of things. Alena, I thought I was ready, but I wasn't, not then. My heart was still with my wife and the family we made, but things have changed. I get it, coming on so strong while both of us were so vulnerable wasn't the smartest thing to do. I should have known better. But, Leen, aside from all of that— what we shared together, that was real. It was much more than the sex."

Michael took Alena's hand and cupped it in his. "Everything I said to you is still true. I love you, Alena. I have loved you for all of these years and I'm just grateful that I was the one you called on…" His voice trailed off as he drummed his fingers against the table.

"I'm not the greatest at this. But all I'm trying to say is that I know you've gone through hell, Leen, but you have to give someone a chance to stand with you. You have to trust someone. Open up to love. People aren't perfect, Alena. You aren't perfect, and neither am I. You've got to learn to love the light with the shadow. I'm not a perfect man, not even close, but I wanted to be there for you."

"Mike, believe me, everything that you're saying to me—I receive it. I know it took a lot of guts to say. And yes, to answer your question, I am tired of being lonely, but you really have no idea what

I'm up against now. It's like I've told you, I have to do this on my own. And I'm doing my best to figure this thing out and stay sane doing it."

Michael cradled Alena's face with his palm.

"I have no idea? Did it ever occur to you that I might be a part of it, Alena? What if God sent me to you just for this? Could that be part of the Divine Plan, Leen? You know, you do have a battle to fight. But I don't think it's as grand as you think it is. I think your biggest battle is the one you have to fight with yourself and it's against your own pride, your own sabotage."

Alena sighed.

"Okay. For the sake of moving forward, let's suppose you're right," she conceded. "I'm sorry for pushing you away then, and for all the times I've pushed you away in the past. Listen, Mike, I'm just trying to do the right things. I'm trying to win this battle, even if it is just with me."

Michael smiled wide.

"I know that and that's what I love about you. Your heart is in the right place. Just know that you don't have to do this part alone. You don't have to keep suffering."

"Thank you, Mike. I understand, and I hear you, really I do. Suffering is what I know how to do. Being on my own, I've got that down pat right along with despair."

Alena let out another long sigh.

"It's over," Michael blurted.

"What?" Alena sat up rod straight in her chair.

"I'm divorcing Lola. My marriage is over, Alena."

"Are you sure that's what you want?"

"I am. I'm absolutely sure."

"Mike, I don't know what to say. I'm sorry."

"Don't be sorry. Everything will be all right. Lola and I agreed to do our best to stay civil, friends hopefully. The boys are having a hard time accepting it, but eventually we'll get through to the other side of this. A new normal."

Michael's eyes were watery.

"Listen, I want you to promise me something."

The air around them stilled and after a long pause Alena spoke, unsure of what he was getting to.

"What is it?"

"Will you promise that you won't send me away again?"

"That I can promise, Mike. I'm here for you, okay?" She offered him a hopeful smile.

"Good. Thank you. I needed to know that, Leen. And now that I've said my piece, what's been going on with your...um...journey?"

"Oh, that," she took a bite of her salad. "Well I'm definitely not the woman I was when you left. I'm releasing more of the old Alena every day. Something is changing in me, for good. I mean, how could it not? I just wish the doubtful side would go first though. I mean, look at this; I begged God to show up and in all her magnificence, she showed. Out of seven billion people in the world, she came to me! She put a mirror to my face and showed me my Savior. Sometimes I feel so ashamed that I'm still questioning any of it. If I'm so great, why do I still feel like me, so afraid and so small?"

"Don't be so hard on yourself. I don't know what more to tell you except to look back in that mirror, Alena, and have faith in the person you see there. You got this. They chose you for a reason, right? Accept it."

"How sweet are the lips that share wisdom with those that seek to know. The Divine Essence that flows from the heart that has been embraced by wisdom is sweeter than Milk and Honey."

SUNRISE

CHAPTER 19

Alena thought of Michael's words deep into the evening. She wanted to be sure, about him but mostly about her initiation. She wanted to know exactly what the Beings of Light had chosen her to do. She needed the next steps. She closed her eyes and spoke the words that came to her.

"Yeye Oshun? Mary Magdalene?" she called. "Come to me now, please. Tell me, what does all of this mean?" she whispered. "Show me what you want me to do."

She quieted her mind just as Gloria had taught her, and drew in deep, long breaths: letting her chest rise and fall into a meditative rhythm. With ease, the right words came to her.

"I am that I am. I call you in. I am ready."

She spoke the words slowly and let them hang on her lips. As she did, she could feel something happening.

The smell of sweet burning herbs reached her nose, and she opened her eyes to find a single milk-white dove perched on the arm of her sofa. She fixed her eyes on the creature, then it flew into her open hands, and at once, Alena found herself standing before a great ancient temple.

Hieroglyphs of Isis, Osiris, and Horus were carved into its massive walls and towering stone pillars. She walked through the temple's hulking pylon where a stately Nubian woman stood waiting. Her long, braided hair hung down her shoulders, and she wore a gauzy white linen tunic that fell to her ankles. Alena's eyes fell on the familiar amethyst amulet hanging at her throat.

"Welcome, Sister. I am Tabiry." The high priestess greeted Alena, and her hand gently clasped her shoulder.

"Who are you? Where am I?"

"I am your guide in this realm, and this is Philae, the Holy Temple of our beloved Mother Isis. We have been expecting you, Alena. Let us go inside with the others and prepare for your invocation."

What invocation? Alena thought. She had many questions, but she didn't think this was the time to ask them.

Inside the temple, the incense of myrrh hung heavily in the air. The clinging melodies of flutes, cymbals, and sistrums flooded the court. Bouquets of flowers and a banquet of fruits were piled high in the shrine. Tabiry offered Alena a copper goblet of sorghum wine and commanded a band of priestesses to bathe and dress her for the evening's event.

They bowed their heads gracefully and poised their ebony arms to gesture the way through a grand hall bedecked with carvings of voluptuous goddesses. Inside an opulent chamber room, the priestesses helped Alena bathe in sacred herbs and anointed her wrists and throat with frankincense oil. She was dressed in the same fine white linen tunic they all wore.

"You must not gaze directly into Mother Isis' eyes, sister," one of the priestesses warned her softly. "Not until she allows. To do so would be like beholding the sun."

Tabiry clapped her hands to signal the start of the invocation, and the music fell quiet.

"On this evening we invoke the full and complete presence of the Great Mother Isis herself. We call upon you, Holy Mother, to help your children and bless your daughters of this temple with your mysteries."

With a wave of Tabiry's hand, thousands of flames bloomed from their golden torches, setting the grand room alight. A colossal statue of a winged Goddess Isis stood in the center, her outstretched lapis vulture wings spanning across the entire width of the room.

The other priestesses joined Tabiry in preparing for Isis' blessings. Their chants to the deity flooded the temple. As they prayed from their hearts, the temple walls shook, and the stone floors quaked beneath their feet. The enormous statue cracked open, offering a flood of blinding white light.

Alena and the priestesses sunk down onto their bellies and prostrated themselves before the broken relic. From it, the great goddess Isis appeared. Alena's mouth dropped open at her might and brilliance. Her skin was as rich and black as the silt of the Nile, wondrous as a swath of starless night sky.

A crown of twelve gleaming stars sat atop her head, and a cloth of beaming sunlight cloaked her body. Around her neck lay a resplendent gold collar encrusted in jewels. As Isis drew closer, Alena saw that they were not jewels at all; they were planets orbiting within the piece. She shielded her eyes from the impossible depths of Isis' lightning-like gaze just as the priestesses had advised.

Just then, Isis turned her attention to Alena. "And who do we have here? What have you come for? Or do you even know?"

Alena's mouth was suddenly dry, and her voice muted. She kept her eyes under the covering of her forearm.

"Daughter, do not be afraid. You are free now to gaze upon me; no harm will come to you." Alena slowly lowered her arm from her face, but kept her eyes trained on the temple floor.

Isis laughed gently. "Ah, perhaps what you need is a bit of privacy." She gestured toward Tabiry and the other priestesses.

"You may leave us," she instructed, and in the blink of an eye, they were gone. Alena stood alone in that great room, face-to-face with the Goddess Isis who was both terrifying and stunning.

Isis beckoned Alena to come closer. "Come, daughter, speak to me."

"I don't..." she began, and then she cleared her throat hoping to find more of her voice. "I don't know exactly why I'm here...Your um...Highness."

Isis released a deep laugh, cocking her head this time as if musing over her small child struggling through their first words.

"Alena Ford, you have come so that you may learn," she said with such certainty that Alena felt it in her heart. "I will give you the secrets of the ages. I will give you the power you seek."

Alena obeyed, and on trembling legs, she stepped forward to Isis. "You needn't be afraid of me. Do you know who I am?" she smiled. Without waiting for a response, Isis began, "I am the Nubian Queen who has descended from the Heavens. I am the same God of your forefathers Abraham, Isaac, Jacob, and David," Isis said in a thunderous voice.

Right, I don't need to be afraid at all, Alena thought.

She mounted her throne and struck the temple floor with her mighty staff, enchanting it. Instantly, the stone floors transformed into a pool of dazzling black cosmos twinkling with a sea of stars and orbs of mighty planets before them.

"And, my daughter, I have come so that you may know the truth of humanity, the truth of your creation, and the truth of your divine mission on the planet earth. Hear it with your heart."

"Because the bee is influenced most of all by cosmic forces, by communing with the bee, the entire cosmos can find its way into human beings, assisting them in stepping into who they truly are."

THE SHAMANIC WAY OF THE BEE

CHAPTER 20

Alena's heart was busy fluttering as she darted a glance at Isis. The deity's face was beautiful, yet stern, as she met Alena's widened eyes.

"You did not expect me in this form, I presume?" A slight smile spread across Isis' face. "Well, what say you?" she waited for Alena to break her silence. "Speak your truth, and be warned, I can already hear it."

"It feels—" Alena paused as she thought about it, "well it feels a little…blasphemous," she said timidly.

"Of course it does," Isis rumbled. With that, a fiery shooting star flared in the pool of cosmos as if to mark her disappointment.

"Tell me, do you believe that human beings were created in the image and likeness of God?"

"Yes, I do." Alena answered quickly.

"And you, both black and woman, do you believe that you too were created by God?"

"Yes."

"So then how could it be that the God of humanity would mirror only one image of our creation, the white and the male? How did an African woman as God become an abomination in your eyes?"

Alena shifted uneasily under Isis's piercing gaze.

"I just never thought of God as a woman, much less as a black woman like me. I guess, to be honest, I thought of us more as a follow up."

"We did not create woman as a follow-up to man. Woman was our completion to creation. You are our final being that brought balance to the earth and perpetuated our handiwork."

"I see," Alena nodded understanding.

"You and your human family have been made to believe that the only God of this universe is a white man with flowing hair. It became a law in your world that those who do not fit into that physical image be denied holiness, denied their full citizenship of the Kingdom of Heaven. Lies and false doctrines!" Isis let her words settle for a few moments.

What Isis was saying was right in line with what Gloria had told Alena about the Black Madonna painting, but this time the words pressed far deeper into her understanding. Still, Alena's mind struggled to keep up with the avalanche of wisdom that was all but crumbling her old beliefs.

"I have come so that you may know my true face. It is infinite," Isis continued. "I am neither male nor female, white nor black—but all, Alena. We are all aspects of the one almighty God. I come to you now in my feminine form, for I am the feminine aspect of God. I am the Great Mother of All Creation. I am your Dark Mother, the Dark Matter whose love for you is so potent that it holds the galaxies together just as it holds your very cells together."

For several moments, Alena could only stare at Isis in stunned silence. Finally, she managed to form a halfway intelligent question.

"Then what is the point of race at all since it's been so divisive? If we're all the same, why not make us look the same too?"

"A-ha!" Isis gave her a satisfied smile. "Now you are getting somewhere."

Alena grinned too, relieved.

"You are not the same. In heart, mind, and spirit, of course all of our children are equally divine. Yet you are different, with a different responsibility. We made you that way."

Isis anticipated the perplexed look Alena gave her.

"Skin color was never meant to be divisive. It is the expression of the diversity of God's perspectives. It is a physical marker of a universal collaboration with every aspect of God that is contributing to the one universal mind." Alena's confusion grew deeper as Isis continued.

"I am God expressing as myself, just as you are an aspect of God expressing and experiencing as yourself, as black and woman, one called Alena Ford. Your unique God perspective is crucial to the collective God experience, just as crucial as say, God expressing and experiencing as Asian and man—like the Buddha when he still walked the earth."

"I still don't understand."

"*Rays* Alena, not race." Isis answered and then willed a glass object to appear in her palm.

"I want you to look here. What do you see?"

"It's a glass prism. Am I right?" Alena answered flatly, not expecting a geometry lesson.

"You are correct. And see here, what happens when a ray of white light passes through the prism."

"A rainbow?"

"Yes! When the beam of white light refracts through the prism, it separates into a spectrum of colors, a rainbow of rays. It is the same with the heart of God, the Divine Heart," Isis said and then waved her hand over the pool of cosmos. In its watery black depths, seven beautiful beams in seven different colors appeared.

"In the beginning, God, the piercing white beam of light, breathed forth seven rays of light, the rainbow, from the Divine Heart, which would be—"

"The glass prism." Alena finished, beginning to see Isis's point.

"Yes, exactly. Each ray of God's light contains the qualities and virtues of God, just as each of the rays in that rainbow contained the white light, and the white light contained all. They are Blue, which is the first Ray, Yellow, Pink, White, Green, Gold, and Violet, which is the final Ray." As Isis spoke, their colors shimmered in the cosmos, dazzling Alena.

"Now, from the dawn of time, our Divine Plan was and remains to be to create the Heavens on Earth and man in God's own image. As above, so below. To complete the Plan, every soul group of humans, or *race* as your world calls them, is given the distinct destiny of anchoring one of these Rays of God. To do this, the root race is sent to embody a different attribute of God on planet earth through their human experience. This is the order of creation."

Alena's mind raced, attempting to make sense of these revelations from Isis.

"So what are those attributes?" she asked.

"We are getting to that," Isis answered with a gracious smile. "But first, do you understand how the human family is all one, with quite different, yet equally important destinies to fulfill on Earth?

"Yes, I understand."

"The diversity of humanity is quite necessary to the delicate balance of the Universe. Each race and the Ray that it depicts is imperative to the Divine Plan. There is no supremacy or exclusion in God—all are perfect and divine. Any soul's insistence on division, or dissension, is proof of the Shetani's demonic infiltration within them. As long as human beings remain divided, and compete for the Light that they already possess, humanity as a whole will never ascend. You should also know that there are villains and victims in every soul's story, for every soul on earth has incarnated at some time into every Ray of God. Now, to the attributes."

"Black people's attributes." Alena added eagerly. "Can we start with what Ray black people are from?"

"The souls that have incarnated in black bodies are the children of the Blue and Violet Rays. The Blue Ray is the first Ray of divine light, the Alpha Ray. It is the Will and Faith of God, and the source of all the other Rays. The Violet Ray is the seventh and final Ray of divine light, the Omega ray. It is the Freedom of God. The Black race is the beginning and the ending, the Alpha and Omega… the original people beginning the race of man on earth.

"With this truth comes a heavy responsibility and great sacrifice. These sacrifices have manifested as the massive struggles that the Black race has had to overcome over the span of human history. This race was called to anchor these Rays and set an example of how to master them with integrity, unconditional love, and undying compassion even in the face of grave adversity."

Alena bristled. The latent, private fury that had burrowed deep inside her began to rumble up and make itself known. With its presence, she quickly lost her fear of Isis along with her poise.

"Why us?" Alena blurted angrily. "Why did we have to struggle the hardest of any other of these 'Rays,' and why did God…why did *you* allow us to go through such terrible things? Especially the slavery that still exists today—the mental slavery and racism!"

Alena instantly regretted her tone. "I'm sorry to argue," she said, "It's just so hard to understand. To accept."

"No apology needed," Isis said, smiling proudly. "You hold an ancient fire, Alena. You are a warrior for the truth and have been so for centuries. That is just what is required of a victorious Bridger, one of the reasons why I chose you to join my Tribe."

Isis spoke gently and tenderly. "To answer this, we must begin at the beginning. Are you willing to see the past differently?"

Alena slowly exhaled a breath she did not realize she had been holding. "I suppose. That's why I'm here, isn't it?" she said more boldly.

"It was from ancient Mother Africa that you have come, the birthplace from which all civilizations have emerged, the highest level of civilization ever known to man. Africa has been known by many names—Mu, Kush, Nubia—but it matters not. Her land, your land, was the true Garden of Eden."

Isis offered her hand to Alena. "Daughter, come with me," she commanded. Alena reluctantly stepped forward.

"Let the honey overflow in infinite tongues..."

"ODE TO THE BEE", PABLO NERUDA

CHAPTER 21

Isis gripped Alena's hand and slammed down her great staff. In the next instant, they were plunged into the pool of cosmos, descending at the speed of light to an odd and ancient planet Earth.

They soared over oceans and seas, mountain slopes and flat plains. Alena was spellbound, her eyes barely able to take in the surreal sights expanding before her. It seemed they'd arrived in paradise. The land was wild with life of every kind, colored in every hue of the rainbow and beyond, some that no human eye had beheld since this early dawn of time. The buildings and technology that jutted up from it made that of modern earth look ridiculously primitive.

This must be Heaven, Alena mused in her mind, scanning the sprawling wonders.

"No. This…is Mother Africa," Isis answered, reading her thought. "She was always a continent of great power, abundance, and wealth—the blessed womb. The magnificence you see here is the full potential of the earth in all her glory, our original intention for this planet and for our children." Isis' staff landed them down gently.

"This is what is known today as the Sahara Desert. As you can see, it was once a pristine stretch of luxuriant land, not the dry and barren place it was reduced to. Its great beauty was matched only by that of its people. Your people," Isis said.

Alena was again astounded, this time at the dark-skinned inhabitants of the terrifically strange place. They were a brown sea of beauty, majesty and divinity. Bold yet humble and full of joy.

"My people," Alena repeated, faintly smiling at the thought that she could have hailed from such a glorious lineage.

"We made a covenant with these first people that as long as they followed God's law, upheld it, and continued to rule in love, then they would always have dominion over this heavenly earth."

"So…how did we lose all of this?" Alena dared to ask.

As if to answer, Isis' staff whipped them up through the atmosphere and then brought them back down to a great valley. Towering over the valley was a lush tree dripping with sublime fruits, each ripened to perfection. Their rinds were rich in hues of the sunset with sapphire blossoms bursting from the tree's bright blue branches of light.

"This is the Tree of the Knowledge of Good and Evil." Isis announced.

"Wait, the Tree of Knowledge? From the *Bible*?" Alena paused to take in the beauty of the tree.

"I will let you decide that," Isis answered. "In the beginning, there were no bounds on the first people, only that they obey the Law with trust and surrender. The Law expressly forbid eating of the Tree. To eat of the Tree was to ingest the knowledge of good and evil, which was judgment that belonged only to God. In doing so, the people forfeited the promise of the Tree of Life, that which bears the true fruit of God's splendor. Now blinded by disobedience, humans could only cleave to their humanness."

The landscape then changed dramatically. The beauty of the land and the people was disintegrating into ruin.

"The Shetani envied God's favor over humans and thus tempted them even further away from their divine inheritance, the earth. Once the first people broke the covenant, their disobedience unleashed the Shetani and the dawn of suffering."

Alena looked around to see that the mighty civilizations were no more. Once bountiful, the land was now littered with the corpses of great beasts and humans alike, scorched by the sun. Sorrow fell over those who survived.

"In grace, we urged them to repent from their error many times, and to remember themselves. Yet they fell prey to the Shetani's contagion of darkness and chose instead to live independent from God and God's law. They pilfered Mother Earth for her riches, and exalted wealth and power as their new God. Their sense of separation from God extended of course to their fellow brother and sister, and soon enough they could kill with ease for a mere nugget of gold. What they did not understand was that death only begets more death, not just for themselves but also for their children's children. So began the sorrowful era of humans playing God and the Shetani urging them along, the Great Fall. It was the birth of war and division on earth, and darkness fell over Mother Africa's holy land."

"So is this why we're struggling so much now?" Alena asked. "Is this why we're the most hated race on earth?"

"As the elders of humanity and the chosen people, you had sworn in the covenant to keep the sacred things of God, and to destroy the enemies of the Light. Yet," Isis said sadly, "the chosen ones chose against their true power—love. It was a stain on human life that would need to be redeemed, by prophesy. Even if that prophesy meant pain."

Before their eyes, the lands once green and teeming with life shriveled into the yellow desolate sands of the Sahara Desert.

"With their gift of free will, those chosen people, the Tribe of the Lion, disobeyed God's creed and broke the covenant. They soon forgot who they were, and the Shetani has helped ever since to hide all trace of their divine heritage. Atonement was required for their disobedience. It was a prophecy that had to be fulfilled, and we could

185

not intervene. That early defiance caused a rippling curse through humanity, and it had to be purified to set the Divine Plan aright."

Alena thought about what she had learned in church and what Mary had taught her about the beasts in her heart. Isis' words were beginning to make a lot more sense. Then, surprising her, she also thought of the black curse her father had always warned her of, the one that had helped to break him, and devour his sense of freedom.

"So are you saying that we're still plagued by that "defiance"? Is this why we've been the damn scapegoats and the whipping horses of the world for over four hundred years?"

"Just as the beloved Christ endured persecution, suffering, and rejection to demonstrate the Will of God, so have you. In order to anchor God's Will, you first had to demonstrate the consequences of going against it. In order to anchor God's Freedom, you first had to demonstrate its opposite— enslavement."

"But why would we have to endure enslavement? We had nothing to do with those ancient times! If you are God, couldn't you have made an intervention of some kind? I don't mean any disrespect, but that just doesn't seem right or fair to me, Isis."

Alena's eyes pricked with angry tears and they slowly made their way down her face. Still, she was willing to be as relentless as a pit bull until she received an answer that satisfied her.

"My daughter, you are our first-borns, our beloved eldest children. We have always loved you deeply and fully—greater than a human being could ever perceive or imagine." Isis engulfed Alena in her mighty arms.

Alena rolled her teary eyes, unconvinced.

"Your suffering causes God even greater suffering. We have never left your side, nor have we ever stopped loving our children the same as we did when we first forged the covenant.

"But you could still *allow* it?"

"What we allowed were causes to render their effects, and choices to meet their destinies—all with love and grace."

"For how long was it necessary? Four hundred years of torture, Isis! Four hundred years and the pain from slavery still lives on with us! In case you haven't noticed, they're still hunting us down there on earth. They're killing us off when they can't control us and we're dying from broken hearts."

Isis ignored her outburst and struck her staff against the enchanted floor once again.

A sick feeling heaved in Alena as Isis's magic took her to yet another time and place. Under her feet were the worn wooden planks of an old ship. A slave ship. Alena flinched as cold Atlantic waters sprayed her face.

"The Black race was not brought to the Americas as slaves. You were sent there by God. What the Black race has done is hailed by all of Heaven, Alena. The depth of your victory is far greater than the treachery of enslavement. The strongest and most noble souls from your Ray agreed in the spirit realm to usher in the New Earth by becoming the catalyst for the passing away of the old Earth. This agreement was a new covenant with God, the purification, in which the Black race would anchor the Blue and Violet Rays in the New World through their human experience of enduring and then overcoming slavery. As it is written, the Black race went on to serve their enemies in a place they knew not for four hundred years."

Sorrow and rage pressed hard against Alena. She tried to bear it. To be strong in that moment, she felt, was the least she could do for her suffering ancestors. They moved to the belly of the ship, and there they were—shackled and pressed flesh-to-flesh in filth.

Isis continued, "When those mooring ropes were loosed and the slave ships set sail for the Americas, the New Blood Covenant was also set forth. A new mercy. The heinous and brutal captivity of those noble souls at the hands of their own African brothers and the Caucasian race, the children of the Pink and White rays, was truly a holy work of sacrifice that has served all of humanity in its spiritual evolution. It also served as the springboard for the return of the Black race to their rightful place and destined path." With another crack of her great staff, Isis and Alena returned to the temple.

"Now, I must tell you that some of the souls that came forward from the Blue and Violet rays and into the Black race had origins outside of planet earth," Isis announced.

"Are you talking about... aliens?"

"I am. Yet not in the misguided and negative way that your world has constructed them. These souls stepped forward from other stars and planets to join forces with planet Earth and fortify the consciousness there so that a New Earth could indeed be possible. They set out on a quest of love to help accelerate planet Earth's evolution. The star Sirius was one of those assisting stars.

Alena frowned, not understanding.

"Those loving and noble souls came to Earth with a far more advanced consciousness than the younger souls that were there, and thus, they came with much needed expertise in surpassing the human condition in order to reach ascension. Their advanced wisdom and fortitude has been key in assisting Earth to fulfill the Divine Plan and move forward in ushering in the New Earth. You are one of those great Sirian souls, Alena."

Alena sucked in a breath. "Are you telling me that I'm not human, Isis?"

Isis smiled. "Of course not, my dear. You are quite human. You've just got something a little...extra." Isis winked, and then moved on quickly.

"You must understand that it was for the depth of your spirits and hearts that you and the rest of these souls were chosen for this mission. God and the entire company of heaven revere you. Your majestic power is unmatched. You are still a chosen people, now in a strange, yet *appointed* land. Do you hear me? You and your people are there by divine right, purpose and destiny. You *belong* there."

Alena nodded proudly.

"Despite appearances, America is the stage that we chose for humanity's ascension to be completed. They call it a melting pot, we call it a cauldron of all Rays. It is right on your soil that the first wave of humankind will return back fully to its original, divine state, and all of the earth will follow suit. This is the reason why this experience of slavery occurred in the Americas.

Isis touched her palm to Alena's shoulder.

"Although it was almost unspeakable, the suffering that you and your people have endured has shaped you into the crown jewel of this age. Black people's enslavement was the impetus for anchoring God's Freedom, Faith, and Will for all of humanity. You will lead the earth and continue to be the spark for the greatest change yet," Isis explained. Her face glowed joyfully.

"As with all things, the term of suffering has come to an end. The generations of the Tribe of the Lion have paid their debts for disobedience, and atonement is complete. With the new covenant fulfilled, a new day has come. You and all of those who have been last during atonement are first once again. The mission of the Blue and Violet Ray remains the same. Turn back to the same indomitable spiritual power that you stood in during those first Golden ages—with love and integrity—and usher in the New Earth."

"Please, Isis. Tell me, how are we to do that? Even if we're all of the glorious things that God says that we are, the fact remains that we're still the most hated. We're still the most disrespected and abused. If we have all of this favor, why does it feel like such a curse to be born black?"

"You still feel that you are cursed?" Isis turned to her with a grave look. "You are not the only Ray that suffers, daughter, but you are the only one with this unique charge on your life. How can that be a curse? You are not and have never been under a curse. You of human and ancient Sirian blood are under a blessing. Have you ever wondered how despite all of the strife your people have been dealt, you only continue to thrive? Evolve? Inspire?" Isis continued without waiting for a response.

"The greatest lie the Shetani ever defiled humanity with was the idea of the inferiority of the Black race. It was engineered like a virus and implanted into your consciousness. They will always try to convince you to despise yourselves and forget your heritage. But remember this: the truth is that God hid the Word in the Tribe of the Lion and the unfailing Word, not a curse, is always with you. As consequence for this truth, the Shetani hotly pursue you. This is why you have been hated." Alena was now galvanized with pride, in her people and in herself.

"Your birthright is stamped on your soul. Take your rightful place, Alena. Then help them to do the same." Isis commanded. "Your humanity has been tested so that you can model for the world what humanity is supposed to look like. You and your people will turn back to your power and accomplish your mission by first mastering yourselves. Purge out every residue of unworthiness and any hint of the Shetani's reign from your own individual being, and then, unify as one. You are the Bridger who will help to make whole that which has been torn asunder. You will teach the human family to unite and stand together against the Shetani. The Era of Rebirth is upon you. The Age of Magic has returned. The tools and powers that were sealed away from you are being returned as well."

"She moves from flower to flower but she does not sip nectar. Rather, she devours the blossom with all her senses; inhaling the fragrance, savoring the taste, absorbing the color."

THE SHAMANIC WAY OF THE BEE

CHAPTER 22

"Mrs. Ford? Hi there. I'm Amy Wannager, pleased to meet you." Alena gave the mousy looking woman a polite smile and then looked around the CCP office. It was shabby and small with towers of boxes almost reaching the ceiling. A lone poster of a sad looking woman and her child was framed on the stark tan wall.

"I am sorry for the short notice. We had an appointment open up at the last minute and thought we could get you started sooner rather than later. Can I get you some water or something? We're out of coffee."

"Good to meet you as well. No thank you, I'm fine."

"Great, then please have a seat and let's start with a quick overview of the program," Ms. Wannager said, sitting down behind her desk.

"My fees are being paid for by a grant awarded to the organization. Whatever charges exceed your allotment within thirty-eight hundred dollars will be considered pro bono. To preserve grant funds applied to your case, the Crisis Project may ask for you to participate in various conservation practices, like agreeing to receive and submit documents via email to reduce waste and costs or to keep phone calls with your representative as brief as possible. And finally, you may be tapped as a volunteer in the future as well. Do you have any questions?"

"Maybe one." Alena wondered if she should tell Amy that this had all been a mistake and that she had never applied, or was this a gift from the Beings of Light. Who could have sent in the application for her? "Out of curiosity, what made you choose my case?" she asked.

"We receive thousands of applications in any given year, so our selection process is more of a lottery. After a rare influx of funding, we were able to sponsor twenty additional families this quarter. Your submission was pulled, and you certainly met our guidelines for aid and, well, there you have it."

"I just... I can't believe it. It's a prayer answered."

"Well Congratulations. Will you agree to these conditions?"

Alena nodded. "Yes."

"Please sign and initial here," she said, pushing the contract across the desk, which Alena signed.

"Perfect. All right, so I've looked into your file, but I like my clients to tell me about their situation and what they're seeking in their own words."

"I'm seeking full physical custody of our daughter, Maya. There was infidelity on my husband's part throughout the marriage. He had an affair and left me for the other woman."

"And how long ago has it been since you separated?"

"It's been about nine months now since he left. What he failed to mention on his way out was that our home was in foreclosure. The bank took it a short while after he left. Around the same time, I was laid off, and we ended up moving quickly to my current address. Things were rough financially, but I was staying afloat."

"So what was the custody schedule after your separation?"

"My daughter was living with me. When my husband finally came out of hiding, he demanded to see her, so I let him, no overnight stays though. It wasn't until I was uh… attacked and landed in the hospital that he took over and insisted she stay with him. I didn't want to make things worse, so I didn't fight him. I was served for the hearing and here I am, seeing my daughter on weekends only."

"I see. I need full disclosure, Mrs. Ford. Would there be any reason at all that your husband would be fearful of keeping your child in your care?"

"Well, the neighborhood I live in would be the only reason. But as bad as it looked with my incident, it really isn't as terrible as he, and others, made it out to be. Maya was still going to a great school, still getting her homework done, and being the happy and well-adjusted kid she's always been. He was the one who shut my finances down, and it's not like I didn't have a great income before my situation changed.

Alena put her palms out.

"Outside of those reasons, no, he has no need to keep Maya out of my care. I'm not on drugs, I'm very well educated, and I've got a career of my own."

"Yes, of course. We just have to look at everything, just like the other side will," Ms. Wannager explained.

"So, what do you think? Do I have a strong chance of getting my daughter back?"

The attorney leaned back in the chair. "Well, we've got some pretty strong arguments to pry this thing open. The judge in your case appeared to have been biased in his decision, and frankly, Mrs. Ford, this is why we exist. I've seen several rulings that strip rights and time away from a capable and vice-free mother in favor of a wealthier, better represented father. The fitness of the custodial parent is one of the court's considerations. But I don't think the judge adequately weighed the most important facts.

"You were the child's custodial parent and acted as such up until the point that you were hospitalized. There was a precedent set before he strong-armed visitation away from you. From what I can tell, there doesn't appear to be any evidence presented by the plaintiff that your daughter suffered educationally, medically, emotionally, or physically while in your care. While your residence and financial situation were not ideal, at no point were you deemed unfit to be the child's custodial parent."

"Ms. Wannager, I've already told the judge these things and he didn't care. What makes you so sure that this will change anything?"

The lawyer sighed. "Can I be frank with you, Mrs. Ford?

"Of course."

"With all due respect, you went in there unrepresented. Going pro se against a hard hitter like your husband's attorney was the equivalent of going to the hearing wearing a dunce cap on your head. As unfortunate as it is, the truth is that sometimes what we call justice is all about perception. You appeared to be in a position of weakness, and you were railroaded. We're going to do this my way now, okay?"

Alena nodded.

"So, we'll do a couple of things here. We'll argue that it's in Maya Ford's best interest that she be returned to her mother. In addition to the stress this separation has caused her, she is a growing and developing child that needs motherly care at this crucial stage. We'll show the court that at the time of the ruling, you were in the midst of a diligent search for work and in the interim have successfully obtained employment adequate to support your child. Now with the uh… personal violence that you sustained it would be advisable that, if at all possible, you relocate as well to complete this picture of redemption. Is that a feasible option?

"Yes, I just have to find a place with an affordable rent."

"Good. The sooner you do so, the better. Now, how far are you and Mr. Ford in the divorce process?"

Alena shrugged. "I haven't filed and as far as I know, neither has he. The only papers I've received were the ones for custody."

"Hmm, that's quite interesting. He's aggressive in his pursuit for Maya, yet has not made any effort to dissolve the marriage. He may have been thinking ahead. It would be pretty hard for you to get alimony or child support if he's the one with primary custody at the time of dissolution. I would also advise that we file immediately."

Ms. Wannager shuffled some papers on her desk and made a note to herself.

"These custody matters, in addition to any claims for support or alimony, will all need to be addressed. I will, of course, represent you in the petition. Can we get you full physical custody? I don't know. Dad obviously is very involved and certainly ready for a fight which, Mrs. Ford, really is a good thing as long as he's a good father. Is Mr. Ford a good father?"

Alena nodded. "He is. I don't see much of their interaction these days, but he's always been a great dad to Maya. And Maya, as much as it used to hurt me, she's a bit of a daddy's girl. She loves her dad and he loves her, fiercely."

"Good. That's great. The bulk of clients we serve here have had to worry about protecting their children against a father's violence, abuse, even molestation. Sad stuff. Well, Mrs. Ford, I'll certainly fight for full custody, but even if you end up getting at least a joint custody arrangement that doesn't limit you to weekends, I'd consider that a win, too."

Alena gave a hopeful smile, although the thought of joint custody still stung.

"I'm confident that we've got something solid here. I'll be contacting Mr. Ford's attorney to get a feel for the possibility of mediation. Stranger things have happened with these cases. Okay? So, we'll stay in touch."

"The taste of honey on the tongue is a lightness, a quickening, a deep emanation of the sun's light as all of creation bears witness and answers."

SONG OF INCREASE

CHAPTER 23

That evening, Alena was restless. She had already paced the living room, made two cups of tea, and tried to read a book. Finally she had resigned to just sitting on the couch and closing her eyes. As she sat there, she felt the familiar beckoning pull that began as a tingling at the crown of her head, through her spine, and then traveled through her heart. Her eyes fluttered closed, and the space in the center of her eyes had begun to buzz. The blackness behind her eyelids filled with light, and then images. She was peering through her third eye, and this time, without a wormhole.

Once again, Alena found herself transported. She was standing at the great jewel-encrusted door of her Queendom, her heart. Alena shuddered and braced herself to behold the frightening dark world of her heart as she had before.

At her silent command, the door opened once again. But this time, the most marvelous, grand palace Alena could have ever imagined greeted her. Its brilliant crystalline walls were made of translucent pink quartz and stood at least sixty feet high. The floors were vivid green jade tiles and glistening emerald slate. Solid gold columns rose from them, jutting up into the palatial archways above. A sweet fragrance of tuberoses permeated the air.

There Mary Magdalene stood in a rose quartz archway, as serene and radiant as before, with an endearing smile welcoming Alena.

Alena grinned excitedly as Mary enclosed her in an embrace. "I'm so glad to see you again!" Alena exclaimed.

"Welcome back, Beloved. I know yours has been an arduous and exciting journey."

"I'm grateful for every moment of it, Mary."

"Well you should be very proud, Alena. You have done marvelous work in clearing your heart, Dear One. Well done. What you will receive here during our time together is the most important key," Mary said as she led Alena through the labyrinth of her heart as she had before.

They ascended one of the spiral stone staircases swirling to the upper chambers. There was no more darkness and the once slime-drizzled walls were pristinely pink with no sign of the Shetani's beasts. Mary and Alena returned to the chamber that held the great Emerald Table.

"You've been working diligently, yet there is one final lesson awaiting you here," Mary said, motioning Alena to approach the table of her heart.

"All creation began with and flows through the black woman. You are the keys to the New Heaven on the New Earth. You must unlock the door, and then change will be assured. We are the Black Madonna, we are the Great Dark Mother emerged as one. Me, you, Isis, Oshun, our daughters—we are the Watchers, the Healers, the Bridgers, and the Guardians. We will end the Shetani's reign and division of the Rays. We will bring oneness and harmony to all of the Great Dark Mother's children who heed the call. There will be even more assistance for you to bring this massive change, as there was for me. A divine partnership." Mary placed a hand on Alena's shoulder. "It's time you heard my story, Dear One."

"I was a High Priestess of the Great Mother Isis. One evening, I lit my candle for her, and she came to me. For many years after, I attended her mystery schools. When the time had come she told me that I was one half of the same soul, that the other half of my soul walks among the earth in search of me to join together and serve the will of God together in a mighty way. The divine sparks placed inside of us were once one kindling fire, and we were Twin Flames. Two halves of one whole with the same life mission.

"We were separated to experience our own individual spiritual enlightenment. We would be cleaved together once again in due time. For many, many lifetimes we learned our lessons, felt the joy and pain of humanity, and perfected ourselves, separately.

"As our enlightenment grew with every incarnation, the distance between us shortened. We were being prepared for a lifetime together in which we would both fulfill our divine destinies. When my divine flame reunited with his, our fire served to free all humanity from the noose of the Shetani's curse of sin and death. Our divine union ushered in a powerful change for humanity. You, too, will find such a Twin Flame in your lifetime, Alena." What Mary said next surprised Alena even more.

"Alena, what do you know of the Holy Grail?"

"Not much. I just remember in the *Indiana Jones* movie that it was a really special gold cup. One that all of the villains were willing to kill for."

"A lost treasure?"

"Yes", Alena answered.

"Ah, such as this one?" A beautiful golden chalice dotted with aquamarine and olive green jewels appeared in the palms of Mary's hands.

Alena had never actually watched the entire movie, but the cup seemed to fit the splendor of the reviews she'd heard.

"Yes," Alena's eyes widened with wonder. "Probably just like that! Is that...is that the Holy Grail?" she stammered, her voice catching in her throat.

With a clench of her fist, Mary crushed the chalice until it was dust in her hands. She blew gently, sending the remaining golden powder scattering into the air.

"No, it is not. Christ cannot be held in the material yearnings of man and will never be found in wicked pursuits. Such power, such force, cannot be possessed like a common trinket."

Alena was a bit disappointed.

"The Holy Grail is neither a golden relic nor a chalice from which Christ imbibed. It is not even my womb as some have pondered. There is but one hiding place for the Holy Grail, a destination that requires a journey from the head to the heart. In man's arrogant quest to possess it, that which is in plain sight was hidden away. For it has been commanded, seek ye first the Kingdom and all shall be added unto you." Mary looked deeply into Alena's eyes.

"Would you like to know the true Holy Grail, Dear One?"

"Yes, of course." she answered hopefully.

"Come, follow me, and I will show you."

Mary led Alena from the Emerald Table and down another great hall.

"The treasures that man has searched for lay only in the heart. Those who have cultivated unconditional love and victory over darkness also assure a most cherished gift, the fifth chamber of the heart. While most humans only fully develop four chambers, your dedication to your healing has cleared the way for this portal to be opened."

They came to the fifth and final chamber door. It had been locked shut at her first visit. This time it sprung open at their approach. Mary opened her arms to the vision that awaited.

"Alena, behold the Holy Grail, the fifth chamber of your heart! It is here in your heart that the Kingdom has come. This throne room of your Queendom is the one true vessel for your Lord, the Christ."

"Did I just hear you right?" Alena slowly realized what Mary had said. The Holy Grail was right there in her heart.

Inside was an enormous sprawling room, each of its massive walls and ceiling were covered in twinkling blood red rubies. At the center of the boundless garnet tiled floor, a blazing white, sapphire blue, and rose-pink fire roared, its flames licking the soaring red heights of the room.

"This is your Divine Fire of Three; love, wisdom, and power. The Divine placed this ever-burning fire within every soul prior to your descent to earth from the Divine Heart. It, like you, is eternal." Mary spoke slowly and deliberately. "And so," she said, "is He," directing her eyes toward an image of a man that had suddenly appeared in the center of the Fire of Three. She then watched Alena intently as she beheld the vision.

Alena stood entranced with her mouth open. His eyes were as bright as sunbeams, blazing with an unimaginable depth of purity and love. His skin was as dark as burned brass, and a fiery ray of white light roared around his head.

"No. It can't be," she mumbled. Alena lifted her eyes to his, and then quickly threw up an arm to shield them from the painful blaze of light he emitted. His brilliance was too piercing for Alena to behold.

"From your Holy Grail, this blazing altar for the Christ in your heart, you shall draw all unto you," Mary said quietly.

The muscles in Alena's trembling legs went slack and folded under her. There on the smooth coolness of the jeweled floor, Alena bowed before Him. "My Lord," she stammered weakly.

Mary helped Alena back to her feet. The vision of the man was gone.

"Whoa!" Alena stood motionless trying to process the experience. "Whoa! Whoa! Whoa!" was all that she could seem to say. Her eyes glazed over with disbelief.

Mary smiled, pleased. "Christ is God's light and love, Dear One. He is the gateway through which the human and the divine worlds meet. His dwelling place is here. Invite Him to make a home out of your heart."

"Can we just slow down for a minute, please? That was Jesus? In my heart? *Jesus!*"

"Yes, Alena," Mary affirmed. "He has been waiting for you to awaken, as we all have."

"Well can I speak to him? I have so many questions, so many things that I want to—"

"He is always with you," Mary assured midsentence. "You may speak to him at any time. He will be waiting with love. Receive him. For now, we must move on. There is something more that you need to see."

Mary Magdalene gestured for Alena to step closer.

"I am going to give you something, a gift. Would you like to have it?"

"From you? Of course, Mary. I would be honored."

Mary then dipped her hands into the Divine Fire of Three and a small yet fierce flame burned where the golden chalice had sat. In the next moment, they both were standing in Alena's living room.

"Look out of your window and tell me what you see." Alena looked through the window.

"Buildings, trees, the street, sidewalks, a red Mazda without any plates double parked in front of that black truck," Alena said.

"Is that all?"

Three young black men were gathered on the front stoop of the apartment. Alena shrugged and rolled her eyes.

"Neighborhood guys. I don't know them, but I see them around that same spot all the time." She squinted for a better look.

"One of them looks like the thug who robbed me. They're probably dealing drugs or bragging about some woman."

"Yes. Is this all that you think of them?"

"Well I don't *want* to think of them like that. I really don't. But I've lived here long enough to see that there are good people, and then there are these guys. Maybe if they didn't act like such gangsters trying to be warlords and talked like they had good sense and respect for other people, then, well, maybe they wouldn't have half the trouble they bring on themselves." Alena remembered Ms. Wannager's words. "Or the perception."

"I tell you the truth," Mary said. "You have not seen them clearly. Come close to me." Mary instructed. "Close your eyes and brace yourself. This will not hurt you."

She pressed the still burning fire from her palms into Alena's sealed eyelids.

"Now open your eyes and look at your brothers once more," Mary commanded.

Alena did so and was astonished. The men were no longer clad in sagging jeans and oversized jackets. They were kings, dressed in luminous metallic robes. A pulsating pillar of light surrounded each of them, and a radiant pink arch of light emitted at least thirty yards from each of their hearts.

"They're magnificent." Alena said in an awed whisper.

"The gift I have given to you is true vision, temporarily. It will last only during our time together, and then it will be yours to earn. What you can see now in these souls are their true selves, god kings walking amongst you. This is how we Beings of Light view each of you. They may present as disrespectful, menacing, and selfish, but it is only because darkness has fallen upon them and lulled them to sleep."

Alena nodded and looked even more deeply at each of the men.

"They have identified as that darkness, by themselves and by the world. Theirs is the same darkness that dwelled in you before you became aware and purged it out. They have pain just like you did. But you see, neither their light, nor yours, can ever be destroyed.

"This is the crux of your work on earth. You must see beyond the illusions and help humanity to see beyond them also. Alena, your robbery experience was a clarion call, an awakening. It seized your attention when nothing else would. You had to lose everything to gain yourself and be drawn into an illusion to discover the truth. As you know, it is the Shetani's plan that you harbor hatred for yourself and those that look like you. These men are no different than you were."

"I can certainly see that now," Alena said repentantly.

"You are the lamppost that will help restore all of humanity, including your brothers, to their true selves, the kings of light that they truly are. As you liberate yourself, you will liberate all. Are you ready for this?"

"I hope I don't sound ungrateful, Mary, but how? Why would the entire Black race, let alone the entire world, even listen to me? What could I say to make them believe? I keep hearing that I will do great things—and I'm very honored to do them all—but how, Mary? I'm never told how I'm supposed to work all of this… magic."

Mary brought a finger to her lips to quiet Alena's doubt.

"Begin by trusting yourself. Acknowledge the miracles you have created thus far."

Immediately Ms. Wannager and the grant came to Alena's mind.

"Your work has already begun with you. You are only uncovering what already is. It is not necessary to know how, you only need to be ready and willing. By the time your initiation is complete, you will be well equipped. Farewell for now, Dear One."

"Each drop of honey contains the rising helix, which invigorates humankind through its spiritual forces. Honey filled with spiritual forces kindles the heart of fellowship."

SONG OF INCREASE

CHAPTER 24

By Friday evening, the anticipation had climbed steadily until Alena's heart was on the verge of bursting. She could hardly contain herself when she saw her daughter waiting in Gramercy Park with Gabriel. "Mommy!" Maya squealed, running in her stiff new boots.

She threw her arms around her mother and hugged her tightly. Gabriel gave Alena a nod that almost seemed remorseful and walked to his car. Alena relished in the warmth of Maya's petal-soft skin and the candy sweet smell of her hair, curled wildly around her face. Holding her again felt like rain to a long arid earth. Maya was breathing quickly. Her little shoulders shuddered as her excitement turned into sobbing. Alena kissed her cheeks then gently stroked them.

"I'm here. Mommy's here, baby."

Maya pressed herself so hard into Alena it was as if she believed she could eventually press back into the sanctuary of her mother's body. For the first time, Alena felt chosen. Though the desperation in her daughter's embrace almost broke her heart, she knew she had been missed.

"I'm so happy to see you, baby!" Maya slowly loosened her grip, and Alena dried her face.

"Mom, I missed you so, so much," Maya gushed. "I love you so much, Mommy."

"You would never understand how much I love and miss you, Maya. It's more than anything I can describe on earth, my love. But we're together now," she said with a broad smile. "And now… it's time to have some fun!" she said, tickling Maya.

Alena spent the weekend half-loving, half-atoning, and staving off sorrow. She vowed to unearth any sadness that may have lodged itself into her daughter. They carved jack-o'-lantern faces into two fat pumpkins and drank hot cider with cinnamon sticks in them. Alena was whipping eggs into cupcake batter when Maya said suddenly, "I don't like Miss Brittany, Mom. All she does is have her fancy parties and tell me to keep quiet while she's having them. 'Dress pretty and keep quiet like a good, proper young lady.' And Dad is gone all the time. I hate it, Mom."

Alena stopped whipping. She placed one hand on Maya's arm and lifted her small face with the other up to meet her eyes.

"Are they hurting you? Is anyone hurting you, Maya?"

"No, Mom."

"Is she mean to you? How does she treat you?"

Maya shrugged again. "She's all right, I guess. I don't think she wants me around though. It's like she tries to pretend I'm not there at all."

Alena cupped her hand over mouth and breathed deeply. She closed her eyes and called on Mary and Oshun. She called on strength and mercy. She called on God and all of the celestial promises of peace for her child.

"Mom, I want to stay with you. Please, Mom. I want to stay here. Why can't I be with you again?"

"Soon enough, baby. Let's go have some fun! I'm going to get ready and then we'll go to Ms. Gloria's, okay?"

Alena had been in the bathroom for less than five minutes when she heard Maya yell, "Mom, where did you get this? It's so cool!"

Maya was peering into the golden Mirror of Truth. In the reflection, she was a young woman many years into the future. She was dressed in a violet gown and seated upon a throne among a crescent of six others. A sea of priestesses bowed before them. Then a regal looking woman went to place a crown on Maya's head, and as soon as she did her throne filled with blackness.

"Oh my God!" Alena gasped, and then the phone rang, her mother.

"Hey Ma."

"I'm glad I caught you at home," Dinah's grave tone gave her pause. She knew what it had to mean.

"You doing all right? How's Maya?"

"Yes, I'm doing good. Maya's doing well, too. Is everything okay?"

"Look, Lena Jae, it's your father."

Alena's heart sank and she braced for her mother's inevitable words.

"He doesn't have more than a day or so. If you want to say your last goodbyes then you should come now."

Alena tried to ignore the sudden fear that tightened her body. "Okay, Mama. I'll be there as fast as I can."

"All right."

"Ma?"

"Yeah?"

"Are you okay?"

"I don't know, Lena, trying to trust in the Lord."

Alena willed the lump of anguish back down her throat.

"I'll see you soon. I'm so sorry."

Alena's hand quivered as she dialed Gabriel. "Yes?" he answered calmly.

"Gabe, my father is passing away. I need to leave for Maryland and I want to bring Maya with me. She's hasn't met my side of her fami—"

"Of course, Alena," he said before she could finish. "Of course she can go. I'm sorry to hear about your father."

She could hardly believe how civil he was being.

"All right, thank you for understanding. I'll let you know when I get back."

"Okay Alena. Take care."

Alena blinked out of the shock of Gabriel's sudden decency and went to make travel arrangements.

"Maya baby, we're taking a trip to Maryland. Something's happened to my father, Grandpa Linny. He's very, very sick so we have to move fast. I want you to meet him before...never mind. So I want you to pack three days of clothes really quick, okay?"

Maya nodded and began stuffing school clothes into her princess suitcase.

"Mom, is Grandpa Linny going to die?"

"Probably so, honey." A tear fell, and Alena wiped it away hurriedly with the back of her hand.

"Mom, is Grandpa Linny still a bad man?"

The question alone seized Alena's tongue. "No, Grandpa isn't a bad man, baby. I should've never told you that he was, it wasn't for little ears."

Maya hugged her mother. "I don't want you to be sad, Mom."

"I know, baby. Go on and get ready, okay? We've only got a short while to make our train."

"Mom, if he isn't bad then why didn't you ever want me to visit Grandpa Linny and Grandma Dinah before?"

"Remember I told you before, Maya Bear, we had a lot of big people problems and…and it just wasn't a good time for you to know them yet."

"So it's a good time now?"

"Yes, Maya. It's time now, that's all that counts."

The taxi arrived at the hospice, and they carted their luggage past the lobby. Alena saw her sisters Agatha and Syreeta in the hallway and felt the weight of their shocked glances. They must not have expected her. Alena was shocked, too. They both looked so different—fully grown women with lives of their own that had not included her in years. Syreeta was fleshier now. Her body seemed to carry at least sixty extra pounds since the last time Alena had seen her. She prayed that neither of them would greet her with anger.

At the end of the hallway, they all stood facing one another. A brooding patchwork of shame, love, and grief stretched over the Johnson sisters. Underneath its shadow, they all stood in tear filled mourning of the past and present. They embraced as a family, though with anxious tenderness, speaking nothing of the churning that lay just beneath.

"You both look great," Alena finally said. "You do, you look wonderful. I'm so...I'm sorry we're having to come together like this. I'm sorry for everything, for staying away…"

"Oh be quiet," chided Agatha. "Don't be sorry. You're here now. We're together. Now is not the time to feel sorry, Lena, so don't, okay?"

She rubbed Alena's back with sisterly affection and sighed.

"You've always been our Lena Jae, no matter what."

Syreeta averted her eyes from Alena's. Her tears had forged two long trails in her makeup.

Agatha turned to Maya.

"Oh my God, is this my niece?" she cooed. "Look at this beautiful child! Look at that face. You're all grown up. I'm your Auntie Aggie and this is your Auntie Reeta. We've been waiting to meet you for a long, long time."

Maya smiled timidly, awkward under all of the attention. Agatha bent down and gave her a loving hug then turned back to Alena.

"You should go on in. He's been waiting for you. We'll be out here. The doctors don't want us to crowd him. One at a time. Randy and Mama should be back any minute. Ma had a little bit of a breakdown, so he took her to get some air," she said.

"We'll go in then. I want Maya to see Daddy." Both Syreeta and Agatha shot Alena quizzical looks as Alena held Maya's hand and walked toward her father's room. Before they entered, Maya jerked her hand out of Alena's grasp.

"Mom, I don't want to. I don't want to say hello. Please," she was tugging on Alena's arm, starting to panic.

"Maya, come now, don't you want to see your grandfather?"

"I can see him from here, Mom."

"It's probably frightening to see him like this, Lena," Agatha said. "No worries, I'll take her to the lobby. I think I've got some games on my phone, sweetness. Why don't you come with Auntie Aggie?" She then led Maya down the corridor.

"Thank you," Alena mouthed to her sister and stepped into the room.

Her father lay limp on the hospital bed, barely looking anything like himself. He had grown even frailer than before.

"Daddy," Alena whispered. She held his hand, and this time he didn't flinch. He grasped hers back.

"Lee?" he was too weak to speak her name fully. "Yes, Daddy, I'm here."

"I love…" he uttered. His dimming eyes stared through hers, and then grew more and more vacant as if he were in a lingering dream.

"I love you too, Daddy."

"Ready to go home." His breathing grew fainter and fainter.

The life left in his eyes was dimming. He was fading.

"Doctor! I need a doctor!" Alena screamed. Though she knew it was too late.

"Daddy! Daddy!" she screamed. Begged. Her father clenched her hand and she felt his life fading away under her fingertips.

"Lord, forgive me my sins." He abruptly drew in a sharp breath, and then pushed it out with finality.

Suddenly a huge plume of the black smoke formed from her father's breath and curled into the ceiling like the ink from a squid. It hovered over his lifeless body for a few moments and then dissipated, giving way to a blue glow that filled the room. Brilliant azure and gold light surged through and around him, embossing an ancient otherworldly symbol into the surface of his skin over his heart.

Alena let out a gasp. The light glared from the bed, growing brighter and drenching the room, banishing the smoke to nothingness. The Shetani had finally released their captive. His coal black irises gleamed silver, like bursts of starlight beckoning from another world. There was magic in them. There was kindness and beauty and promise restored in every part of him, and Alena could now see her father clearly. The glyph emblazoned on his chest smoldered brightly with a sparkling blue-green light. It was electric, alive.

She realized that she was still holding his hand and watched in awe as the light radiated down his hand and into her own, until every wall of every vein and capillary in her was lit up with the iridescent glow. Alena looked at her reflection in the medical equipment. Her skin looked as if marbled with blue stardust. Her face was illuminated as well, and her eyes gleamed with silver just like her father's.

From his flesh to his heir's, a deep-seated ancient power surpassing earthly limitations clapped down into her like lightning kissing the earth. She heard Isis' words, "You are not and have never been under a curse. You of human and ancient Sirian blood are under a blessing." Her father gently closed his eyes. He had given his final gift to his daughter, the last of his light, the Sun of Sirius.

"The honeycomb signifies that which is interior to the physical, in which is created the choicest of nectars. If you reflect on this, you will unlock the secret we carry."

THE SHAMANIC WAY OF THE BEE

CHAPTER 25

Alena's father's funeral was a small affair. She spent most of it clenching her sisters' hands, trying to convince herself that it was all real. Though when she finally allowed her eyes to fall on his dead body and really view it and study it, something quite unexpected occurred to her; she realized she would never again have to carry the weight of his secrets. She would no longer have to be loyal to his pain or to the life she had lived because of it. Neither would he.

"You all right, Reeta?" Alena asked her sister, who was sitting in their mother's cramped living room alone.

Syreeta only shrugged, staring ahead.

"Mind if I sit in here with you?"

She shrugged again. Alena settled into the small space left on the sofa next to Syreeta's ample hips.

"Folks left enough cakes, pies, and casseroles here to feed an army didn't they?" Alena said.

"Well it is a repast, Lena. You know people and funerals. They try to help you feed the grief away with all that food I guess."

"How's Ma doing?" Alena asked.

"Sleep now. Those nerve pills she's been taking finally put her out."

"And how are you doing, with everything?"

"He's in the ground now, ain't he? It is what it is."

"Interesting way to put it, Reeta. Well, I wanted to tell you that we're going to head back for New York soon. Maya's got school in the morning and I've got work."

"Must be nice." Alena could hear the bitterness in her voice.

"What's that supposed to mean?"

"Nothing. It don't mean nothing. Make sure you wrap Maya up good on your way back. Sounds like she's catching a cold or something."

"Thanks, I will."

"You got a precious little girl, Lena. Besides being bright yellow, she looks a lot like you. Smart like you, too. You should've heard her at the hospice. She was telling us all kinds of things, talks like a little woman."

"Thanks, Reeta. Maya's my heart. I'm surprised you don't have any of your own yet. You always loved kids."

"Ain't worked out like that for me." Her chest heaved with a sigh. "Look here, I'm going for a smoke and a walk. If you see Aggie before I do, tell her Mr. Dean will be looking for that check for the flowers and he'll be here any minute."

"Okay, I'll let her know. So the service isn't paid off?"

"No. The funeral home let us piecemeal some of it here and there. But don't worry yourself. Mama, Aggie, Randy, and me got a system. We know who's got what 'til it's all taken care of."

"Why didn't anyone ask me to help out?"

"You really want to ask that question, Lena?"

"I'm his daughter, too."

"Well, Ma said you were in a bad way, things weren't all that rosy for you in New York and to leave you out of it. So don't worry about it. We're taking care of what needs to be done like we've been doing all this time. It's not like it would be any different just because you decided to pop back up all the sudden."

"Well damn, Reet. Guess I deserve that. I knew it was coming at some point." Alena leaned slightly towards her sister.

"Reeta look, from the bottom of my heart, I'm sorry, okay?"

Syreeta wrinkled her face but was silent and cold as a stone.

Alena reached for her sister's hand. "I'm sorry for leaving you, for cutting you and everybody off like I did. I just want you to know that I love you. I had to leave to save my life, Reeta. Did you hear me? I'm telling you that I am sorry!"

"Of course, I heard you."

"And? Do you accept my apology?"

"What you want me to say? Would it make any difference? Or you just want to feel better about yourself now that you ain't got that pretty little fairy tale up in New York no more?"

"What I want is to have my baby sis back. I've missed the hell out of you, Reeta."

"I'm going for a smoke," Syreeta said, her voice faltering. "Reeta? Come on, please say something. Anything."

"Your baby sis, hmm? It was pretty hard for me to tell we was even still sisters. I don't even know you no more." Pain radiated from her face and her body. "You left me alone for eight years, Lena."

Tears were pooling onto Syreeta's bosom.

"It's me. It's Lena Jae. I haven't changed. Talk to me. Please," Alena pleaded, guilt raking through her.

"All right, fine. You want me to say something? What about my life? Huh, Big Sis? Did you ever think of how mine was gonna get saved? You left me alone for eight years! Almost a whole got damn decade. And for what? What did I ever do to you, Lena? What, because I ain't speak out against what he did? Because I didn't say nothin' when you did? How was I supposed to, Lena? I had no voice! I had nothing left! I couldn't speak even if I wanted to."

Syreeta had buried her face in her hands. "I ain't even wanna think about what Daddy did to me, let alone hear it come out of my mouth. He broke me, Lena, down to the ground."

Alena draped her arms over Syreeta and pulled her close. It was as if no time had passed between them at all, and they were girls again.

"He knew I wouldn't have anywhere else to go," Syreeta continued. "He knew I wasn't strong like you were. I wasn't perfect like you, with a knight in shining armor and a big law degree. I've never been and I still ain't. But at least back then I had you. You were the only one I could tell. You knew I couldn't expect Ma to do anything. And do you remember what you did when I told you?"

Alena nodded sadly, her own face streaked with tears.

"You held me. You held me like a little baby and you told me I was still a good girl, a good and pretty girl, and none of Daddy's sins on me were ever gonna change that. You gave me love, Lena Jae. You made me feel human again. You was my big sister. Then you just left me. Bad shit happens to little girls who ain't nobody's little girl. And that bad shit hurt like hell."

Syreeta pushed her sleeves over her wrists. They were lined with wounds she had cut into them.

Alena gasped, "Reeta! No!"

"A psychopath. That's what they all think I am," Syreeta said. "I'm fucked up in all the ways a woman can be fucked up. Can't keep no job. Can't keep no man. Can't have no kids. I can't even off myself right, and I'm 'bout big as a horse. Useless." Syreeta shook with sobs as more and more tears drenched her.

"My God, Reeta." Alena gently traced a finger over her sister's scars. "Why did you do this to yourself? If I knew you were hurting this bad I would've taken you with me. I had no right to try to force you to back me up in front of Mama and Daddy. You were nowhere near ready."

Syreeta shook her head slowly.

"Sometimes the pain's like sipping from a fire hose. It just rises up so fast and so strong that it drowns me. It swallows me up, and I just gotta do *something* with it," she sniffed bitterly.

Alena held Syreeta's face in her hands, wet cheeks against her palms.

"I know my sorry just isn't good enough but please, please forgive me. I should never have punished you for making a choice for yourself. Listen to me. Listen to your big sister, Reeta." Alena wrapped her lips tightly around every syllable as if her words were bricks building a fortress around her sister. "You are not fucked up. We just had some fucked up people raising us. Daddy hated himself, so he came for us. Ma didn't love herself either, so she let him."

Syreeta didn't look convinced.

"It didn't have a thing to do with who *we* are. There's nothing wrong with you, Reeta. You were the strong one, not me. I ran away, but you stayed here with all those demons and you're still here, still standing."

Syreeta frowned and shook her head again.

"I ain't interested in being strong. I just wanna be loved, Lena. Why can't nobody see that? I just wanna be loved for me."

"You *are* loved, Reeta. I love you. Ma sure doesn't know how to show it most times, but she loves you, too. We've been stuck in a mess, this whole family. We're finding our way out of a shit storm that's been here way before we were even born. But I know one thing for sure. You have everything it takes to make it out, Reeta. You aren't the only one who's been under. I almost killed myself, too. It's a trick, Reeta, a trap. This whole world is rigged for us to fail, that is, if we don't wake up and open our eyes. I'm going to show you the truth. Soon. I'm back now. I'm sorry for all the time we lost, but I'm here now and I'm not going anywhere, okay? In fact, why don't you think about coming to New York with Maya and me?"

Syreeta let out a long sigh.

"Thanks, Lena. That sounds real nice and everything. Whatever truth you're talking about I sure could use, but I don't need you to help me escape, sis. And don't you go feeling bad about what you made out of yourself. You were right to go ahead and get it. I just want you to see me, be my sister again."

"I'll always be your sister, Reet. I love you."

"I love you, too. And you know what, as pitiful as I must look right now, I'm happy. I'm happy that you're back." Both grief and joy reverberated in her voice. "I'm glad I got my niece back."

Alena squeezed her sister's hand. "I'm going to miss you. We'll talk every day, promise? No matter if you're feeling good or bad."

"It's a promise, Peanut Head."

"Well, I should be getting us ready to catch the train home." Alena dried her face and was about to stand when Syreeta gently tugged her back.

"Since we're being all Kumbaya and honest with each other right now, let me ask you something and tell me the truth."

"Ask away, Reet."

"What happened in that room when Daddy died?"

"What do you mean?"

"Lena, don't play with me. You were freaked out when you came out of there, and it wasn't because of grief. I could tell."

"Daddy died right in front of me, Reeta, holding on to my hand for god sakes. Of course, I was freaking out."

"He said something to you, didn't he? A deathbed confession or something like that. Whatever it was it was huge, I can see it in your eyes even now."

"Reeta, drop it, please. It was just a lot to go through was all."

Syreeta kept a suspicious gaze on Alena but let it go.

"All right, well, let me give my niece some kisses before y'all leave. When you're ready to stop keeping your secrets, I'll be here to listen."

How fragile and painfully beautiful life is, Alena thought. On the ride back home, she made her decision. As soon as she had the chance, she would gather up all the rest of her suffering, lay it down, and let it burn.

"The queen bee carries on the work for which she is annointed."

SONG OF INCREASE

CHAPTER 26

When Alena and Maya returned to New York, it was time to give Maya back to Gabriel for the week. She'd wished she would have Gloria to lean on, but she was away visiting her daughters. Alena clung to her daughter's hand until she climbed into her father's car. The sight of Maya waving goodbye behind the car window struck her to the heart.

Alena painted a wide, brave smile on her face for the both of them and waved back. Unexpectedly, Gabriel got out of the car this time and walked toward her with Maya looking on.

"Alena, hold on. Can I talk to you for a second please?" She was shocked at both the request and by the strange gentleness in his voice.

"What is it, Gabriel?" she answered.

Even the ruthless spark she'd come to expect in his eyes had been replaced with something else, shame maybe. Guilt. She sensed his unease with it.

"I just uh… I want to offer you my condolences for your father, again. I'm sorry for your loss, Alena."

"Thanks, Gabe. Really. It means a lot," she answered with a polite half-smile, and then turned to leave for her apartment.

"Wait," he called behind her suddenly. She turned back to face him. They stood for a long, uncomfortable moment while Gabriel seemed to be deciding what to say next. This was the first time that Alena had ever seen Gabriel appear to be anything close to humble, and she could barely believe it. Yet there he stood, looking regretful.

"I don't hate you, Alena," Gabriel finally said. "I mean, I know that you must hate me for..." his voice trailed off and then came back in clumsy spurts. "Anyway, what I'm trying to say is that...you're a good woman, Alena. A good uh...a good mother. I've never denied that. I know it's uh...hard to believe coming from me, but I never meant for things to end up like this. I'm...uh...Well, I'm sorry that it did." Gabriel looked unnerved by his own words.

As he was speaking, Alena could *feel* him. Straight into his heart. It was as if she had somehow entered into it. She felt the misery that he tried to keep hidden, the darkness. Then an epiphany came to her. Her brokenness had called to his. It must have been why they had forged such a perfectly dysfunctional union.

Something came over Alena, and she decided to tell her absolute barest truth to her husband. Pride tried to stop her words, but she slipped free of it, of everything.

"Gabe, I always wondered why you started acting like you hated me. Why you treated me like you did and said the things you said. It tore me apart. But I'm clear now that you were just reflecting my own hatred and my own forbidden thoughts right back to me. Our marriage was a part of an old, very sad, and very lost me. I held you responsible for my grief. I made you responsible for making me good again, loveable. Of course, you couldn't make me lovable."

Gabriel shifted uncomfortably as he stood listening.

"It was my work to see I already was," she continued. "I felt like a burden on you that you wanted to get rid of, and now, I see that's exactly what I was. I put a heavy, heavy load on you Gabe and I'm sorry... No one could have done the things you did to me unless their heart was broken, just like mine."

Alena then felt the release of Gabriel from the core of her heart, and the unhooking of the cords between them. Shackles unlocking. The entanglement she mistook for love had finally unraveled. Floodgates of freedom burst open, and it made her feel so light and brave.

Gabriel looked dumbfounded by her truthfulness, docile almost. After several moments, he mumbled awkwardly, "That's quite an epiphany, Alena. We've got to be going... Goodbye." His face flushed as he turned back for his car.

"Gabriel?" Alena called after him. "Yes?"

"You can still change the way things end up. You can make it right, now.""We'll talk soon, Alena. Take care."

"You can make it right, Gabe!" she called out after him again. "It's not too late." With his eyes downcast, he pretended he had not heard her plea. He climbed back into his car and drove away.

"What does this honey do? It creates sensual pleasure, upon the tongue in particular, and when imbibed it creates a circuit of force between sexual power, mind and emotion."

THE SHAMANIC WAY OF THE BEE

CHAPTER 27

Michael greeted Alena with a wide cheerful smile at the front doors of her office building. He'd surprised her with an invitation for dinner at his new place. Something about that smile always felt like home to her. He had brought her a gorgeous bouquet of red roses and white lilies, her favorite. When she buried her nose in them, the beauty of Oshun's grove came to her mind. The walk to his car was only two minutes long, but he found the chill of the evening a fine excuse to draw closer and drape a possessive arm around her. Thirty minutes later, they had arrived at Michael's new home in Harlem. He pushed open the weathered bronze door to his brownstone.

"Welcome to my humble abode," he announced.

Alena could see that inside was anything but humble. She glanced around his apartment. Just about every corner reflected a

Michael she never imagined. He was well traveled, that much she could tell. On one shelf of a massive oak case tribal necklaces made of brightly colored shells and beads were mounted elegantly on stands. On another, three very ancient looking monkey masks were etched in red pigment.

"Wow, Mike! This is amazing! Who knew you were so damned National Geographic."

"Funny and thank you. I hoped you'd like it."

"I love it. This is the most gorgeous bachelor pad I've ever seen."

"I'll give you a tour after dinner."

"Speaking of, what's for dinner?" Alena asked. "I don't mind admitting that I'm starving."

"For you, Madame, tonight's special is paella," he gave her a mock curtsy. "I made it last night so I'd only have to heat it up," he said with the easy smile that Alena had come to adore.

He took her coat and the thick cardigan she wore underneath it and hung them up for her. He then went to the bar and opened up a bottle of wine and poured two glasses.

"I brought this just for you. This is from a vineyard one of my clients owns. I told him to give me the finest he had. Now I'm not much of a wine connoisseur. It's supposed to be good is all I know."

"Well, I'm sure you made an excellent choice. Thanks for thinking of me."

"Merlot with violet and plum notes," he said in a mocking falsetto.

"Oh stop it, Mike." Alena giggled.

"I'd like to make a toast," Michael said, raising his glass. "To new beginnings." His eyes latched deeply onto hers.

"To new beginnings!" Alena repeated, then sipped the wine. "This is delicious, Mike. I'm glad you brought it for me," she teased.

"I'm glad you're here." He took a sip of his glass, then smiled.

"It *is* good. Why don't you enjoy it while I heat up dinner and set the table?" He then disappeared into the kitchen.

She saw that he had an impressive collection of artwork, too.

Lola must have really changed him, she thought. "Mike, I had no idea that you collected. Why didn't you tell me?"

"Eh, not really. Just a few pieces here and there. We split everything down the middle. These are all I really wanted."

One piece was a lithograph of a sturdy Mexican woman bearing a sheaf of calla lilies on her back. Another struck her as soon as she saw it.

"And who's this one by?" It was a painting of a couple, black in color, their flat faces meeting one another, cheek to cheek.

"That's James Lesesne Wells. It's called *Twin Heads.* You like it, do you?"

"I do. Hmm. Twin Heads, like Twin Flames," Alena said.

"Huh?"

"Twin Flames. Two lovers, two halves of the same soul with the same life mission."

"Oh. Well it was expensive as heck, that's all I know. I like it, too."

"And I see a trumpet, do you still play?"

"You remembered," he said with a grateful smile. "I do. I play a lot more now that I've got a much quieter house."

"So? Can I hear a few notes? I bet you're still great."

"Sure." He picked up the instrument and played a snippet of a song for Alena—*What a Wonderful World.*

"I knew you'd still have it. That was beautiful, Mike."

"Thank you." Mike returned the trumpet to the shelf and took Alena's hand to lead her to the dining table. He helped her into her seat then sat down across from her. "Beautiful song for a beautiful woman."

Alena looked down at her plate. "Your paella looks good. Everything looks great actually. I had no idea you were so… fancy."

Michael dug into his food, and Alena did the same.

"Well thank you. I've been inspired by a special elegant someone," he said with a wink between bites. "And you ain't seen nothing yet. If I play my cards right, she might bless me with her Upper East Side style and really turn this place into a palace."

"Very funny." Alena grinned. "I'm impressed, that's for sure." Michael looked down at his plate. "I'm hoping I can always impress you with more than that," he said behind a half smile. "You have my mind going crazy with all of that mahogany beauty over there."

"Mike?" Alena said quickly to hide her blush.

Michael shrugged. "It's the truth. Maybe one of these days you'll let me bask in it every day."

His comment moved Alena to an uneasy silence. Michael picked up his fork and continued eating amidst the silence that ensued. "I need to be sure that whatever we do, that it's what's best— for both of us," she said finally.

How is Maya doing?" he asked, sensing her need to change the subject.

"Not the greatest actually. Her teachers are saying that she's been very distracted lately, not getting her assignments done. Of course, we know why. I'm worried about her to be honest. All of this must be so hard on her. Her life changed in the blink of an eye. It's been hell for me as a grown woman. I can only imagine what she's going through as a little girl trying to piece some normalcy back together."

"And what's Gabe have to say about it?"

"He says she'll adjust. She just needs some time and her grades will be back on par. He hired a tutor. I told him what this girl needs is her mother, and probably years of therapy. He'll throw money at everything except that, the admission that this nightmare he started is damaging her. I talked to him by the way, about things. I got everything out. And I told him it wasn't too late to turn this around, to make it right."

"Everything? And no police had to be called in to break the two of you up?"

"I'm not angry anymore, I let all of that go. I just want my baby to be okay. I know I'm supposed to have faith, but this thing, it's still like an open wound. A mother's wound. I don't know if this feeling will ever go away. The worst thing about being separated from your child is the helplessness. I always have questions without answers. Who's mothering her while I'm stuck over here? What is she feeling this second? Is her heart breaking, or did it already break? Who's being tender and kind with her pain?"

"Leen, I can only imagine what it must feel like as a mother. I'm not even close to getting used to living away from my boys. But one thing I do know is that kids are more resilient than we think."

"I sure hope so. It hurts like hell not to be there to protect her from all of this and do those everyday things we used to do. But I'm determined to live in joy, and I'm doing the best I can."

"I know you are, Leen," he said soothingly. "It's just a matter of time before you get her back, I promise you. You're a good woman. You have more courage than a lot of men out here."

"Thanks. I'm just trying to be patient with this whole convoluted legal process. It's finally looking like it's going to land in my favor, like heaven is rearranging everything. You know, ever since my father passed I'm starting to feel like I gained a guardian angel or something."

Michael gave her a wide smile.

"Speaking of your dad, have you heard from your mother?"

"Surprisingly, yes. Ma's been calling me once a week or so now to check on me, as she says. She's doing a lot better than I expected with Daddy gone. My sisters and Randy have been calling me, too. It's almost starting to feel like I have a family again. Weird."

"I'm so happy for you, Leen. And it'll just get better." His eyes shone with such profound tenderness it was as if he knew what she did not put into words.

"I can finally feel that. Thank you. I've been thinking about what you said back at the café. Nothing that I experienced could've happened any other way. I do accept it. I praise God for it all, every last bit. Even these hard, jagged parts."

"That's what I've been waiting to hear, Alena. Great! I also meant it when I asked you to consider that I have a part in all of this, too."

Alena smiled softly, but Michael's tone and expression had turned serious and her smile left her face.

"What is it? Yes, of course I know you play a big part, Mike."

Michael looked at her as if he had the answer to a question she hadn't yet asked. He gave her an odd look and then shook his head, deciding to keep whatever it was to himself. "Just know that I meant it. I'm always going to be here for you," he said.

"Of course, I know you do," she said after a flat pause before pushing her plate aside. "Well…I think I'm finished with dinner."

"You can't be done eating already, you barely touched your food. I thought you were starving. You didn't like it, did you?"

"Oh," Alena glanced at her plate. "No, it's really good. I swear. I guess my appetite wasn't as big as I thought it'd be."

She stood up to clear the dishes from the table. "Leave them there, I've got it," he said.

"Come on, you've made us a beautiful meal. Let me help you clean up," Alena insisted.

Michael eased the dish from her hand. "No. It's fine. You are my honored guest, m'lady," he said with a playful bow. "Please, relax and make yourself at home." He carried the plates into the kitchen, then returned a few minutes later.

"Mind if I play some music? If you like my rusty trumpet playing, you're gonna love this."

"Sure," Alena said as she sat on the sofa and drummed her fingers against the chocolate leather.

Michael walked over to program his sound system. A few moments later, a jazz number filled living room.

"You like?" he asked.

"I like. Very mellow," she answered.

"John Coltrane, *A Love Supreme*," he said.

"I love it. It's soothing."

"Good. Relax. I'll be back in a bit. You want some coffee or something?"

"Coffee would be great, thanks."

When Michael returned with a tray, the tempo of the music had slowed. He set the coffee down and joined Alena. Closing his eyes, he swayed his head to the melody, then reached over to hold her hand.

"Dance with me?" he asked with a charming smile.

"I don't think so. You know I'm not a very good danc—"

"Aww, come on. Let's dance," he interrupted her. "Just feel the music. This is soul music. Your spirit will take over."

When she stood up and stepped into his arms, he held her closely and gently. They swayed together with her head nestled on his shoulder, the notes of the music floated around them. The feeling and the setting were perfect. Alena's eyes rested on the spray of lilies jutting from his crystal vase. She closed her eyes and tried to lose herself in the sweetness of the moment. She let her hips slowly undulate to the music with shameless sensuality. She let herself indulge the fantasy, and the world fell away from her for a few moments more.

"You are so beautiful," Michael said, looking into her eyes.

He then pulled her closer.

Her indulgence fleeted away. His face was too eager, his body too tempting. She started to feel uneasy under his gaze, exposed.

"You're safe with me, Leen. Okay? Just let yourself feel it," he whispered his cheek against her forehead.

His words set off a creeping insecurity deep within her. They reminded her of his words when they first made love, when he had assured her in the same charming way. "Let yourself just feel good for once." She'd let herself feel good, and like all the other times, she still got hurt.

Alena stopped dancing and pulled away from his embrace. "It's getting pretty late. I should get a cab," she said, stepping away from him.

"A cab? What is it, Leen? Did I do something wrong?"

"No, it's not that, it's just late, you know."

"Did I say something wrong?"

"No, nothing like that Mike. You didn't do anything wrong."

"Tell me, Alena, what is it? Throw me a bone. Does my breath smell?" He cupped his hand over his mouth and nose. "Tell a brotha, I can handle it," he said, a grin forming on his handsome face.

229

Alena laughed. "It's none of the above, just time to call it a night."

Mike stepped back. "Okay, if you insist. I won't call a cab, but I will drive you home."

"Look, we've been down this road before. We know how this thing goes, this whole thing—the romantic dinner, the soft music, the feelings. We sleep together next and a few days or maybe weeks later, we decide it would've been best if we had never bothered," Alena said, sighing.

Mike shook his head. "No! Not this time. Please. What can I say to you, Leen? I love you, woman. What can I say to make you understand that I'm here for the long haul, and I'm not going anywhere?" he asked.

As his words echoed in her mind, Alena realized that Michael was right. She felt ridiculous. Just that easily, she was settling right back into her pattern of distrust.

"I'm sorry. Mike, it's just scary. All of these emotions kicking up, I just need time. *We* need time."

"You don't need to explain." He gave a wry smile that set Alena at ease and settled his arm over her shoulders.

"Listen, it's okay. You want to slow down, we slow down. Nothing has to change. Just be here with me now, okay? Let me be there for you, and with you."

Alena let out a sigh of relief and smiled back at him. "Okay."

"And just so you know, I didn't expect anything tonight. I just wanted you here with me."

"I know. I'm sorry if I offended you, Mike."

"No apologies. Put your mind at ease." He stroked her hair and then the rim of her jaw. "But I do have to admit one thing."

"And what is that?"

"I have been wanting to kiss those pretty lips for a long time. I missed them. May I?"

Alena nodded as he pressed lush, warm lips against her mouth, kissing her deeply. He slid his arm around her waist and pulled her closer to him. She felt a rush of pleasure surge through her body. His scent poured over her, and she reveled in his presence, the feel of his arms around her.

His possession, the strength and gentleness of it, was as exquisite as the easy joy he infused in her. She even dared to contemplate the ecstasy of making love to him, her body exploding under the delicious pressure of his fingertips and manhood. In Michael, she sensed the same inexplicable energy that stirred in her. He was home to her.

"You still want to leave?" he teased. His dark brown eyes glinted mischievously as he tightened his arms around her.

The tension between them made Alena's legs weak. Familiar passion thrummed through both of their bodies. Within minutes, they were naked, entwined right there in Michael's living room, belonging to each other again. Alena gripped his forearms as his body vanished into hers.

Something beyond their comprehension had begun to happen. Pleasure moved through them with such fierceness that it was almost unbearable. Alena clenched her teeth as the ecstasy coursed through every inch of her like raucous ocean waves.

This lovemaking was different. It was ripe with intention, purpose. Of what, neither of them knew, only that they were making a covenant and gave themselves over to it. In a long pulsing moment, they brought life to one another. That hungry place in Alena that always needed to be filled with assurance was gone. Her apprehension at making love to him was gone. Her resistance was gone. Alena was, in fact, whole. Holy. And free.

"By Him in whose hand is my soul, eat honey, for there is no house in which honey is kept for which the angels will not ask for mercy."

PROPHET MOHAMMED

CHAPTER 28

Alena woke earlier than she had wanted the next morning. Her body was still ringing with too much elation to remain asleep. She had taken a very late-night taxicab back home, wanting to wake up in her own bed. She had wanted space to process all that had happened in the last 24 hours. She stared at her bedroom ceiling, replaying the steamy night before over in her mind. Where had they gone last night? What had they transcended? She smoothed her palms over her body, remembering the way Michael's hands had charged it with a sublime rush of sensation. Her bliss abruptly ended with the cell phone startling her out of her reverie.

"Hello?" she answered groggily.

"Mrs. Ford?" It was the attorney Amy Wannager on the line. "I apologize for the early call, but I've just gotten some news I thought you'd want to hear. Good news. Is now a good time?"

Alena flicked on the table lamp, pulled her robe over her body, and sat upright.

"Yes. Yes, now is fine," she answered.

"Well, one of my little birdies gave me a tip, and I poked around at your husband's business records. Looks like he was offloading assets for a slick bankruptcy, painting a picture of distress for the court while he went to hide the real gold. Your penthouse was probably number one on the chopping block. Smells like bankruptcy fraud."

Fraud. The word sent a ping of shock through Alena.

"I'm sure your husband loves his daughter, Mrs. Ford, but this custody issue could have been another business move to keep you out of his pockets. All we'd have to do is demand a complete scrub of every last bit of his bank records in a discovery order from the court, and this could blow up in his face."

Alena listened in incensed disbelief. *He put me through a living hell over money?* she thought. *All of this torture was about his greed?* Rage boiled up inside of her, but she fought it back down. She gritted her teeth and breathed in deeply, reminding herself over and over *Forgiveness is my freedom.*

"Well, I let his attorney know what we came across, financial infidelity, and Mr. Ford's attorney sent us an offer for the settlement this morning of both the divorce absolution and the custody of Maya. Mrs. Ford, he's giving you full custody. Uncontested divorce and an $8,000 child support payment monthly with your agreement to visitation with the father two times a week. This does not even include settlement of assets."

Her anger subsided, and joy swelled in her throat. *She found it! God found it! The way back to Maya.* Alena leapt to her feet, barely able to keep from screaming. In the slimiest way, Gabriel had made it right after all.

"What? Unbelievable. Are you sure? How? Oh my God! Full custody?" she asked breathlessly.

"Yes, it's true, Mrs. Ford. I'm just as surprised as you are. This is a very, very generous level of voluntary support."

"My God," Alena began to sob with joy and relief. "It's over, it's finally over," she said, smiling through her tears.

"Almost." Alena could hear a triumphant smile fading in the lawyer's voice. "The offer is contingent on an agreement from you that your daughter remain with Mr. Ford until she's remanded into your custody after a settlement meeting next month. I don't know what the extra time is for or what kind of tricks his side may be trying to pull, but they were adamant about it."

"What? Ms. Wannager, I have waited for months for my daughter to be returned to me. I want my child back! If he's agreeing to all this, and we have all of this legal ammunition now, then why should I have to wait any longer? For him to find a loophole or change his mind? Don't we have the power now?"

The attorney sighed. "I realize it may be frustrating, but this is still a win. What's crucial here is that we get you your daughter back in the end. Please try to be patient. Any wrong move is ammunition. To keep our win in tact may mean that we've got to play their game for just a little longer.

I told his attorney that I would pass the offer on to you. He's given us until the tenth of this month to take it. So I'll give you a few days to mull over it, and we can regroup on Monday, all right?"

Alena paused for a few moments. She decided that this was a victory and a gift from God, no matter what Gabriel may try or what battles there were left to fight, it would remain so.

"Of course I'll take it," she said.

"Great, so can you be in my office to sign the acceptance, let's say, tomorrow afternoon?"

"I will see you then. Thank you, Ms. Wannager! Thanks for everything! Goodbye."

To add to the sweetness of her good fortune, Allison had given Alena the day off as a reward for her hard work on her latest project. She decided to pay Gloria a visit that evening when she returned. She had not seen her since her father's funeral. Inside, her immaculate apartment was hazy and reeked of burning leaves.

"Come on in, honey, excuse the smoke." Although she smiled in her usually warm way, Alena couldn't miss the subtle weariness and trouble in Gloria's eyes. Her mood dropped like a stone.

"It's sage. I've been cleansing and purging. A storm is coming this way. A wicked one."

She lifted her worry-filled eyes past Alena and through the window lined with potted morning glory plants. "Oh, yes, a storm is brewing, Alena. I can feel it, like before. Just can't see it yet." With her finger, she gently tapped the space between her eyebrows, her third eye. Her mouth pulled into a slight frown.

"Time is short and they're on the move. We'll just have to stay vigilant and ready," she said, trying to lighten her voice. She crossed the room to the kitchenette for a hot teakettle.

"Let me pour you some of this new tea. It's bush tea. Abiola brought it back from her trip to Johannesburg for me. Tell me, how are you, dear?"

Alena stirred honey and condensed milk into the bitter tea and then stared into the swirling liquid.

"It's been a little hard, but I'm okay.

Regret is what's hitting me the hardest. I wish I would've gone over there again, while he was still alive. Even after all of these years of hating him, I realized how much I still loved and needed my dad. I knew he was dying. I should have gone back and at least told him that I'm trying my best to forgive him."

Gloria patted her knee. "He knows. Your father knows, honey. Everything is just as it should be, remember?"

"Yes, I do remember. There's something else, and it's been harder to grasp than the regret. What's replaying in my mind the most is what he gave to me before he died."

"What did he give you?" Gloria asked as she sipped her tea.

Alena paused for a few moments to give the experience words. "Power."

Gloria nodded knowingly. "By way of light?"

"Yes. I should have known you'd know right away. I guess that was what was going on. Transference of power by way of light. A lot of it."

"Very good."

"Is it, Gloria? I have so many questions. Who was he? Did he know about me and my initiation this whole time? Anyway, it was unreal how it all happened. The Shetani were there. They came right out of him, right before he passed. And before that, this strange symbol showed up on his chest and the thing *lit up*. It sort of looked like markings I had seen in Isis' temple, but not exactly. I have a good feeling you know what it was."

"Hmm. It isn't my place to speculate, but I believe what you have seen is one of the three sacred symbols. Your father clearly carried the blood. As do you."

"The blood? Uh, you want to fill me in? And what symbols, Gloria?"

"In time, Alena. In due time. Something tells me that it won't be long before you learn the meaning of what your father has given you."

"Of *course*," Alena said in frustration. She cocked her head back against the plush sofa. "How could I forget, that's how this thing goes. Wait and learn." It was then that Alena remembered the vision that Maya had in Oshun's mirror. In all the excitement of her father's funeral, she had completely forgotten.

"I almost forgot. Something really weird happened with Maya, too. I had her with me when my mother called me with the news. She got into my things and found Oshun's mirror. She was looking into it, and I saw her in the reflection, but it was of an older Maya. She was a young woman sitting on a throne in the middle of six other thrones. Someone was crowning her. And then all of the sudden a dark cloud of smoke or soot fell over her, and her throne was empty."

Gloria's face knotted with confusion.

"Can it be? Can the Oracle be the heir of a Bridger?" she whispered aloud to herself.

"Gloria, watch out!"

Right then, a gust of gray-black mist had surged into the apartment from the ceiling, taking on a gruesome, beastly form. The creature lunged toward Gloria, crushing the teapot as its hulking fist tried to descend on her. Gloria raised her amulet to it and commanded it to flee. It slinked away as quickly as it had come, disintegrating in the light she had summoned.

"Your arm, you've been hurt."

The shattered glass had etched a long scrape along Gloria's forearm. Alena held a napkin to the thin trail of blood.

"Wait. How did it hurt *you*? They can only hurt you if there's a breech in your heart."

Gloria's expression suddenly turned dire, and her eyes flashed with a fearful revelation. She thumped her fist hard against the table, rattling the teacups.

"Never mind that! It's the child! The Shetani are going after Maya! Here, take this." She walked to her credenza and pulled a velvet pouch from its drawer, then coiled an odd necklace into Alena's palm. "It's a talisman I made for your girl. It's got a shard of the spirit crystal in it. Kiss it! It needs your motherly imprint on it."

Alena did as she was told.

"Now call your husband, Alena! Call Gabriel! Hurry!"

Without another thought, Alena furiously dialed his cell phone number, but it kept sending the call to voicemail.

"No answer! No answer!"

Alena's panic was ratcheting up, her eyes frantic.

"Come on! We'll go to him! Hurry, child, hurry!" Gloria pleaded.

Gloria called a cab. Inside it, Alena continued to call Gabriel's number until finally she heard his voice on the other end. "Gabriel, is Maya okay?" she panted.

"Alena! I've been trying to call you! Something's happened to Maya, she's had a… a seizure or something."

Alena's chest seized.

"Oh my God! *Is she okay?*" she wailed.

"She's unconscious but still breathing on her own. Her vitals are stable. They're running tests now."

"Where is she, Gabe?"

"Presbyterian, Children's Unit. Third floor. Hurry."

The taxi ride to the hospital was almost unbearable, a breakneck blur of city lights and sharp turns. Her racing thoughts swallowed up all awareness of the sounds and sights around her. She tried to push aside the sickening dread creeping in as she prayed with Gloria.

Gabriel's eyes were feverish and desperate with worry when Alena and Gloria rushed through the hospital doors. "Gabe! How is she doing?"

He was relieved to see her but looked uneasily at Gloria. "She's okay," he answered weakly.

"This is my neighbor, Ms. Chukwu. I believe you two have already met."

Gabriel nodded politely toward Gloria. "Hello."

"What happened to her, Gabriel?"

"Alena, I…I don't know. She was fine, all day," he explained. "Everything was normal. She'd just had her bath. She'd gotten in bed, and I was about to tuck her in for the night. One second she was her regular self, and then just like that, she became… delusional. She started talking gibberish. I didn't understand. It was as if she was fighting someone off, screaming 'Get away from me, my mother will find you. My mother will know and find you.' It made no sense."

He looked at Alena. "Do you have any idea what she was talking about?"

"No," Alena lied, and then she glanced at Gloria, who was clutching the amulet around her neck.

"I thought she was playing a horrible joke on me at first, and I was waiting for her to knock it off. But she wouldn't stop. She kept screaming it over and over. Then her eye, her eye rolled into back her head and she started convulsing. And then she fainted." Gabe had a horrified look on his face.

"Oh God. My poor baby. What did the doctors say?"

"She's still not conscious, stable but unconscious."

"What room is she in?"

"308. They're getting another room ready for her observation, and when it's available, they'll move her."

"I'm going in."

"Wait, they told us to sit tight and let her rest while they analyze the scans. The doctors should be back around any minute, and then we can go in with them."

"I need to go to her, Gabe, *right now.*"

"All right I'll go with you," Gabriel said. "I'd like to see her alone please."

Their anxiety and tension hung in the air. "Huh?" Gabriel said.

"I just want a minute alone with my daughter. I'm going to let her know that her mother is here."

"Okay. Fine. Remember the doctors said—"

"I know what they said," she said, cutting him off. "I've got it. I'll be only a few minutes, I promise."

Gloria squeezed Alena's hand and whispered sternly into her ear. "Fear *not*. You know what to do. You know how to save her." Gloria grasped her amulet tighter as Alena hurried into Maya's room.

"I'll be right outside," Gabriel called out behind her.

Alena sensed them instantly—a damp black smell wafting from underneath the door. She threw it open then ran to Maya. An oxygen tube murmured under her nose.

"It's me. It's Mama, my angel," she cried out. "I'm so sorry I wasn't there to protect you."

Maya looked so small and fragile. There was no doubt the Shetani had descended on her precious child. Their putrid stink lingered on her. Alena closed her eyes and breathed in a prayer. She then reached deeply into her heart, drawing from her fires of wisdom and power there. Opening her eyes again, she armed herself against the beast's heavy malignant presence. Her palms began to throb with rings of heat, and her hands and arms glimmered in gold and azure light. Steely cold air crept along the nape of her neck. Alena's hands clenched into fists.

"*Show yourself!*" she demanded. "Show yourself *now*, demonic cowards! It's me that you want, come for me!"

Wide streaks of pitch-black smoke crawled down the walls, seeped from Maya's bed sheets, then dripped into a pool in the floor before gathering itself together as one dark beast. Alena steeled herself.

"You *dare* lay a hand on my child! *My child?*"

Its ember-like eyes formed and latched onto hers. She could feel the vile thing scanning her heart for fear, or doubt.

"You silly, silly girl," it hissed. "So you've learned a few tricks, and you think you're safe, do you? Have you any idea how many Bridgers we've killed?"

The dark beast then struck her chest and jolted her off of her feet, sending her smacking into the wall with a loud thud. The force slammed the breath out of her lungs. Gabriel rushed into the room.

"What in the hell is going on in here, Alena?"

She scrambled back to her feet, ignoring the sharp pain in her back. "I fell... lost my balance. Just wait for me outside."

"Two minutes," Gabriel warned, reluctantly closing the door behind him.

"Hell is just what you will get if you don't give us the girl," the beast hissed.

"You will leave my child alone! You know who I am. I have no fear of you. I will destroy every last trace of you. You have no power over my child and none over me!"

"Ha! Then why do you tremble? Either we kill her now or we take her slowly. What do you think will happen once we invade her mind? Have you ever witnessed mania loose in the mind of a child, Alena? Tragic, we assure you. Deadly."

Alena took a deep breath and steadied her thoughts on truth. "I am Victory. I am Joy. I am Peace. I am Life itself." She repeated the mantra over and over, faster and faster, each time drawing strength from the depths of her heart. Alena placed her glowing palms against Maya's forehead and chest.

She recalled Mary's words from her first encounter with the Shetani. "Heel! In the name of Jesus Christ, you are cast out! Release her and never return! In the name of Christ you are cast out!" she chanted. Her words were gaining new strength and life. Immediately the dark beings spiraled out from her daughter's bed sheets and dissipated into the light.

"Don't you ever even think about touching a hair on this child's head! *Flee and never return!*"

She wrapped her arms around Maya and clung to her for dear life. With her mother's heartbeat sounding in her ears, Maya woke. She stirred and fluttered her eyelids, her eyes cracking open slowly. Alena pushed the tube aside.

"Mom?" she sniffed.

"Maya, baby! Talk to me! Are you okay? Oh, Maya," she whispered, lifting her daughter into her arms. "You gave us such a scare."

"I'm fine, Mom," she said, looking around the hospital room. "Where am I? Where's Dad?"

Alena breathed out with overwhelming relief and doubled over. She sobbed at the sweet sound of Maya's voice and the realization of how close the Shetani had come to taking her daughter from her.

"Oh, my baby. My precious, precious baby. I'll explain later, honey. I'm going to bring your father in. We've all been waiting and praying for you to wake up. Just one thing, do you remember anything strange happening to you?"

Maya paused, then nodded. "What do you remember?"

"The monsters."

"They're gone now. Do you hear me? They will never hurt you ever again, I promise you that, okay?"

Maya nodded once again.

"Baby, how did you know? How did you know that I would… protect you from them?"

"Mom, you and Dad want me to choose, but I already chose both of you. I chose you as my mother because you're the best. You're the strongest. I knew that they would come, and when they did, you would make them go away.

Maya's words mystified Alena. *What else does she know, and how?* She then remembered the talisman Gloria had given her.

"Maya, listen to me carefully. I'm going to put this special necklace on you, and I need you to keep it on. Don't you ever take it off, not even in the bath, okay? Do you understand? Never."

Maya nodded.

"You are Mama's brave angel. If those monsters ever come back, this will protect you. It's me in here. I'm right here with you. Always."

"A maiden who carries the seed of the drone has been awakened—not by mating, but by a sovereign language within the code that calls her forth. Pregnant with a virgin birth, the expression of God's love speaks through her, and thus, she bears the drone into being."

SONG OF INCREASE

CHAPTER 29

It was late February when the rains began, soft and steady at first, then a winter monsoon. It was as if even the weather was preparing for something significant. Spring was slowly arriving and with it, as the clock ticked closer to the Spring Equinox, the opening of the Cosmic Door. Gloria hadn't spoken of it. Deliberately, it seemed. Any time Alena brought it up, she'd simply nod and say, "Due time." Alena could not deny that with each passing day she felt the magnitude of what was to come. With Gloria remaining oddly silent on the matter, she nestled into the comfort of her nights with Michael. She could not deny it. As guilty as she felt for it, their romance was flourishing. That evening, they had sloshed through Manhattan back to her apartment for a home-cooked steak and salad dinner.

The recipe was Venezuelan, Carne Mechada, a dish she hoped would rival Mike's paella.

"I hope this tastes as good as yours," she said. Michael took a bite and closed his eyes as he chewed.

"So?" she asked, her adoring eyes lingered on his face. "How'd I do? Do I get an 'A' or what?"

After a few moments, he gave her a thumbs up.

"Esta es la más deliciosa carne mechada que he tenido des de mi abuelita. Es oficial. Tienes que casarte."

Alena laughed heartily, letting her head fall back. "Show off! Now you speak Spanish, too? The surprises just keep coming. You know I have no idea what you just said, but I'll take it as a compliment," she said, beaming.

"I said that this is the most delicious Mechada I've had. It's official, you must marry me, Alena," he joked.

"I'm so happy that you really like it. I spent three nights perfecting it for you."

Michael leaned over to give her a congratulatory kiss. "All that for me? Am I a lucky man or what?"

"You are. But it's also a special occasion."

"Yeah? What are we celebrating?"

"I was going to wait to tell you until it was official, but you know how bad I am with secrets. I'm going to be moving soon! I've finally saved enough for a deposit, and if all goes well, Park Slope will be me and Maya's new home!"

"That's great, Leen. You did it."

"You don't sound all that excited. This is huge! We're finally on our way to a whole new life."

"Of course I am. I'm very proud of you too—you know I am. But it's just that I was thinking...hoping, maybe you and Maya could live here instead of all the way out in Brooklyn. I want to take care of you two. Plus, it's closer to her school, and like you said, I set it up pretty lovely. For you."

"What? Mike, thank you for thinking about us, but you know I can't move in with you. Especially not right now."

"Leen, we have something strong, don't we? Something solid?"

"Yes, we do and it's amazing. And new, Michael."

"Then why are you fighting it so hard Alena, I want to lay the world at your feet. I want to protect you."

"It's not about that. What kind of mother would I be? You couldn't even begin to understand the weight that's sitting on me right now. I'm fighting off the courts *and* the supernatural to save my daughter, Mike. I almost lost her, for god sakes."

"You may be surprised at how much I do understand." His eyes locked on hers. "Alena, I need to tell you something," he said strangely.

Alena smiled and skewered a sliver of tomato with her fork. "Oh goodness, is it bad news? Don't tell me you're pregnant," she joked.

"No, but it did happen after we made love." Alena drew her head back slightly and searched Michael's face. He took in a long inhale. "The morning after, I woke up to this incredible...I don't know....*brightness*. And then, I wasn't *me* anymore. It was like I didn't have any senses, just the awareness of this light, and somehow I knew that I was a part of and it was a part of me. It was God. Alena, God came to me. He or *it* told me that I have a destiny, a contract that I haven't fulfilled yet. It said that I'd been here before, on earth, but this time I needed to finish my assignment."

Alena stared at him in confused wonder.

"I'd been feeling things before, but it's like I got this huge download from heaven, and I could see the world clearer than I'd ever seen it before. You remember that kid they shot over in Crown Heights last summer?"

Alena nodded.

"A cell phone. The police claimed they shot him because they said they mistook a sixteen-year old kid's phone for a gun. We know that was bullshit. They murdered him. But why? Cowardice? Of course. Racism yeah, but it was deeper than that." He took another deep breath.

"Remember when I told you that I'm sure I'm a part of your journey?"

"Yes." Alena remembered the conversation and the awkward moment well.

"Well something is happening here, more than meets the eye, and I think it has something to do with what you've been going through." Michael crossed the room.

"I started seeing *them* that morning, too. Alena, I can see them just like you can," he said abruptly. "The Shetani."

The blood drained from her face. She swallowed hard and brought an involuntary hand to her mouth.

"And they're exactly how you said. Creepy sons of bitches. They smell god-awful. I've watched them slide in and out of people. They take them over and make them…do things. Today I watched one slink into a dude on the subway, and the minute it slid in, he starts talking crazy and threatening people on the train. We're just hosts to them, the weakest of us. That cop? A host. Most of the American government, shit, the worldwide government? Hosts for the Shetani. This is spiritual warfare out here. But I'm sure you already know that. I'm not telling you anything new, it's just…Wow. This is what you've been seeing all along, Leen?"

Michael's words dumbfounded Alena. Michael draped his hand over hers.

"You all right? I know this is a lot. I never in a million years thought I'd ever be the one saying anything like this. But hey, now it's your turn to get weirded out," he said with a half-smile.

"I…I'm listening Mike. Just go on, please," she stammered. Michael continued.

"Whatever this thing God gave me is, it's giving me this immediate knowing on stuff. Like, now I know why things like the shootings are happening, especially to black men. And I know why we're here. My purpose is the same as yours, Alena. It's to help everyone else see God in themselves, to help them remember who they really are. My brothers and I have lost something. It's a vital part of who we are, and for whatever reason, I'm here to bring it back… working with you. If men knew where they came from and the power that they have, then they would understand why those cop hosts are trying to kill them."

He paused and looked in her eyes. They had a tinge of disbelief in them.

"Alena? I know, it must sound crazy as hell to you, coming from me."

"No, of course I don't think it's crazy. Shocking, yes, I guess this is how you felt when I finally told you everything," she answered.

"And that's not all I've been seeing. I can see lights around people."

"Auras?"

"I don't know what you're supposed to call it, but I can see yours. It's bright purple and blazing around you like crazy. And... spirits."

"What in the?"

Mike nodded, knowing how strange he must have sounded. "You have a whole entourage by the way. Spirits. Your ancestors. And Leen, they're hardcore, too. They wouldn't even let me tell you until I proved to them that my intentions were good with you. They're all around you, Alena, rooting for you. So am I." For a few silent moments, he gazed into her eyes.

"Leen, I... I think I'm a Bridger, too," he said.

Alena shuddered inwardly.

"What did you just say?" She was barely able to get the words out of her mouth.

"I might be a Bridger." Silence filled the room as Michael's words settled over it. Alena finally broke it.

"Wait, just hold on a second. You're seeing Shetani and auras and spirits now? And on top of it, you think you may be a Bridger? Who are you and what did you do to Mike?"

"Leen, I know it's blowing my mind, too, but...maybe some of your...I don't know...magic...got transferred to me."

"Why do you think you're a Bridger?" she dropped her voice to a whisper. Michael undid the second and third buttons of his blue linen shirt and untucked a chain bearing a large, gleaming purple stone inlaid in a setting of five golden cobras.

"When the brightness left, *this* was around my neck."

Alena sucked in a quick, startled breath as she brushed her fingertips over the amethyst, feeling its power surge through them.

"How… how did you get this?" she stammered, her thoughts still jostling wildly in her head.

"Alena, I have no clue. None. It's like some kind of switch got turned on in me through you, and now the floodgates are opened."

"I don't get it! Did you go through a painting, a mirror? You haven't met one Being of Light?"

"No, I haven't gone through any of the things you did. I don't understand it either, but I feel like this is all meant to be."

Alena's eyes were riveted on Michael's amulet, examining it. With hesitant fingers, she gripped it carefully and then turned it over to study it further. There were symbols intricately carved into its prongs, symbols similar to those burned into her father's chest. Her thoughts were racing.

"Gloria! I have to speak to Gloria! Mike, just give me a few please, I'll be right back," she interrupted and rushed down the hallway to 3A.

"Hi Gloria, how are you?" she said breathlessly when Gloria answered.

"Hey, honey, are you all right? Come inside."

"Yes, yes I'm fine," she said quickly. Gloria watched as Alena scurried through the door and stood at the sofa.

"Well you're looking a bit antsy there. What's the matter?"

"Gloria look, there's someone I'd like you to meet. Michael." Her words were coming in a rush.

"Your gentleman friend, the tall handsome fellow. I've seen him," Gloria answered, eyeing Alena.

"Can I bring him by? I need you to… look at him for me."

"What is this about?"

"Gloria, he just told me that he may be a Bridger. I thought you might be able to take a look at him, maybe get a read or something on whether it could be true. Can't you sniff this sort of thing out like you did from me?"

"A Bridger. Hmm. Well why would the man make such a thing up?"

"I don't think he would, I just don't understand it. Gloria, he's wearing an amulet. An amulet! And it looks almost exactly like yours. Where the heck did that come from? How can this be? All of the sudden he's talking about seeing Shetani, ancestors, and auras. No visits from Mary, or Isis, nothing of the sort. Just one day, poof, he's got powers and an amulet from thin air. Can he really be a Bridger without going through the initiation that I've been going through?"

"The two of you have been intimate, I presume?"

"Yes, we've uh...been...intimate."

"Of course. Osiris returns through the sacred cauldron."

"English please, Gloria."

"Simply put, your womb is his portal, Alena. You initiated him with it."

"But we've had um...relations...before and he never turned into a Bridger then."

"He's always been a Bridger, but only now have you been standing fully in your powers. Your womb is the temple at which he received his."

"My God." Alena breathed out.

"And love, well, it is the most potent and ancient catalyst in the universe."

"I...I'll have to come back later. Thanks Gloria." Gloria grinned as Alena shuffled out of her door as quickly as she'd come. Michael barely waited for Alena to close the door behind her.

"So what did she say?"

"Mike, you are a Bridger." She'd recovered from her shock enough to smile.

"Yes! I feel it so strong. Just like you are here to anchor the Black Divine Feminine, I think I'm here to anchor and resurrect the Black Divine Masculine. It's fate, Alena, it can't be explained. Divine intervention. Everything happens in its own perfect time, right? God just saved the best for last."

He pulled her close and gently pressed his lips to her forehead. "From the moment I saw you back in school, I knew. I knew that I would always be with you. I've probably waited lifetimes."

He brought each of her hands to his lips, kissing her knuckles. "Can't you see, Alena? We're Twin Flames. We're back together to bring massive change to this earth. Again."

And with his words, Alena remembered suddenly—the sweet feel of Michael's spirit, his smile, the call of his soul to hers—every cosmic detail of lifetimes past came flooding back to her. It was at that moment that she knew, without a doubt, that what he said was true, he could see her. She had waited, too. She had waited for lifetimes to be seen, truly seen by his knowing and adoring eyes. There in all her clothes, she was naked before him, more vulnerable than she had ever been to any man in her life. She laid bare and open to love and to life as he gazed devotedly into her and bore witness to her light. He wrapped his strong arms around her, enveloping her in his protective warmth. Stillness. Heartbeats. Elation coursed through her body, rushing joyful tears to her eyes.

"I won't ever let you go," Michael said softly. "I'm going to be the man that you and Maya need."

He held her tighter than ever, their bodies, and spirits, leaning in as one.

"Mother of all beginnings. Hold me. Gather me. Feed me with the honey nectar from the hive."

ANNE BARING

CHAPTER 30

It was the evening that Michael and Alena made love as two Bridgers reunited that it happened. She had drifted to sleep in his arms, and in the next moment, she stood between two enormous emerald obelisks, back in Isis' temple. Isis towered before her, wearing a broad collar of yellow gold, and her staff in hand. Her earlobes bore earrings made of moon and star. In her eyes shone the heartbeat of the cosmos.

"Daughter, you have accepted the quest required of you and so begins the advent of your ascension. With you we are all well pleased." Isis swept her hand toward a crowd of thousands of light beings smiling upon Alena. Alena stood motionless, her eyes surveying the angelic-looking guests before her and the wonders of the temple. It was even more magnificent since Tabiry and the priestesses had first ushered her through it. In the center, a massive pillar made of solid amethyst throbbed with power, the Crystal of Isis.

"Now, daughter, understand that you have only reached the midpoint of your initiation. Yet it has been decided that you shall receive the powers that have since been presented to you."

Isis turned to the crowd.

"Council of Ancients, Brothers and Sisters of the Great Cosmic Light," Isis began, "The time has come when we choose another great being in human embodiment. Our daughter shall take her place in the fulfillment of the Divine Plan. She will lead the first string of humanity on earth to usher in the New Earth. She will restore all that the Shetani have sought to destroy in the human world."

Isis turned to Alena. "Honor your Dark Mother," she said. "And all of those who have given their human lives for the Plan, by honoring yourself. To you, I give the Power of Transformation."

The Beings of Light roared with sounds of celebration, returning to silence when Mary Magdalene appeared at Alena's side.

"Dear One," Mary said with a broad smile. "You have heeded our call obediently and walked through the open door to your destiny. Keep your faith only on the Christ within your heart. Draw your power from the Divine Fire of Three that is ever aglow inside of your Queendom. Teach your sisters and your brothers to turn away from the illusions of your world and to destroy the Shetani once and for always. To you I give the Power of the Heart"

At that, Oshun appeared in cascading skirts weaved of gold and a garland of hibiscus and jewels crowning her head.

"My daughter, show your sisters the way back to their honey wisdom. Show your people the way of unconditional love, compassion, and joy everlasting. To you I grant the Power of Joy."

Isis began again, "Blood of Isis, wisdom of Isis," she said. A strange gold instrument materialized and hovered midair, its sharp point fashioned into the shape of an Ibis' head and beak.

Isis pricked Alena's finger with it, drawing a sole carmine drop of blood. Next appeared a small, gold sarcophagus richly adorned in carnelian and lapis with ancient looking symbols engraved into it. Isis held it reverently in the palm of her hand.

"This is your womb, my daughter," Isis said to Alena. With a few mysterious words from Isis, the box opened slowly. From it, Isis withdrew a glorious amethyst amulet and upon its stone, she placed the single drop of Alena's blood from the instrument. Once her blood met with the jewel, it pulsed with a glow of the three powers she had been granted. Isis placed the amulet around Alena's neck.

The amethyst's illumination against her throat set off a million points of light that pierced into her flesh and past the boundaries of her body. She felt the powers course through her like a flash of three fires snaking from the tips of her toes and flaring out through the crown of her head. A deluge of violet fire rained down on her, and she stood joyfully engulfed in the divine flames.

"Kneel," Isis commanded.

Alena fell to her right knee and bowed her head.

"What have you learned? Confess it with your tongue," Isis said.

"I have learned that I am divine, Mother," Alena answered without effort. The words spilled easily from her mind's eye to her lips.

"What have you seen? Confess it with your tongue."

"I have seen my divinity," Alena answered.

"What shall you do? Confess it now with your tongue."

"I shall show your children that they, too, are divine, Mother."

"Yes, you will lead them back to their origin." Instantly Alena's hand began to glow with a blinding blue light.

"Ah, your inheritance," Isis said, acknowledging it. "The Sun of Sirius. Your father's mission is your mission. The Shetani's poison was what he chose, and in the end, he let it overtake him. In his evil ways, he strengthened you, Alena.

"Your father helped you to cultivate a well of compassion within you, deep enough to hold the suffering of others and transmute it with your power to heal. He lacked good character in this lifetime and forced you to find your strength so that you could carry on the torch that he could not bear in his lifetime. We need you to know that underneath the darkness, he was a light-filled and valiant soul. He still is. He gave in to the Shetani's madness, but his original intent was to fight for the Plan. Only the family blood, the pure Sirian blood, can hold what I am about to impart to you."

A legion of Alena's ancestors raised their hands, and she saw that their hands glowed, too. They, too, bore the Sun of Sirius.

"The Sun of Sirius is the seed of light that was lent to earth so many years ago after the fall of man. It is a purifier. And now, in addition to your new powers, we shall grant you the Flame of Restoration. With this gift, your very touch holds the power to restore original sacred memory from the Divine Heart. It can return the brain to the memory of divinity, of one's original glory and divine purpose. In your hand is revolution. You hold the power to return the consciousness of the Black race to its original, intended glory. My daughter, you are hereby exalted to my Tribe. Welcome," Isis announced, and Alena was crowned.

A roar of applause and cheer echoed throughout the Council. Isis rapped the ground five times with her staff to conclude the Initiation. Five, the number symbolizing great change.

"The sun's eyes are bees that weep honey; the honey in our heart comes from tears of village indebtedness."

LONG LIFE, HONEY IN THE HEART

CHAPTER 31

The morning was swathed in an uneasy stillness that Alena had sensed in her spirit before she even opened her eyes. It was the morning of the Spring Equinox. The energy thinned the air and seized the winds, rousing her from a sound sleep. She rose and peered through the window to the blackened mounds of winter's final snow. Leafless trees lined the streets. Clouds lumbered slowly over the sun.

Even the sidewalks were sparse and quiet. This was her moving day. After nine months, she was leaving East Church Street for a beautiful brownstone apartment in Park Slope. As she stepped out into the morning air, Alena filled her nostrils with the sharp cold of the new day. She felt it again; something lurked just beneath the calm. She tried to release the feeling as she dropped Maya off at Gabriel's and went about her day.

That evening, when she returned to her old neighborhood for the final time, Alena was greeted by a cacophony of screaming and wailing, both from sirens and from the people. It was coming from a growing mass of people just a block from her apartment. Their eyes were aghast and fixed on the sidewalk. She pushed her way through the chaos trying to peer over their heads.

"What's happened here? Excuse me, I live here. What's happened?" Alena asked anxiously.

"Damn Pigs shot another kid. A baby." One of the neighborhood women spat with disgust as she shook her head in disbelief. "Killed a goddamned baby."

Alena felt a tug at her coat. One of the neighborhood boys she'd seen from time to time had grasped her sleeve. "Miss, over here," he said. Alena let the boy lead the way to the opening in the crowd, and her eyes were horror-struck, too. There on the sidewalk,

Benjamin's small body lay where he had fallen after a police officer's bullet pierced his heart. The concrete was stained with his blood.

"My God! Oh God, please no! Takeah's son!" she cried out. Her hand flew over her mouth. A wave of nausea gripped her and bowled her over to her knees. "No! Not BJ!" Alena's wrenching cries joined with those of the swelling crowd rushing behind her.

One of the men yelled. "Where's the ambulance? Where the fuck is the ambulance? Can't they at least put a sheet over him and give that boy some dignity? See, they don't give a fuck about us! Out here killing us off, don't care who goes down. Any other goddamn day five-o be swarming this bitch in five seconds. This shit is bullshit, man. They want us all dead, and they ain't gone stop 'till we extinct." The crowd yelled back in agreement.

Alena looked up to see Takeah restrained by two officers. Horrified disbelief twisted her face. "My baby, they killed my baby…"

Takeah shrieked repeatedly, her eyes fixed on her boy. The misery in them was all too familiar.

Alena fought her way through the swelling crowd and rushed over to her. Gloria was not far behind. Worn with grief, Takeah tottered on her legs until the weight of her limp body started to fall to the ground. Two men helped to catch her before she hit the ground. Alena grasped her arm, and Gloria fanned her face with her scarf.

"Please, bring her with us. Quickly," Gloria whispered urgently. The two men raised Takeah to her feet and whisked her through the crowd behind Gloria. A woman, a mother without hope. Robbed. The sense of injustice boiled inside of Alena so wildly, it was as if her own child lay dead in the street. She felt that at any moment it would break through her skin and detonate the world.

"Get her in here. Bring her in here, please. Lay her on the bed. Yes, just lay her right here," Gloria instructed the men into her apartment. "Thank you, brothers, so much."

"It's the least we can do, ma'am. It was bad enough she had to see her boy shot up like that, then the cops got the nerve to treat her like she the criminal. It's a damn shame. They better pray Bengy's peoples ain't get they badge numbers or else they gonna be some five-o turning up missing. Anyway, you call us if you need us.

My name is Brotha Ski, that's my number here." He passed his business card to Gloria. It read, "Ski's Imported Oils and Such."

"Thank you," she said before they turned to leave.

Gloria pulled Takeah's shoes off, tucked her under the blanket, and laid a cold compress against her forehead. Takeah whimpered and turned her head to vomit.

"Shouldn't we call someone?" Alena said frantically. "An ambulance? She looks like she's in shock."

Gloria swatted away her words with a wave of her hand and shook her head.

"Those doctors won't do a thing for her except give her a night's stay in the psych ward and send her home with some Valium. Just let her rest here for now. If she needs more attention, then we'll call. What she really needs right now is love. And prayer."

"Does she have any family we can call to help comfort her? Bengy!" Alena cried, fresh grief weakening her voice. "Does someone have her boyfriend's number?"

Gloria waved her hand again and shot Alena a shut-your-mouth glance. "The man who almost killed you? Think straight now! If that boy isn't still in prison, he's already on his way here, I'm sure. What I'm not sure of is how much help he's going to be to this poor girl if he gets here." Gloria peered through the blinds onto the courtyard and shook her head slowly. The crowd had grown even more after the coroner had finally taken Benjamin's body away, and the officers demanded they disperse. Night had fallen over them along with their thickening grief and anger.

"This neighborhood is going to burn to the ground if that Bengy fellow and his friends have anything to do with it. These young people are tired. And for what they did to little Benjamin…" Gloria's voice trailed off, and her expression darkened. "Time is up, the Shetani are busy." Gloria gestured toward Takeah.

"Tacky's mother is gone, and all I know of is a grandmother in Guyana and a few girlfriends from the neighborhood. We're all this girl has got right now," Gloria said.

"Oh God. Oh my God, I can't believe this is happening. I…I'd just seen BJ and Takeah the other day, Gloria. She was just so proud, so proud of her son. How is this happening?"

"The Plan," Gloria said sadly and quietly.

"What?"

"The Divine Plan, Alena. Have you forgotten? The Cosmic Door opens tonight once the Grand Cross forms."

A dark feeling crept over Alena. Of course, she had not forgotten, not for an instant. With all of its mystery and Gloria's outright silence about it, this day had loomed heavily over her. What she knew for sure was that this was the ancient vendetta that Isis had warned her about. Benjamin Jr. was the Shetani's bait, the sacrificial lamb to begin the final battle.

"They're trying to stage an uprising to stop the Plan. A race war," Alena said.

Gloria nodded gravely.

"Keep your third eye open. Keep your heart open. Be on guard," Gloria urged.

"Michael," Alena whispered, suddenly remembering that he had been waiting for her. "You know, my… boyfriend. He was supposed to help me move the last of my things tonight. God, he must be worried sick by now."

"Why don't you give him a call? And maybe you should think about going with him. It's not safe here, and it's only going to get worse."

"Gloria, I'm not going to leave you or Takeah here. You know that. No. If you stay, I stay." She held Gloria's hand tightly. "I've got my sword ready."

On the other side of the wall, the city filled with the wailing of sirens and shouting and chaos mounting by the minute.

"I'm not going," Alena said defiantly. A faint smile crossed Gloria's lips and then quickly faded. She scanned the apartment for any sight of a shadow and sniffed the air for any scent of the beasts. "I'm going to call Mike. I'll be right back, okay?" she said as she headed for the hallway.

"Be careful. Do you hear me? They want you, Alena. Badly." "I'll only be a few minutes, just letting him know I'm all right."

Gloria nodded. "I'll see to Takeah."

"Babe!" Michael answered on the first ring. "Are you okay?"

The roads are closed off, there are barricades, and the cops won't let anyone in or out. Cameras everywhere. Are you all right? I've been calling you like crazy!"

"I'm fine, honey, I'm all right. My friend Takeah, it was her son they killed. Shot him in cold blood for nothing. He was just a baby, Mike." Alena started to cry.

"I'm getting you out of there, okay? Go to the barricade on the top of East Church and meet me there in five."

"I can't, Mike. I can't leave. My friend is here with me and she doesn't have anyone else except for my neighbor and me. She's not doing well either, I can't just leave her like this. Mike, please listen. I'll be okay. We're locked in tight. No one is going to attack the buildings. The worst thing they'll do is loot the stores. Please go home. It's not safe for you out here. The cops just need a half of a reason to put a bullet through another black man. Please. Turn around. I'll stay on the phone with you while you do."

"Leen, are you crazy? I'm not leaving you alone in that zoo! Brothers are out here talking about an all-out war. They don't give a damn about looting. They want blood for what the police did to that kid. They're talking bodies, Alena. The boy's dad is apparently a heavy hitter out here. If his mother is in that apartment, what makes you think they won't carry their war right up there where you are? Come on, babe, you can bring them with you."

"Takeah's not in any shape to go back through that crowd."

"Look, just please meet me at the top of East Church, okay?"

"Michael, I'm sorry but—"

"Alena, please don't argue. Five minutes."

"All right," she answered, knowing there was no convincing Michael otherwise. She would show him that she was fine so he'd go home, then she could rush back to Gloria and Takeah.

"Five minutes," Michael repeated.

Alena made her way down the stairs and pushed the front door open slowly. Just beyond it was a swarm of people. Angry people. The scarlet spot where Benjamin's slain body had laid was already bordered with candles. And then, she saw guns. Guns. Men from the neighborhood had guns. The police had guns. Their faces were hard and cold, prepared for war, yet still fearful. Alena's breath sped up, and her pulsed raced.

Oh my God. How the hell was she going to push through all of that to get to Michael? There was no way she was going to put Takeah through the trauma of that crowd and no way she could she leave her and Gloria in all of this mess. She couldn't. She closed the door and ran back up the steps before calling Michael back.

"Baby, I can't do it. I… I'm sorry, I can't. They have guns out here. They're ready to die. The police. These kids. They're ready to kill, Mike."

"Alena, baby, please. You have to get out of there. Do this for me, Alena. Do it for Maya. Leen please, listen to me," Michael pleaded.

"I am. I'm doing this for you and for Maya. Michael, I love you. Deeply. But I feel this in my bones, this is where Isis wants me to be, right here. No running. No hiding. I'm staying, baby. I'm sorry if you're upset with me. Go home. Please, Mike, go home now. Something is happening here… something that has been waiting for a long time. I'm going to check on Gloria and Takeah now, okay? I'll be just fine, I promise you. Call me right away… when you get in your car, okay?"

Alena went back inside Gloria's apartment.

"How is she doing?"

"She's awake, going in and out. I gave her some herbal tea that'll keep her calm at least through half the night. She's talking some. She said she'd sent him to the store for a pack of cigarettes, the same as she had any other day. The boys said the police mixed him up with some older kids that robbed the place. They say they thought those Marlboros was a gun." Gloria beat her fist against the table.

"My Lord! My *Lord!*" she cried, clutching her heart. Her breathing was labored, and she looked physically pained, as if she was responsible for Benjamin's death. Alena had never seen or imagined this depth of despair in Gloria. Her grief drenched the air, and for once, Gloria's kind eyes were unreadable.

"Innocent! He was just an innocent little boy! He's got nothing to do with this!" she seethed into nothingness before collapsing onto the sofa chair.

Alena rushed to her side and clasped her forearms.

"Gloria!" Gloria was deflated, her face buried in her hands, shoulders bobbing with sobs. "Gloria, stay with me. Are you okay?"

Tears covered her face. It was the first time Alena had ever seen Gloria cry. Alena squeezed her hand. Gloria was silent. Weak.

"You need some rest yourself. Why don't you lay back on the sofa? I'm going to put some tea on for you."

Without lifting her head, Gloria said, "Now isn't the time for rest," she said with a hardness that startled Alena. "They are coming, Alena. Me, I've got too much fear in me to conquer them. That was the breech in my heart that let that beast in. That's why it was able to scrape my arm. But you're strong now. It's your time."

"How can you of all people be fearful, Gloria? You are a rock."

"Because I love you, honey. I love you like my own. I still have a mama's fear for her child. Get my Bible out of the bedroom. It's on top of the dresser nearest the window." Alena obeyed and returned with the large book as quickly as she could.

"Read me The Lord's Prayer."

Alena hurried through the aged pages to the Book of Matthew and began in the most soothing tone she could muster for Gloria.

"Our Father in heaven, hallowed be your name. Your kingdom come, your will be done, on earth, as it is in heaven.

"Give us this day our daily bread, and forgive us our debts, as we also have forgiven our debtors. And lead us not into temptation, but deliver us from evil."

"Psalms. 23:4," Gloria commanded with her eyes closed, tears flowing, and head grasped in her hands.

"Yea, though I walk through the valley of the shadow of death, I will fear no evil: for thou art with me; thy rod and thy staff they comfort me," Alena read.

"Yea, though I walk through the valley," Gloria repeated.

Alena lifted her head from the passage and stared at her.

"Yea though I walk through the valley." Her voice was gaining strength.

"Yea though I walk through the valley of the shadow of death I will *fear no evil!*" she screamed. Takeah stirred in the bedroom.

"*For God is with me!*" The raw power in her voice alarmed Alena. Had Gloria lost it?

"God is with me. *God is with me!* God is with us. God. Is. With. Us. God is with *you*, Alena." She finally lifted her tear-stained face to Alena's. "Blessed are they who are pure in heart, for they can see God. Do not let the Beasts blind you." Tears welled in Alena's own eyes as she felt the magnitude of what was coming to pass.

"Come," Gloria said. Alena's eyes were wide as she walked to Gloria and knelt in front of her. Gloria cupped her hands around Alena's face. Her eyes were ravaged with exhaustion, yet hopeful.

"Go. It is time. Go out there. You will know what to do." She planted a soft motherly kiss on Alena's forehead. "Go and fear no evil." She touched her fingers to Alena's heart.

"There is one last thing you must know, Alena." A somber look clouded her expression. "Maya is the Oracle. She is the one. If the Darkness enters that door tonight...if they get past you...they won't stop until they destroy her. I'm so sorry." Gloria collapsed into deep sleep.

Alena felt her heart sink as she stood in silent prayer, willing the creeping terror from penetrating it. She slipped out of the apartment quietly and pushed the building's doors open for what may be the last time.

"Mike!" He was standing on the stoop ready to turn the handle. "How did you make it past the barricade?"

"I told you I wasn't leaving you here by yourself."

He kissed her gently. "This is my battle, too, just as much as it's yours. We are going to stop all of this, together. Come on. It's insane out there. Let's go in and get your friends."

Alena curled her fingers around her amulet resting against her skin. Something like a smile tugged at Michael's mouth. They walked into the courtyard where the moon was crouched low onto the horizon. It was nightfall, and the same corner shop where young Benjamin Jr. had been gunned downed was ablaze, just as Gloria had said. Suddenly, the dismal night sky broke open and mourned with them. Heaving sheets of cold rain pelted the earth.

Despite the rain, hundreds of people demanding justice by any means still clogged the streets. A fleet of police cars had descended on their block. Their red and blue lights pulsed through the darkness. Armored in riot gear and shields like soldiers on a battlefield, a wall of police officers stood ready to charge against the crowd. "GO BACK TO YOUR HOMES! GO BACK TO YOUR HOMES NOW OR WE WILL DEPLOY TEAR GAS," an officer screamed into a megaphone.

Then with one act, the chaos began. "Fuck the police!" a man yelled and hurled a glass bottle toward the officers. The moment its green glass shattered, loud, raucous cries rang through the night as both walls of people surged forward toward each other. The Shetani began to uncoil from their hosts and show themselves to those with the power to see. Wide streaks of the darkness seeped from the hearts of the protestors, and from the hearts of the police officers, swelling with their anger, bitterness, wrath, and pride until their evil presence completely coursed through the city. The Shetani's deathly black void then shifted into its beastly shapes. Alena glimpsed each of them in terrifying clarity.

"God, give me the strength to do what you've asked me to do. Please, protect my child," she prayed.

More were coming. One by one, the torrent of demons swarmed in like a rolling sea of bats in their wretched forms: Fear, Dissension, Bondage, Jealousy, Malice, Murder, Rage, Spite, Cruelty, Bitterness, Greed, Poverty, Torment, and Cowardice.

The creature's ear-chattering shrieks rang through the air, battle cries from the pit of evil. Their wicked stench descended. The beasts all concentrated on Alena through the menacing red orbs of their eyes, waiting to devour her when the time was right. Their gaping mouths snapped at her with razor sharp fangs as they spit fires onto the buildings.

Alena refused to allow any fear to infiltrate her. The black formless shapes merged into one another and materialized as one gargantuan beast looming before her. Her eyes swept up to the creature's impossible height and determination flared in gaze. It loped toward her and within seconds it was upon her.

"Do you think you can defeat us? We are infinite. We are legion." It was reading her heart and reading her every thought. "You will die now, fool! Now, should we crush you or shall we have them pierce your heart with a bullet as we commanded they do to the boy?"

It laughed evilly before baring its teeth and snapping its jaws before her face.

"Leave her alone!" Michael bellowed, standing in front of Alena with his hands shaking with fury. "Get back! Move!" Michael warned her.

He tried to hold up his arms to defend her, but one of the police officers seized him by his throat. "Get over here, boy. Ha! Lover boy is it? You think you can save her? You think you can save them, nigger?" The whites of the officer's eyes went black. The Shetani behind those eyes howled with haunting laughter.

"Never, boy! Never!" the thing sneered. It vacated its human host and revealed itself, then shifted into dark wisps of smoke that coiled around Michael's wrists and legs.

"I can't move! In the name of Chr—" A final dark wisp wrapped itself around his mouth, silencing him.

"You can't fear it, Michael! You have to believe! Fear no evil. You are the truth, you are the light!" Alena urged.

Rooted to the spot in which she stood, Alena gazed defiantly back into the boiling viscous red of its eyes. They were void of any life. Absolute nothingness. Alena refused to give the beast any of her power—none of her fear, none of her heart would it ever have again.

"Heel! Heel in the name of Christ!" she screamed.

In one swoop, it grabbed her throat, claws digging mercilessly. Alena felt the scathing pressure and then the warm scarlet trails of blood spurting from each point of her skin the creature had pierced. The beast threw her several feet to the ground. Before she could get up, it grasped her by the arm and ripped its fangs through her flesh, searing through the tendons and leaving gnashed skin flapped open to the white shell of her bone.

None of this is real! But how was she feeling every agonizing sensation? The beast growled and smiled its evil smile at her.

I fear no evil. I fear no evil, Alena chanted in her mind, willing her emotion to stay centered on what was true. She groaned in pain as rainwater battered her face, trying not to look at the grisly wound the beast had torn into her arm. It stung like hellfire. Despite it, her face was transcendent with a fiery boldness. The beast lunged on her and snapped again. This time the clutch of its powerful jaws threatened to snap her arm and tear it from her shoulder. She closed her eyes and pushed its fearsome image from her mind.

"This is not happening. They cannot kill me." Despite the searing pain in her arm, she would not submit to the illusion.

"No! It's not real!" she panted through clenched teeth.

At that, the beast wrapped its hand around her throat. No matter how vivid the illusion of it was, no matter the pain, she steadied her thoughts and her feelings on truth. It took everything in her to remain there. Yet behind the dark shroud of the beast's unrelenting hand, Alena was running out of breath. The scene before her was fading to black, and she felt the panic of her last breath leaving her body.

Alena blinked the rain out of her bleary eyes and glimpsed Gloria a few yards away, hobbling toward her to help her from the beast's grip. She was determined, yet still weak. She'd fought her exhaustion to make her way to the courtyard, not able to bear to leave Alena and Michael to fight alone. The beast brought its monstrous fist down on her as she approached, hitting her with enough force to send her flailing until she lay motionless on the asphalt.

"The Darkness is passing." Gloria rasped, sweat pooled above her lip. "Gather your strength, Alena. See only God."

The beast's grip tightened. In the dreamy chasm between life and death, Alena remembered her father's gift. She called on all the power in her Sirian blood.

"Daddy! Daddy…" she tried to squeeze from her throat. In the next moment, a blazing hand holding a sword of gold pierced the beast between its eyes and instantly it released Alena. She closed her eyes against the incoming bright light. The hand belonged to a mighty warrior, his breastplate like a fortress of sunlight. The warrior then touched her arm where the beast had nearly torn it from her body. Alena kept her eyes on the beauty of his ethereal form. It was shining illustriously against the black void, like a guardian angel. Though she had never seen the entity before, her soul and heart recognized its presence. The holy warrior was her father. As she felt the warmth of his loving light wash over her, she felt her own power rising. Her father, her real father, had come to help her.

An orb of roaring orange flames sat in the south of the sky, a searing, brilliant white star perched at the north. The planets were settling into their foretold positions. The Grand Cross was almost formed.

"The door! They're going for the Cosmic Door!" Gloria warned with all she had left.

Then came a sound that froze everyone in place. What began as a low grumble of thunder broke into a terrible cracking that pierced the air and drew all eyes upward to the rainy sky. It had turned an almost impenetrable black as the Shetani's army descended with fury.

A new gargantuan beast formed from the mass of demon servants, rushing in to besiege Alena and infiltrate the Cosmic Door. It was even more monstrous than the first. As she remembered who she was, Alena's magic began to pour from her. She raised her hand to the beast, and her true strength was revealed. A glow pulsed around her entire body like the sun's corona.

As Alena reclaimed her power, so did Michael, and the restraints of darkness dropped from his wrists and ankles. A flash of intuition hit them both in the same moment. *Join together as one.* "Take my hand!" Michael shouted to Alena, who had already begun running toward her. The earth quaked, and the winds became almost unbearable, whipping up earth and debris into a wall of haze before them.

Hand-in-hand, they rushed through the haze to Gloria's side and Alena took her weak hand into her own. The instant they embraced, a jolt of unified power surged through each of them. Bars of light beamed from each of their amulets and soared miles into the cosmos, piercing through the vortex of the darkness. Together they had forged an arch of protection over the earth. Peering into those cosmos, Alena could see now that they were not alone.

Legions of angels from the North, East, South and West had descended from their angelic kingdoms. The Beings of Light, her father, the holy Sirian warrior, and the ancestors joined in with them and crackled down like bolts of lightning surrounding her, and brilliant white veins of power cut through the night.

They arched their blazing bodies over their people to fortify the lighted fortress that Alena, Gloria, and Michael's powers had created. A mighty violet orb then took up its station in the West of the sky, the star of Sirius. There was only one more planet to rise and complete the formation.

Alena felt the sharp pain in her arm recede to nothing, and the wound was no more. The jagged flesh was now smooth and new. The glow around her hands intensified, and light pulsed from them even more brilliantly. Her power was magnifying by the second. She felt it rattle her teeth and rage with the force of her words.

"I am the resurrection of the glory! Leave them alone in the name of Christ! Flee from here! You have no power!" Alena commanded in a soaring, powerful voice.

Just then, a smoldering red orb settled into the east. All four arms of the Grand Cross of Initiation had been set, and the New Heaven and New Heaven's door began to stretch open from the center of the formation. From the flames of her heart, Alena summoned a force that surged through her. The force sent a peal of thunder bursting through her limbs. The Sun of Sirius blazed in her left hand, the Flame of Restoration in her right.

Alena directed her hands toward the beast, and the glow died in its eyes. At her command, it was bound in the pillar of golden flames she had summoned. A terrible screech rose from the beast, one so shrill and haunting that everyone stood still and silent. It broke through the dark skies and rode out on the storm winds. Then its writhing body began to burn. The flames grew, shooting out several feet into the air. Alena could feel the heat of the blaze on her face. And then, just as quickly as the flames had risen, the beast burned into nothingness. Breath and life returned to the city. The rains stopped and calm rested over all of them. At once, she knew that in that space and in that time, she had changed everything.

A silver finger of lightning tore down the center of the sky, splitting it in two. Each half gave way like two great curtains, revealing a golden river of light.

Alena also knew that it was time to speak the truth, starting with the massive crowd that had gathered. *"Hear me!"* she cried. Even her voice was new.

The sea of people obeyed and stood statue-still, transfixed by the mere vibration of her voice. The gift of true vision that Mary Magdalene had once given temporarily was returned to her. In that hushed fold of time she saw and felt into one thousand hearts at once. They were dull and broken from years of serving as vessels to the Shetani.

"You must remember yourselves!" Alena cried once more, this time casting the fires she had created into the crowd. With her enchanted flames, she bestowed true vision to the people.

With that, the lightness of peace and hope now purified each one of their hearts. One by one, the bonds of illusion the Shetani had placed on them were broken. With the Flame of Restoration, their divine senses were returned to them. With true vision, they could see themselves and one another as holy kings and queens after centuries of blindness.

"Listen to me!" Alena screamed, resplendent in her full power. "You have been lied to. You have been deceived for generations. I have come to remind you of the truth. I have come to return you to the glory that you have forgotten. You must know that for eons you have been fed an illusion. Lies. Look around you." Alena gestured to the still burning buildings and charred remains of the community.

"This is just what they, the dark forces, want you to do, to destroy yourselves with their darkness. I know you are tired of the injustice of this world. The cruelty! The war waged against you! The war waged against even your children! I know that you are enraged, and you have so many reasons to be. But please, understand that that police officer is not the true enemy. We are not each other's enemies. The entire human family has been pitted against each other by an evil force called the Shetani. Their mission is to destroy God's Divine Plan for a New Earth by destroying us, the Black race. It is a mission achieved by creeping into the hearts and souls of those who seemingly hate you. But it's over now. We are free!"

The crowd turned to look at one another, nodding and cheering in agreement.

"Their hatred for you is hatred for the truth, for your birthright to the throne of God, and for the Great Dark Mother of All Creation," Alena continued. "Underneath their fear of you is their deep longing to be a part of you. Those infected by the Shetani do not understand how viciously they destroy themselves in their quest to destroy you. Hear me! No matter what we have been told, no matter the amount of brutal dark forces that have been trained against us, we belong here, and our victory is assured." Alena felt her power growing even stronger as she looked out to the crowd.

"We are the first and the last, sent here by God and the Beings of Light. We are the portals through which this planet will receive Heaven on Earth, god kings and goddess queens walking on our consecrated land. You must know that we are rightfully on the very land that God has ordained to us, to save.

"America is a hallowed ground, our hallowed ground. Our sacred work is here, to live as God's Freedom, God's Faith, and God's Will, and to show humanity the way to victory."

Alena thrust both palms toward the ground. The Sun of Sirius and the growing forces within her struck the earth with a sonic boom, breaking the wet ground open.

"It's the Shetani who try to bury you in hardship in order to make you believe that you are powerless, cursed, and alone. Let the lies that claimed that you've come to this land only for servitude and suffering be burned away from you tonight. Today we will finish the mission that our ancestors began. The battle is already won. It is already done! We only need to stand. It is up to us to bring it forth. Come. Follow me!"

From the fault in the earth, a bridge of fire emerged and arched through the golden opening in the heavens. It was the bridge of freedom. The Era of Rebirth had begun.

The End… For now.

ABOUT THE AUTHOR

Malena Crawford is a Washington, DC-based writer and a graduate of the George Washington University. She is the founder of the Black Divine Feminine Reawakened movement and facilitates workshops on personal development, empowerment, and anti- oppression across the globe, most recently in South Africa and Ghana. *A Fistful of Honey* is her first novel and she has completed an accompanying self-development workbook entitled *A Fistful of Honey THE WORKBOOK: A Guide to Awakening, Healing & Creating Your Honey Sweet Life* and life planner entitled *Your Next 90 Days on Your Throne* exclusively available now on her website. She is also the founder of **The Honey Experience Charm School for Goddesses on the Rise.** If you would like to read more of her work or sign up for more insights and exclusive offers, visit her here:

Join the Family on the Website:
www.MalenaCrawford.com
Email & Love Notes: malena@malenacrawford.com

Text:
Text to Join Newsletter: Text the word "HONEY" to 66866
Facebook:https://www.facebook.com/TheBlackDivineFeminineRe awakened

Instagram:
https://www.instagram.com/malenacrawford/

Facebook:
Join the Honey Experience Facebook Group for support & teaching at https://www.facebook.com/groups/thehoneyexperience/

If you are so moved, please consider leaving a review and sharing with a friend so we can get Alena's story into more hearts!

AUTHOR'S NOTE

Writing *A Fistful of Honey* has changed my life. It helped me to heal in ways that were unimaginable to me and I will be forever in gratitude. This book began as an answered prayer. After witnessing the exoneration of a murderer, the man who shot and killed a young, unarmed black teenager named Trayvon Martin, I was livid and full of questions. How could this level of blatant injustice still exist in 2013? Why did it seem that black and brown people always on the receiving end? How can black people keep their sanity and hope despite this foolishness?

I was also afraid for my people, especially my brothers. I prayed intensely, demanding understanding and most of all, a solution. The answers that I received came to me steadily within a four year journey, a deeply spiritual one. You are now reading some of the insights that I received. If the story of little Benjamin, Takeah, Gloria, Alena, Maya and Michael has affected you in any way, please share your inspiration with the world so we can change it.

If you are questioning your value in this world, especially as a person of color, please know that the truths in this book are real. You are more than worthy and you more than matter. You are a key that the world needs. If you are in the midst of your own healing journey I urge you to keep going. If you are on the verge of rising into your power, I urge you not to think, but to stand. Now. Right now. We only need to stand.

In Gratitude,
Malena Crawford

READER'S GROUP DISCUSSION QUESTIONS

1. Discuss the theme of motherhood in the novel and the term 'motherless daughter'. How has motherhood shaped Alena and Dinah's lives? How does Gloria's presence affect Alena's plight as a 'motherless daughter'?

2. What is the role of race and identity in the book? What do you think of Crawford's methods of raising the issue of police brutality?

3. Alena Ford holds some scathing judgments and prejudices against her own race as shown in her attitudes toward her new Brooklyn neighbors. Do you think classism and 'respectability politics' are significant issues in the Black community?

4. Self-hatred is a common thread in Alena Ford's journey. Discuss how the effects of colorism and racism have shaped her choices. How have these affected you in your life? How did this book make you feel?

5. Several examples of disempowerment occur in the novel. For instance, Gabriel accuses Alena of being a bad mother for moving her child to Brooklyn. While she is recovering from her injuries in the hospital, he takes Mya and is able to gain

custody of her. How does the book treat disenfranchisement? How might the story be different without it?

6. How would you describe Alena and Michael's relationship? Do you think Michael truly loves Alena? Why or why not?

7. Mary Magdalene tells Alena that "All creation began with and flows through the black woman. You are the keys to the New Heaven on the New Earth. You must unlock the door and then change will be assured. We are the Black Madonna, we are the Great Dark Mother emerged as one." What did Mary mean by this? Discuss black womanhood through this lens.

8. Of the 'thugs' gathered in front of the apartment Mary Magdalene says this, "I tell you the truth," Mary said. "You have not seen them clearly." She enchants Alena's eyes so that she can in fact see them clearly and tells her to 'open your eyes and see your brothers once more." Alena does so and is astonished to see that those men who appeared as menacing criminals were "kings, dressed in luminous metallic robes." Why do you think Crawford created this lens of divinity for Alena to see these men? Discuss how society may have trained us to view black men.

9. What was Oshun's grove a symbol for? How does Oshun help Alena return to herself? Can you imagine your own experience with Oshun?

10. How does Gloria's presence in the story affect how it unfolds? Why do you think Alena's wellbeing is so important to her initially, and does her motivation change over the course of the novel?

11. Alena's devastation over the early loss of her innocence seeps into every aspect of her life, including her marriage and her relationship with her daughter, Maya. Discuss the role of trauma and recovery, and how trauma can be passed down through generations.

12. Discuss the relationship between secrets and truth in this story. Almost all of the characters keep secrets. Whose actions are justified and whose are not? Use examples from the book to illustrate your points.

13. Discuss Michael's character. Michael is the only male character whose perspective is shown in the book. Do you think this is significant? Why do you think the author chose to knight him as a Bridger? How does it affect your feelings towards him?

14. Throughout the novel, Gloria and the deity characters (Isis, Mary and Oshun) say things like, "The Black woman is the mother of all humanity." Does this ring true to you? How did this affect the story for you?

15. After years of denying that her husband raped her daughter, Alena's mother finally admits, "I knew he did it soon as you told me when you were little girl. I did a terrible thing. I was a shameful woman, pitiful, and I'm sorry. I'm so sorry for what you went through." Is this apology enough for what Alena endured? Discuss why you believe Alena decides to forgive her mother after so many years of neglect and after her life was so deeply affected by Dinah's choices.

16. "I'm fighting because she couldn't, but now I can. I can create a completely new world. I have the power now. I can say yes or no to life. I have a choice. We all do. We've just forgotten. They're telling me to go back for what I thought I lost. It's still there. It's always there because, truly, nothing is ever lost in spirit. There are no more shackles, no more Massa Johns.," This is said by Alena to Michael shortly after she returned to the present from her experience as a slave in the antebellum South. She is slowly realizing her connection to Sarah and eventually also realizes the parallel between Master Ashby and her husband Gabriel. To what extent, if any, do you believe racial oppression continues to shape our identity and reality today?

17. Alena answers her mother with "What did I do, Mama? What did I ever do to become the sacrifice? I just wanted to matter. I just wanted to be worth your protection and your love, his love'. Discuss how black women and girls have become the 'sacrifice'.

18. Alena's mother goes on to explain her choice to deny her husband's acts of incest and rape with "I was so scared. Our family would have been broken up. He would've been marked a monster and sent to jail for a very long time. But I swear, I didn't choose him over you. Baby, please believe me. I swear it on my own life." She pulled Alena back and stared into her eyes, pleading. "I was too weak to stand alone, to stand up to him, and too weak to stand by you and Reeta, my baby girls. I hate myself every day for what he did to you."

Discuss how the cycle of abuse and trauma is perpetuated by those who do nothing.

19. Discuss the ways in which the title A Fistful of Honey encapsulates the relationships within the novel. What emphasis do we place on our own kinship?

20. Crawford ends the novel with Gloria, Michael and Alena succeeding in opening the Cosmic Door and leading others to walk across the bridge to the New Earth. How do you imagine this New Earth would be like? What do you believe would be different?

21. Consider the following quote from Isis' character: "The Black race is the beginning and the ending, the Alpha and Omega… the original people beginning the race of man on earth. With this truth comes a heavy responsibility and great sacrifice. These sacrifices have manifested as the massive struggles that the Black race has had to overcome over the span of human history." What do you think of this statement? Discuss what Isis meant by the "Alpha and the Omega".

22. Alena has a painful secret concerning her father, Linwood. She is resentful towards her entire family and her mother especially because she believes that Linwood's wellbeing was more important to them than her humanity was. Discuss the effect of this secret on Alena and the other members of her family. Do you believe that these effects plague the Black community as a whole? How?

23. Crawford makes bold assertions about religion and human history throughout the novel. In one passage, character Isis claims that she is the Nubian Queen who has descended from the Heavens and tells Alena," I have come so that you may know my true face. It is infinite," Isis continued. "I am neither male nor female, white nor black—but all, Alena. We are all aspects of the one almighty God. I come to you now in my feminine form for I am the feminine aspect of God. I am the Great Mother of All Creation. I am your Dark Mother, the Dark Matter whose love for you is so potent that it holds the galaxies together just as it holds your very cells together." Discuss this perspective of God being a black woman.

24. Do you believe Alena found her 'Honey'? Have you? What does 'Honey" mean for you?

25. What did this story stir in you? How has it challenged you?

ACKNOWLEDGEMENTS

It is my great honor to express gratitude to all of those who both directly and indirectly have made this work a possibility. I thank God, my angels and my ancestors for pushing this story through me. I thank Jaqueline Freeman, author of one of my favorite books *Song of Increase* for giving me her blessing to use its quotes. There is magic in the honey and in our bee family, and she has captured it all in her beautiful words. I thank each and every one of my readers for supporting and sharing this work. Thank you for all of the heartfelt messages sharing how the story has touched you. It is my absolute favorite part of this process. Thank you for your feedback, and reviews. May you all be blessed richly!

Many thanks to each and every one of the "Crawesome" Crawfords! Mama Carrie thank you for always being supportive of my gifts and dreams and my love for writing at an early age. Daddy thank you for teaching me that I need not follow anyone else's ideas but my own. Folayan, Kemba, Kenya, Candace Mickens, and Kela Harris thank you for all of you tireless reading and rereading even when I know I drove you all crazy. Thank you for being so gracious and loving through it all. Folayan thank you for your genius, if it wasn't for your keen Virgo eye this could have gone very differently. I would not have been able to birth this book without you big sis! Imani, Kwame, Joe, Ayanna, Kaisan, Kobe, Elijah, Raine—I love all of you!

Adara, my beautiful baby girl, thank you for your patience with your mother through this writing process and for being so excited for me even when I'm sure you would rather have gone out to play. You are my reason for finishing strong! Thank you Michael M. for your shaking me out of my ruts and being my inspiration throughout this writing process. Thank you to all the mamas and the Iyas who helped rudder my ship! You know who you are!

To Sheree Renee Thomas, one of the best editors and writers in the world and John St. Augustine my book coach, a huge thank you for helping me to unearth the story that must be told. From my heart to yours, this project would not have been possible without your midwifing, hand holding, and holding the vision of completion for me from day one. Thank you Rev. Chris Bazemore for your undying wisdom and support! Thank you to all of my glorious teachers and those gracious enough to read in my rough stage. Thank you to Ginny Weissman, Natasha Brown, Tressa Smallwood, Josiah Davis and Lucila Pulido. A deep bow and thank you to Octavia Butler and all of the writers of color who opened the door for stories like this one.

Thank you once again to my all of my ancestors and to my grandmother Sudie Hopkins who reminded me that my purpose gave me an early clue when you sent my published poem to me. What a gift and a beautiful woman you are! Thank you Jesus and Yeye for walking with me every step of the way! Thank you Dacia Stephenson, Juanita Holmes, Margie Pridgen and Linda Crawford Strickland, even though you are no longer here I knew it was you all along. I love you so much, thank you for teaching me to live for the gift that is now.

To all of my sisters, the Bridgers across the globe, thank you for being you!

29012488R00174

Made in the USA
Columbia, SC
03 November 2018